PRAISE FOR
BLACK CHUCK

"A stunning work of prose—poetic and haunting, tender and gritty—this is a remarkable novel."

—**Andrew Smith**, Michael L. Printz Honor
and Boston Globe-Horn Book Award–winning author

"Superb debut novel; the pain and angst of both Ré and Evie is palpable, and the struggles they face within their respective relationships are real and nuanced…This is a brutal, heartbreaking, and yet strangely uplifting novel about the consequences of lies, the gravity of love, and the courage it takes to prevail over self-condemnation."

—*Booklist*

"Atmospheric…Ojibwe mythology and language add texture as the mystery surrounding what really happened to Shaun, and who—or what—is at fault, deepens."

—*Publishers Weekly*

"McDonell provides a strong sense of character for each of her players, drawing them to a crashing conclusion through a series of impactful events. The author also displays an adeptness in handling themes such as inevitability, loyalty, and guilt, making this a read that sticks in the gut…This book delivers on a stirring psychological drama fans of Carol Plum-Ucci's *The Body of Christopher Creed* and of the CW's *Riverdale* will tear through."

—*School Library Journal*

"McDonell deftly handles a surprisingly complex narrative…Her characters are well developed and well deserving of empathy while not always likeable…*Black Chuck* surprises at nearly every turn; it's a powerful debut."

—*Quill & Quire*

"Dynamically complex characterization and storytelling…brooding and absorbing."

—*Kirkus Reviews*

"A gritty, dark mystery...McDonell captures the characters' diverging paths with heart and talent, exploring the secrets we keep from others and ourselves, and the decisions that determine who we are."

—**Amy Mathers**, National Reading Campaign

"A beautiful and painful novel...McDonell's background in creative writing and poetry is evident in this excellent debut novel...A strange, brutal, heartbreaking, and strangely uplifting novel about lies, love, friendship, courage, and the struggle to overcome guilt. Recommended."

—**Rob Bittner**, *LitBit* blog

"This novel is Orca at its most mature. The characters are living on the edge, with such raw intensity that it is painful to remember that they are still teens...As these four teens struggle with their demons, we are pulled through their living nightmares by McDonell's harrowing depiction, and hope for their sakes that they can each find their road."

—*Resource Links*

"A book unlike anything I have read before...McDonell has developed characters who are diverse, multidimensional, and flawed, which makes them relatable...Highly recommended."

—*CM Magazine*

"A darkly atmospheric story, filled with heartfelt, yet perfectly-flawed characters. I loved it."

—**Ash Parsons**, award-winning author of *The Falling Between Us*

"*Black Chuck* is easy to get lost in, haunting, hard not to think about. This story is compelling, chillingly real and sad. Timeless, yet contemporary. A pleasure to read."

—**Genevieve Scott**, author of *Catch My Drift*

"McDonell has captured the brashness and insecurity of adolescence in this gravel-splattering joy-ride."

—**Karen Nesbitt**, author of *Subject to Change*

REGAN
McDONELL

BLACK
CHUCK

ORCA BOOK PUBLISHERS

Library and Archives Canada Cataloguing in Publication

McDonell, Regan, 1974–, author
Black Chuck / Regan McDonell.

Issued in print and electronic formats.
ISBN 978-1-4598-1630-5 (softcover).—ISBN 978-1-4598-1631-2 (pdf).—
ISBN 978-1-4598-1632-9 (epub)

I. Title.
PS8625.D774B53 2018   jC813'.6   C2017-904574-1
C2017-904575-X

First Published in the United States, 2018
Library of Congress Control Number: 2017949715

Summary: In this gritty young adult novel, Réal struggles with his guilt over a friend's
violent death and his feelings for the dead boy's pregnant girlfriend.

*Orca Book Publishers is dedicated to preserving the environment and has
printed this book on Forest Stewardship Council® certified paper.*

Orca Book Publishers gratefully acknowledges the support for its publishing programs
provided by the following agencies: the Government of Canada,
the Canada Council for the Arts and the Province of British Columbia through
the BC Arts Council and the Book Publishing Tax Credit.

Cover images by Getty Images and Shutterstock.com
Edited by Sarah N. Harvey
Design by Rachel Page
Author photo by Guy Glover

ORCA BOOK PUBLISHERS
orcabook.com

Printed and bound in Canada.

21 20 19 18 • 5 4 3 2

For the boys I didn't love
And the one I did

I

R

Réal hunched into his old jean jacket, running a cut lip between his teeth and not looking anyone in the eye. Beside him, Alex Janes flicked a silver coin between his knuckles. Eyes pinned to his dirty boots, jaw set so hard it could crack, Alex looked like he could barely keep his lid on. Like he was about to explode. Across the sidewalk, Sunny kicked her heel against a broken chain-link fence, talking with a speed that killed any chance of getting a word in.

Compared to his friends, Ré felt weirdly quiet, weirdly still—even for him.

Past Sunny, on the other side of the chain link, mist rose off North Cold Water Collegiate's pretty green football field. It was a bright, sunny, almost-summer morning just like any other, and Ré was thinking, Nothing. Nothing on earth gonna make this day go easy.

Sunny shook her long black hair. "I'm not telling her. Hells no," she said. She'd tossed her backpack in the dust at her feet and was staring down the hill with red, swollen eyes. As usual, it was all about her.

"And anyway," she went on, "someone for sure went over there last night, right? I mean, one of her other friends—she has other friends, right? God, I can't fucking believe this. I seriously can't be the one to tell her—"

Réal closed his eyes and pressed his back teeth together, the sound of her voice starting to grate. "Jesus," he snarled. "I'll tell her. Just shut up already."

Sunny narrowed her eyes on him. "Nice," she said. "First words you've spoken all day. Glad you decided to join us, dickhead."

He stared her down, mouth closed, and she just stared back, stone cold.

"She's here," Alex said. He'd stopped rolling the coin and rubbed his thumb across its corrugated edge.

Down the long hill, Evie Hawley emerged from the mess of yellow buses and kids fighting for parking. Réal could see the big black headphones covering her ears, dark hair like a curtain over her eyes. As she got closer, he saw that dreamy, other-planet look pasted to her face. As if she didn't already know. As if no one had told her last night, when the kids had found it. Sunny's words echoed in his head. *Somebody* got to her before now. We *can't* be the first—

Sunny pounced on Evie, yanking the headphones off.

"Hey, wha—" Evie pulled back.

"Oh my god, are you okay?" Sunny blurted out.

As Evie glanced at each of them, Réal looked away quick. He swallowed. She didn't know. She really didn't know. "*Câlisse*," he swore under his breath.

Evie shook Sunny off and pulled her backpack from her shoulder, stuffing her headphones into the front pocket. "What's going on?"

Sunny's eyes widened. "Didn't your mom tell you?"

"Mom's on graveyard," Evie said, flicking her hair over her shoulder and scanning them all again. "I haven't seen her in a week."

Sunny turned to Réal, and he felt something dark and poisonous whirl up in his gut. Goddammit, Sunny, he thought, flashing her a look of pure evil. She just twisted her jaw and glared at him, pressing him to step in. *You promised.*

He shoved his fists deeper into his jean-jacket pockets, pulling his shoulders to his ears, hoping to disappear. Nothing, he thought, not even *Sunny*, is gonna make this day go easy.

He took a long breath. His eyes fell back to that field. And then, because there was nothing else he could do, he just opened his mouth and said it. "Shaun is dead."

❖   ❖   ❖

E
Evie buzzed like a bell struck by a hammer. She stared at Réal, but he just looked away over the fence, bomb dropped.

She turned to Alex, whose face crumpled instantly as the words all tumbled out—the bloody grass, Shaun's belly torn open, the police dog, the kids all coming across that field at twilight, screaming. "He had no shoes on, man," Alex said, his voice a broken mess. "Who would take his fuckin' shoes?"

The backpack slipped from Evie's hand. Her eyes went wide, but she saw nothing. Her ears rang—she heard nothing. *"No way."*

She'd been with Shaun just days ago. Nursing fries and bad coffee at the Olympia, talking about—what? It all left her head the instant that word came out of Réal's mouth. A blown fuse, a bulb burned out.

Pop.

Crack.

Dead?

Shaun Henry-Deacon? *Fearless frickin' Shaun Henry-Deacon?*

A picture of him across the table from her, lips mid-sentence, sea-colored eyes set on hers…He couldn't die. It wasn't possible.

Shaun was invincible.

A picture of him leaping from the fire escape at the Grains, throwing himself, weightless, into the night—he'd done it a hundred times. Never so much as scraped his knee. It wasn't in his nature. Every step he took was total blind confidence, on air or solid ground. That's just who he was.

Shaun Henry-Deacon.

Evie's chest squeezed tight. Her scalp pricked with needles and pins, and the world spun, though she stood perfectly still. *Impossible.*

Alex dragged a grimy sleeve across his eyes. "Fuck it," he said. "I'm not going to school today." He jumped up and flicked the coin into the road, where it skipped off the pavement and *thwacked* into the side of a parked car. "I feel like getting bombed," he said, heading away from them down the hill.

Evie looked to Réal again and realized then that he'd been crying too. Maybe for hours. It had been hard to tell before—dark purple stained his eyes, and the bridge of his nose was swollen and scabbed from some days-old fight. Ré had four brothers, and he was tough as hell. She'd seen him beat up and black-eyed plenty of times. She had never seen him cry.

"Come on," he muttered, pushing past her and heading down the hill.

❖ ❖ ❖

Burned oil and sour milk. That was the smell of Réal's old Buick. Evie stared out the dirty window in the back seat, watching telephone poles slide by, trying not to breathe. The car's soft suspension lurched and bounced over every bump, every hill, as Ré stomped the gas.

In the front seat, Alex lit the bowl of a small pipe, and a moment later skunky, blue smoke filled the car as he exhaled. Evie gagged. She opened her window an inch, and smoke sucked past her face and away. She began to feel carsick, the rotten-upholstery-and-pot-smoke smell nagging at the back of her throat.

At Mill Road, Réal peeled off the highway too fast. Sunny shrieked as the Buick fishtailed dangerously through the dock-yard. At the end of the yard, Ré stood on the brakes, locked tires sliding through gravel till the rubber butted up against the low wooden barrier at the edge of the riverbank.

Evie looked for a trace of the grin Réal usually wore when he did stupid stuff in his car, but his jaw was set hard and tucked to his chest like he'd really meant to drive them all off the bank into the black water below.

"What. The. *Fuck*, Ré!" Sunny screeched, kicking the back of his seat with her pointy boot. She jumped out of the car and slammed the door with a hollow clang, black skirt swirling as she stalked away.

"Jesus, man." Alex laughed. It was a reedy, fearful sound. He punched Réal's thigh lightly, then got out to go after Sunny.

The car's engine ticked as it cooled. Colorless dust whirled around them. Neither Evie nor Réal spoke. She sat gripping the vinyl under her, eyes locked on a broken bit of piping on the passenger seat that barfed up yellow stuffing. She could hear Sunny's complaints bouncing over the concrete past the car.

Suddenly Réal punched the dash hard with his fist.

She jumped like he'd hit her instead. "What the—"

"Shut it, Evie. Don't say it." He flexed his hand as blood began to ooze from his cut knuckles.

"I was just—"

"*Don't*," he growled. Then he softened. "Please. Just don't talk, okay?"

Evie sighed. She slumped back against the seat and looked out at their pretty, red-brick-and-wrought-iron town. The train bridge over the Ohneganohs River cut a black slash through her view. She'd lived in Cold Water for six years, in four different, equally crappy houses. Always on this side of those tracks.

Réal ran a thumb over his bloody knuckles, smearing rust across the back of his hand. Almost too low to hear, he said, "I saw him."

"Uh-huh." Evie was not really listening.

"No. I mean, I *saw* him," he said. *"After."*

Evie turned to look at him. She said nothing, waiting.

Réal pressed a thumbnail into his torn skin and picked back the ragged edge. "He looked like hamburger."

Evie blinked, not sure what he was trying to say. "Why didn't you tell anyone?"

"Because, man," he said quietly, "because it's my fucking fault."

He began to cry. It was a sharp, painful sound, like he didn't do it too often and didn't really know how. He covered his eyes with his bloody hand and shriveled into his jean jacket.

"It's not your fault, Ré," she said.

She got out of the car and left him to cry alone.

Sunny and Alex were arguing on the far side of the docks, voices lifting like birds in the morning breeze. Evie went the other way, climbing down the rough edge of the riverbank to the flat shale below. She kicked through the patchy grass and garbage till she found a good stone to sit on.

Hugging her knees to her chest, Evie looked down into the slick, dark water.

None of this is real, she thought. It's all just some big, dumb joke on me.

Ha-ha.

And instantly Shaun's voice came floating back: "Why would you say that?"

She'd laughed. Sitting across from him at the Olympia that day. "Shaun. Come on. You *love* me? How can you say that *now*?"

"How can I not?" He'd chucked his fork down onto his plate. "What do you know, anyway?"

He'd sat back, crossing his arms over his chest. Despite his nearly elbow-length blond hair and the athletic build of those arms, he had looked exactly like a pouting child.

"Shaun, we're in high school. We have our whole lives ahead of us." His eyes had begged her to shut up, but she'd only looked away. "We're way too young to get married," she'd muttered.

"According to who? Your *mom*?" He'd sneered.

Evie had sighed then and picked at her own plate. She hadn't told her mom yet. She'd been hoping she'd never have to. Lucky Shaun gets out of another jam, she'd thought. I'll just *deal* with it, and no one will ever know.

But Shaun had not followed her script. Shaun was happy.

She'd thought it would be the worst news he'd ever heard. That he might hate her, maybe even break up with her. Instead, he'd dropped the L word. As if that magically fixed everything between them. As if it fixed this. *Abracadabra, girl.*

Shaun had been happy. He'd wanted this. And now he was dead.

Evie looked down into that smooth, black river sliding over the stones to some better place, far away.

Alone. Still in high school. Not quite seventeen, and three months late.

There was no way in hell she was having this baby.

"I wish I'd never met you, Shaun Henry-Deacon," she said.

2

R

He couldn't get it out of his head. Those dusty, bloody tracks trailing out from where Shaun's belly was ripped open, contents spilling into the scrub grass and staining the sandy earth. He'd been dragged some distance across the field by pretty big teeth, taken down like prey, though the footprints were human. Or human-*ish*.

At least, that's how it had looked to Réal, who was no great tracker.

But he didn't need to be—he'd cut across that field to Shaun's since he was nine years old, its dirty footpaths worn right into his muscle. Even with the train tracks, he'd never taken the long way around. Hop the broken chain-link fence and go east along the trail. Stop to chuck stones at the rusty rail containers, spray-painted and tagged by people so far away that their marks were like light from dead stars. Then cut down through Baxter Grains—Shaun's nan lived three blocks that way.

Réal's feet had crunched across those dirty train tracks more than twice a week for nine years. His mom maybe would have killed him if she knew, but she'd never asked. Through dark and snow and rain. Lately, coming back from Nan's drunk and whooping at the moon on Saturday nights. The stones he threw echoing blankly off those rail containers, a sound that made him feel huge and insignificant all at once.

The distance to Shaun's was mapped in his limbs, and he'd been headed that way again when he saw it—the waxy blue flesh all tangled in the grass, the gray T-shirt torn and stained dark brown.

An arc light shone from a pole by the fence along the north side of Baxter Grains. It mostly spilled its cold, blue light into the Grains parking lot, leaving only a thin fringe to fall on the wrong side, the side no one but Réal ever seemed to use.

At the edge of this light, Ré's legs had folded under him.

They'd fought, but that was nothing. They'd fought hundreds of times. Shaun was a fifth brother, a pale fraternal twin. Réal had been coming across the tracks that night to say sorry, that it was none of his business. If Shaun wanted a kid, it was none of his business. He just thought it was dumb. No, maybe just—it was Evie's decision to make, being the girl and all. Shaun was eighteen, but Evie was just a kid. Sixteen maybe. It was fucking *nuts*, but it was none of his business.

When Shaun told him he planned on marrying Evie, Réal laughed at him and got a fist in his ear for it. They'd grabbed at each other, cursing and crashing into the wall of Nan's front room, Réal's tight bundle of muscle against Shaun's lanky, athletic frame.

Shaun's fist smashed Réal's nose, and blood poured out, all down his shirt. Pain tore through his face, and he choked on it. But Réal got a few good ones into Shaun's ribs. Might have even cracked a few. Then Shaun yanked Réal's plaid shirt up like a hockey sweater, buttons strangling his throat, and it was done.

Réal snatched his jean jacket from the floor and left, slamming the front door and running across the field. When he'd gotten away from the rows of wooden houses full of little Nans, he bent and yelled, "Fuck!" as long and loud as he could with his fists balled up and the tendons jumping on his neck, the sound coming out of him all animal. But it hadn't emptied the feeling from his gut.

That night he drove the Buick too fast, music too loud, blood still hot. He'd half wanted to go over to Evie's and yell some more, but he didn't go. It was none of his business. He wished he didn't even know.

A *baby*. Even the word sounded weird and helpless.

He'd finally ran his rage down at the empty dockyards. Sitting on the hood of his car at the river's edge, he'd watched the full moon rise. The liquid white cooled his blood, till at last he was calm. Then he drove home slow, falling into bed without even remembering it.

That night, dreams of awful violence had sat on his chest. He fought with Shaun over and over. Wrenching his gray T-shirt in his fist. Shoving his shoulder into Shaun's chest, knocking the air out. Smashing up against the wall, picture frames scattering. The taste of blood in his teeth, all tinny.

Nobody thought anything about it, Shaun not being at school the next day. It happened a lot, with his nan being so old. And nobody asked Réal about the purple under his eyes, 'cause that happened a lot too. But then another whole day passed and still no Shaun, so Réal had crossed that field after supper, after sundown, to go say sorry.

And he'd folded to his knees just outside the arc light, one hand over his mouth, wide eyes flicking over the meat.

Fuck.

Parts of Shaun looked eaten. Mostly the gut, with its pearly blue tangle of tripe and fat. Not much fat on him, Ré thought. Not much of a meal.

His own gut lurched. He kicked away from the floodlight, back into the scrub of the field, and he puked. Chunks of chewed hamburger, bloody red tomato sauce. Again he puked. Gasping for air, he kicked in the dusty ground to get a foothold, he bolted back across the field, away from what he'd seen.

Back in his room, he found his plaid shirt balled under the bed, the front dried brown. *The same.* Shaun's torn gray T-shirt was the same. He drew breath fast and shallow. His heart skittered. *Shaun was his best friend.* Blood on his sleeves. More than just a busted nose. He looked down at his jeans, his shoes—flecks of brown and rust on those too.

He ran a hand over his mouth and a rubbery, gray piece of puked-up meat came away on his fingers. He stared at it, helpless. *The taste of blood in his teeth.*

He started to cry, and he didn't stop till his face hurt like hell and he could hardly breathe at all.

He'd told no one what he'd seen.

It was another whole day before the kids went through that field.

And now, people who'd never once given a real rat's about Shaun were squawking and hopping like crows on roadkill. Girls he'd never talked to cooed over his corpse like he was some lost puppy they'd secretly always loved—which probably was true, Réal thought, rolling his eyes. Shaun had that effect on girls.

Réal's ears pricked when he overheard Tracey Weatherall tell a small crowd that Shaun used to holler *hey, girl* at her in the parking lot, long arms hanging out the window of his car, blond hair shining in the sun. She said, "He only seemed like a burnout if you didn't know him. Really, he was sweet."

"Ew, seriously?" another stuck-up girl said.

"Well, it's not like I dated him!" Tracey backpedaled with a laugh.

Réal tasted vomit in his mouth all over again.

He eyed Tracey as he pulled books from his locker. She was hot, in a boring way. In a thin-tanned-perfect-white-girl kind of way. Shaun probably *had* hollered at her. Probably slept with her, too, 'cause, well, he was *Shaun*. But she was popcorn. No way in hell did she *know* him.

He slammed his locker door and shoved off in the other direction, leaving the roadkill behind.

It had been two days since they'd found his best friend's half eaten body.

There was a memorial in the gym that afternoon—the last place Réal wanted to be, but the others were going. Sunny had insisted. *For Evie's sake*, she'd said—although he suspected it was really just for Sunny's. She liked calling the shots. Liked the world to spin on her fingers.

Réal and Shaun had grown up together. They'd met Alex in junior high. And in sophomore year, Sunny had swooped down, landing on Alex and making them a quartet.

Scary Sunny. Tall, skinny like a wishbone. Long, straight black hair. *Hot.* Definitely not popcorn. She knew it, too, with her serious dark eyes and a mouth that could turn you into a snake without saying a word. She was the only Korean goth he'd ever met, and everything was a fucking hurricane with her.

And somehow, like this was some darkest timeline slash twilight zone, she'd wound up with Alex Janes. Of all the guys! Not tall, good-looking skater Shaun, who only had to holler *hey, girl* out a car window to get laid, but skinny-legged stoner Alex Janes, son of bikers, grandson of bikers. Nearly three years later, Réal still couldn't figure that one out.

As he pushed through the crowded hall, every third person seemed to eye Réal strangely. He just glared back, irritated, till he remembered his two black eyes going green around the edges. Irish sunglasses, he thought, almost smiling.

A familiar shape floated down the hall from the other direction, and guilt flew through his gut when he saw her. He ducked into the collar of his jean jacket, heart tapping up under his ribs.

Evie Hawley. The final fifth. The last piece of their puzzle of friends. She'd been Shaun's girl for almost a year, but she was so quiet Réal still hardly knew a thing about her. She was just dark hair, big eyes, pretty laugh—nothing like Shaun's usual prey.

There was a word Ré had thought of the first time he saw her sitting in Shaun's car, hair half hiding her face. *Fragile,* maybe, or *insubstantial.* Or *barely there.* But he couldn't remember that word now.

He turned a corner, taking the stairs two at a time and leaving her behind.

❖   ❖   ❖

Alex whistled under his breath. "This is so messed."

Réal grunted in agreement. There were no pictures hung in the gym. Like Shaun's wiseass grin and shitty tattoos would be in bad taste at his own memorial.

He looked around for the girls and found them two rows back, Sunny's arm around Evie, who sat stiff as a cat that didn't want to be touched. Réal turned back to face the principal. "Shaun Henry-Deacon was one of our own," she was saying. "He was just like you and me."

Someone coughed "Bullshit!" loud enough for everyone to hear, and a din of laughter broke out.

The principal only spoke louder into the mic. "He may not have been a model student. He may have even rubbed some of us the wrong way. But these are often the kids who need our care the most." She glanced at the teachers flanking her in folding chairs, some nodding slowly as they looked down at their hands.

Hypocrites, Réal thought.

"He was not honor roll, or star athlete, or class president..."

Alex muttered, "A pain in their necks, more like." Réal nudged him with his elbow, and both boys half smiled.

"...but he *was* special," she went on. "He was *ours*. And as a Northerner, he represents each and every one of *us* at North Cold Water Collegiate. This tragic event stands as a lesson—"

"Say no to drugs!" the same wiseass cracked. A laugh rose up but was choked out fast.

"Mister McKellar, what is wrong with you? One of your classmates has died!" the principal barked, fist landing like a gavel on her podium.

After a red-faced pause, she went on. "As you all know, the police are investigating this incident, and we have promised to cooperate fully. If anyone in this school is found to be working against that promise, there *will* be consequences. As well," she added hurriedly, "grief counseling will be available to any students who need to talk about their feelings."

Kids started snickering about *feelings*. Some outright laughed.

Réal's knee bounced as he tapped his heel against the bleachers. "*Ostie d'crisse,*" he swore. "These idiots don't even know what dead means." A cold finger ran up his spine. *It means having your guts dragged from the bowl of your belly across a field in the middle of the night.*

"Yeah," Alex agreed. "It's not like losing your damn wallet."

And then McKellar made another wisecrack.

"Goddammit!" the principal spat into the mic, and the whole room laughed.

Réal stood up.

He walked down the bleacher row and grabbed McKellar's shirt collar. He popped him once, hard and fast in the ear with a cut fist, not waiting for the kid to get scared first.

Then he waited, fist pulled back, eyes narrowed.

The dazed boy looked up at him, blinking blindly. Then he lost it. He scratched at the hand that held his shirt, trying to wrench it off. "What the fuck, Dufresne!" he yelped, eyes going white. "You frickin' psycho!"

Réal smiled. Then he punched him. Knuckles met orbital bone with a satisfying crack, and McKellar spat that dumb look right off his face.

The gym exploded. Kids screamed, scrambling like pins from a strike, McKellar flailing helplessly in Réal's hands. Réal saw nothing but red, heard nothing but the ringing of a bell as his fist fell again, then again.

Suddenly there were hands on his arm, hobbling him. He jerked, trying to shake them off, but they wouldn't shake. He glared over his shoulder at their owner, thinking, You're next, buddy.

Evie's sad, scared eyes looked back at him.

His jaw clenched so tight it hurt his neck. He tried again to shake her off, but her two hands around his elbow were like a hundred-pound trap.

His nostrils flared.

He dropped McKellar, who stumbled back with a cry.

Ré was tight as a crossbow as Evie pulled him away, down the bleacher stairs. Panicked kids skittered out of their way. Two hundred jaws on the floor, but no one said a word. Not even the teachers stepped in.

❖   ❖   ❖

E

The door clanged shut behind them as Evie pulled Réal out into the parking lot. They got thirty feet before Réal stopped dead. Evie turned to face him, confused.

"What?" she asked. He'd reared back like a chained dog, looking down at her through his lashes. "Why are you looking at me like that?"

But he said nothing, lips sealed in a tight line.

She glanced at his wrist in her hand. It was tan-dark, with a worn old watch on a black leather band. The knuckles of his right hand were bloody and swollen around a large silver ring set with black stone. Evie cringed when she saw it, thinking of that poor kid's face.

Réal was nearly six feet of muscle. A Rottweiler of a boy. This wasn't the first fight she'd seen him start, and she'd never seen him lose. He wasn't called "Psycho Ré" for nothing. He is, she thought, the toughest boy I know. Toughest anyone knows, probably.

"Come on." She tugged him again, half scared a teacher would come out that door and make them go back inside, ruining their perfect exit. "Let's get out of here."

And then he spoke. "*Evie.*" It was a low, warning sound, like he wanted to say more. He didn't say anything though. Instead, she watched his eyes fall to her belly, then away.

A wave of shame rushed through her, hot and red. She jutted her chin, heart fluttering up her throat. So he knew. For a second she just stood there, not sure what to do. Then she turned and walked away as fast as she could.

"Evie, stop," he called after her. "Come on, girl."

He trotted up to her side, grabbing her sleeve, but she yanked away. "What else did Shaun tell you?" she spat over her shoulder.

"He just *told* me, that's all," Réal said, sidestepping along next to her.

She laughed harshly. "Did he tell you he wanted to marry me?"

"Evie, just stop, will you?" His fingers closed on her arm, jerking her around to face him. "He told me what you wanted," he said. "And I told him you were right—and then he busted my face." He grinned, just for a second.

She gaped at him. His nose was back to normal, but dark bruises still circled each eye. Never in a million years would she have thought Réal Dufresne—of all people—would stick up for her, be on her side. Not with this—the last living scrap of his best friend in the world.

She took a sharp, jagged breath. Then she burst into tears.

Réal's face changed instantly, the lines all pointing down. He reached out and pulled her to him, wrapping his arms around her head. She felt his muscle move against her cheek. His shirt smelled like lemon soap.

"If you need my help," he said quietly, "I'm here, okay?"

She closed her eyes and cried, trying not to think at all. Then she said, "Can you please just not tell anyone else? Not Sunny, not Alex. *Nobody.*"

"Yeah. Of course, Ev," he said. "It's your business. I don't even have to know anything about it. Just—whatever you need, I'm here. All right?"

She swallowed, breath shaking out of her as she held back more tears, and she gripped his cotton T-shirt like she was falling off the edge of the world.

After a while she calmed, listening to his body. His lungs, his heart, her eyes closed. She thought of that smooth, black river water sliding over the stones so easy. Just knowing its way without even thinking about it.

She sniffled and pulled away, blinking back fresh tears. He didn't say anything. He just held her shoulders lightly and looked at her so long she felt like she was swimming in his soft, brown eyes.

Then the door at the side of the gym banged open, metal on metal.

At the sound of Sunny's voice, a shadow fell over Réal, and whatever had just passed between them was gone.

❖   ❖   ❖

R

"Hey, guys," Sunny said as she walked around them in a circle. She stopped to look at Réal over Evie's head. "Are you okay?"

"Fine," he answered. He let go of Evie and stepped back. "Just happy that little prick gave me an excuse."

Sunny laughed. "Yeah, McKellar is a punk. I don't think anyone would have stopped you." She glanced at Evie and shrugged. "I mean, you know what I mean. The teachers weren't in a hurry to step in."

Réal laughed too. Then he let out a long breath. He looked down at Evie, shoving his cut hands into his back pockets. The front of his T-shirt was blotched with tears and snot, but he didn't care. His eyes darted all over her. *You okay?* he asked, without saying it out loud.

Evie blinked up at him, smiling weakly.

Réal bit his lips together and knit his brow. These few words were the most he and Evie had ever exchanged. She was so quiet—nothing like Sunny, who was all cackle and screech and easy to figure out. Evie was as alien as they came to a guy with four brothers.

He meant what he'd said though. Whatever she wanted, whatever she needed, he was there. If she wanted to end this baby thing without anyone knowing, fine by him. He'd even pay for it, if she had no money—he didn't know if these things cost money, but he would if they did, one way or another.

It was literally the very least he could do, since he'd killed his own best friend.

3

Shaun lived down the road from her, way past the edge of town, in a house like hers—too small and beat up for good company. His nan was his legal guardian, but she was too old to really govern him, so he was mostly wild.

He'd started coming around Evie's at the end of last summer. The first time, she'd heard the car drive past and a few minutes later roar back again, like somewhere down the road he'd found the courage to knock on her door.

On that first night, Evie had only felt confused. They weren't friends. She knew who he was, because everyone did, but he'd never spoken to her before. She'd leaned on the porch railing, watching him as he talked, blond hair spilling across his shoulders, T-shirt all stretched and faded. He sat on the steps and chucked pebbles across the lawn like he was skipping them on a lake with his big, athletic hands.

He talked about school, but she got the feeling there was something else. Some other reason he'd turned up like this, out of the blue. Eventually, she just said, "Shaun, what are you doing here?" and it stopped him mid-throw.

"Shit. I'm sorry," he said. He looked down at his shoes and laughed self-consciously. "I guess this is kinda weird."

"No," she said. "It's just, I don't know, you never even said hi to me before. I didn't think you knew I existed."

"Yeah. Sorry about that," he said quietly, turning a small pebble in his fingers. "I guess I should go." He dropped the pebble and stood up. "I'll see ya at school," he said, and he left, confusing her even more.

Three nights later she was washing up dinner plates when she heard a car with a loose muffler cruise past. She turned off the water and listened. Sure enough, a few minutes later that engine came down the road again from the other direction and pulled into her drive.

She pushed open the screen door and leaned on the jamb. He was staring at his thumbs on the wheel, then he looked up and smiled, caught.

"Hey," he said, easing out of the car. "I was just driving past." He jerked his thumb at the road as he came across the lawn, but she knew his arrival was no coincidence.

He stopped at the bottom of her steps, resting a foot on the riser and leaning an elbow on his bent knee, his body a question mark. She unhitched herself from the doorjamb, letting the screen door slam behind her, and stood at the top of the steps. They smiled nervously from each end of the little obstacle.

"You haven't been at school," she said.

He grinned and cocked his head. "I didn't think you noticed stuff like that."

"Well, normally I don't, but you said you'd see me there, so I looked for you."

"You did?" He laughed, surprised. His teeth were perfectly straight and white, and when he smiled, his bottom lip slid up to touch them.

"Well, yeah." She shrugged, like it was obvious.

She took a step down and sat on the top stair, her face almost level with his.

He only hesitated for a second, then climbed up and sat next to her.

She didn't say anything; she gripped the uneven boards under her legs, looking off across the field on the other side of the street.

"So," he said, "I guess you think it's weird, me coming here?"

"No, not weird," she said slowly, thinking of his little white house at the other end of the road—they were sort of neighbors, after all. From the same side of town. "It's just, I don't know, why now?"

He took a deep breath and blew it out slow. For a minute he, too, just looked at the fields. Then he said, "What are your parents like, Evie?" And without waiting for her answer said, "Mine are fucked."

She looked at the side of his face, the blond hair tucked behind his ear. "Yeah," she said. "Mine too."

"I thought so." He nodded, tugging at a string of beaded leather that wound around his wrist. "I knew there was something...I don't know, I mean, we live in the same 'hood, and I see you at school a lot. I drive past here all the time thinking I'm just gonna stop."

"I'm glad you did," she said.

"You are?"

"Yeah, I mean—" She shrugged and looked around. "I'm here alone most of the time. It's cool to have someone to talk to."

"Yeah." He nodded, a slim grin sneaking across his lips. "It's cool."

They sat in silence again.

"So, you wanna go somewhere?" he asked after a while.

She shrugged. "Sure."

That night he had taken her to the Olympia Café. She'd never been in before. She'd thought only townies hung out there—kids who actually lived in town, not just clinging to the dirty edges like her and Shaun did.

But the waitress knew him. Her name was June, and she called him *son*. She dumped two greasy menus on their table and walked her big square hips away. Shaun leaned and in a low voice said, "June won the lottery *twice*. You should see her truck."

He didn't look at the menu. He stretched his long arms across the back of the vinyl banquette. Evie anxiously scanned the greasy pages, trying to find something appealing, but she was too nervous to read any of it, so she just flipped through.

"Nothing's good here," he said, taking the menu from her. "Are you hungry?"

"Uh, no, not really," she said, suddenly feeling dumb. "I had dinner before."

She looked around. There was an old drunk at the bar, nursing a beer. A radio played the baseball game in the kitchen, and June leaned in the pass-through, talking to the cook.

The place was dark, with wood paneling and an ugly brown-and-orange carpet. Ceiling fans listlessly turned the air. It was pretty quiet, too late for townie kids to be there—at least, the ones with curfews.

Shaun sat back and turned half sideways in the booth, stretching his long legs out across the seat. He must have stood six foot two in his bare feet.

She'd noticed him as soon as she started at North Cold Water Collegiate. He hung out on the hill with Réal Dufresne and Alex Janes, but he could easily have been a jock. He was broad across the shoulders, lithe at the waist, and he moved with the determined grace of an athlete, each gesture flowing logically from the last. And boy, was he good-looking. Almost too perfect to be sitting across the table from her in real life.

"So, what's wrong with your parents?" she asked, just as the back door of the restaurant banged open.

Sunny and Alex came in from the parking lot. Sunny looking scary and beautiful in a long, black, completely see-through skirt, worn over a shorter, tighter, opaque one, and tall black boots. Alex loped along ahead of her like a witch's familiar.

"H.D.," Alex called, eyeing Evie as they came across the room.

"Janes," Shaun replied flatly.

He introduced them to Evie when they arrived at the table, but he didn't move his legs so they could sit down. "Evie lives down my street," he told them.

"Cool, cool," Alex said, looking at her. "You're a Northerner, right? I seen you at school."

Evie nodded. *Northerner* was local shorthand for their high school, though she was more accurately an Easterner, since the town was pretty clearly divided. Best and Least.

"We were just at the band shell." Alex jerked his head in the direction they'd come from, and Shaun nodded without comment.

After a few minutes Alex and Sunny sat at another table, and Shaun turned to face Evie, taking his legs down from the seat. They talked, and as they did, he watched the other couple over her shoulder. It only dawned on her later that this had been her initiation. That Shaun had wanted her to meet his friends, to stir them together to see what happened.

Lots of girls at school whispered about Shaun. He had a reputation for being kind of slutty, a player. It was a long time before she realized that, although he'd had plenty of hookups, he'd never had an actual girlfriend. At least, not until Evie.

Shaun started coming around most nights after that one. They sat on the top step looking out across the grass, just talking. And then one night he put his hand down over hers, gently but with purpose, and she didn't resist.

"Does your grandmother ever wonder where you are at night?" she asked, trying to ignore the electricity from his fingers.

"Nah," he answered, voice full of swagger. Then he explained, "Nan's pretty old. She doesn't really understand much anymore. Mostly she just thinks I'm there anyway. Like, I catch her talking to me sometimes, but I haven't been around for hours. Once I was even—" He stopped and grinned. "Ah, never mind."

"What?" Evie asked. "Tell me."

"Uh..." He cringed a little, and then he laughed, embarrassed, or at least pretending to be. "I was, uh, with someone, y'know, in my room, and she walked in and started talking to me." He laughed again, this time for real, and shook his head, remembering. "I don't think she even knew there was someone else there."

"You were with someone?" Evie asked, already knowing but not wanting to know what he'd meant.

"Yeah," Shaun said. "Y'know. *In bed*." He cleared his throat and laughed again.

"And she didn't even know it?"

Shaun squeezed her hand. "Yeah, she just walked right in and turned on the light! Started telling me the kitchen drain was slow again. And I'd just fixed it the day before, so I knew it was fine."

The thought of Shaun in bed with someone made Evie shiver. Picturing him naked, wrapped in sheets and legs and long hair, sweating and breathing over some other girl, made her both excited and a little scared. His story dropped the suggestion of sex into the conversation, and now all she could think was, Will we? as it circled them like a shark.

Had he done it on purpose? She looked at the side of his face, behind its curtain of golden hair, and she could see his grin, could almost see the sidelong glance he wanted to throw her.

Yes, she thought.

When he turned his grin on her, it felt like he knew exactly what she was thinking.

"I'm sorry," he said. "I hope that doesn't bug you."

Blushing, she deflected. "What, your grandmother?" She tried to pull her hand from his, but he held tight.

"No, dummy, that I screwed some other girl and just told you about it. Kind of a bonehead move, don't you think?"

"Ah, I uh…" she stammered, then looked away, face burning.

She covered her eyes with her free hand and laughed a little too loudly. She felt like her thoughts—his sweat, his shoulders, the sounds he'd make, his tenderness or lack of it, even his low voice saying the word *screw*—were all over her face.

"Shit, I'm sorry," he said, pulling the hand he held to his chest. "It was just some girl. I mean—it was a long time ago."

"A long time ago?" She raised her brows. "How old are you?"

He sat up a little straighter, clearing his throat again. "Well, I just turned eighteen, but y'know. I been on my own a long time."

Then he bit his lip to stop grinning and said quietly, "That's a really stupid story to tell a girl I like, huh?"

His sweet embarrassment—and the unexpected confession—felt like a disarming spell he carried in his pocket, ready to cast at a moment's notice. She wondered if he'd told this story a thousand times and guessed that he probably had. He'd probably driven past a hundred girls' doors in his rusted old Dodge and sat on a hundred stoops, grinning like he was right now.

But as she looked at his frayed jeans and dirty T-shirt, at the wavy blue lines of his homemade tattoos, she wondered if it was just survival—raising the odds of a warm body to sleep next to.

"Do you ever worry about your grandmother?" she asked him.

"Hells yeah," he said. "All the time. She can't really take care of herself anymore, and I mean, I can't always be there. I worry that she's gonna hurt herself or leave the gas on."

He looked away from her, out over the patchy grass. "She got really sick last year, and I had to leave school to take care of her. That's why I'm not graduating."

"Oh, I thought—"

"Yeah, it's not 'cause I'm dumb." He cut her off, proud.

"But what about your parents?" she asked.

He laughed, one short, hard sound, and didn't say anything more for a minute.

Then he told her, "My nan raised me. My mom visits once in a while, mostly when she's broke. She's pretty messed up. She drinks a lot. She's pretty crazy."

Evie studied the side of his face again. She could see that he'd told *this* story many times too. To teachers, and probably to cops.

But it really wasn't any different from her own—her dad left when she was six, and she had no siblings. Mom had worked nights since Evie was just old enough to be left alone, two weeks on, four days off. She told her story as bluntly as he had told his. They weren't comparing wounds, just confirming what they'd already known—they were from the same tribe.

He turned to her with a relaxed smile. The twinkle was back in his eye, and instantly he was the invincible Shaun Henry-Deacon again. Swaggering, easygoing, nothing-can-touch-him Shaun. The wooden porch, the field and the crummy house all fell away when he smiled, and she could tell by the way he licked his lips that he was going to kiss her.

4

E

Evie couldn't remember what she'd just been doing.

Dead, she thought.

She slid down the wall at the end of a row of lockers, knees folding to her chest.

Dead.

She pressed her skull to the cinder block as she remembered him standing in her driveway, leather jacket and a handful of rocks in the middle of the night.

Dead.

A picture of his smile. Of him landing a perfect kickflip, long hair fanning out in a bright half circle of gold.

Dead.

A picture of him leaping from the fire escape at the Grains, like gravity couldn't hold him...

Evie leaned back against the cold wall. There were too many pictures. First kiss. First night together. First fight.

Second fight. All the rest, until *I love you*. It had all passed by without a sound the first time, barely touching her, and now it all boomeranged back, knocking her lungs out.

She'd never said *I love you*.

She'd only laughed, mad that he'd waited till it was like leverage to say those words. Until they were not words but a bribe—my love for the rest of your life. I'll trade you. I'll marry you. *I love you*.

And now he was dead. She heard Réal say it over and over, bleak and empty. She'd laughed, and now what did she have? Just those three little words. *Shaun is dead*.

She remembered his eyes, sea blue and bright with the sting of her laughter. A wave of acid raced up her throat. She scrambled to her knees and splashed the linoleum with vomit.

"Gross!" someone cried, and suddenly there was a crowd around her that she hadn't noticed a moment earlier. She wiped her cheek with her sleeve. She wanted to tell them all where to stick it, but if she opened her mouth again, the rest of her breakfast would find its way out.

"Oh dear," a voice said, and there were hands on her. Warm, maternal hands pulling her up and away. "Are you all right?" the voice was asking. Evie couldn't answer. She was being dragged down the hall, feet stumbling over each other.

"We'll just get you to the nurse's station," the woman said. Evie glanced at her. She recognized the teacher but couldn't remember her name. Everything seemed to be slipping from her head.

"But my—" Evie craned her head around to look for her backpack, but the teacher didn't slow down.

"We'll get someone to bring your things, don't worry," she said.

At the nurse's station, Evie was given an empty waste-basket and told to lie on a cot. She didn't bother lying down. She hugged the basket and just stared over the rim at a spot on the floor, letting it shift in and out of focus. Eventually a nurse arrived to take her temperature.

"I'm fine," Evie said around the glass rod. "Just ate some-thing weird."

"Well, you're a bit too hot for my liking." The nurse wrin-kled her brow at the numbers. "I'd really like it if you could lie down."

Evie scowled at her, then fell to her side, sneakers still on the floor, empty basket tipping sideways.

"That'll do," said the nurse, going back to her desk.

Evie barely blinked as she stared out the open door into the now-empty hall. All the normal crush and noise of the school had faded, leaving just the lonely squeaks of shoes racing the last bell to class. She could hear her own heart beating in her ear.

Dead. Dead. Dead.

A moment later the phone rang. The nurse murmured into it, pretending not to look at Evie, who stared back, expression-less. When the nurse put the phone down, she had a crease between her brows.

"Sweetheart," she said, "we're having a little trouble reaching your mom."

Evie just blinked. *So?*

"Are you able to get home on your own, or would you like to just stay here for the rest of the day?"

Evie squeezed her eyes shut, trying to decide what would be worse—lying here all day in her puke-stained hoodie or going home, where Shaun's ghost lay waiting. Acid scratched in her throat again.

"*Psst.*"

She opened her eyes. Sunny stood just outside the doorway with Evie's backpack in her hand. She jerked her head sideways, gesturing for Evie to follow.

"I think I'll go home," Evie told the nurse. "I'll just call my mom on the way."

"Well, all right. But take this." She scribbled an absence slip and handed it to Evie. "And you get straight into bed when you get there, okay?"

Evie stood, dropping the wastebasket onto the cot behind her. She shoved the slip into her pocket and mumbled thanks to the nurse. Outside the room, she let Sunny put a bony arm around her. It was more comforting than it looked.

"Where are we going?" Evie whispered. There was no way Sunny was taking her straight home.

"The question is, where do you *want* to go?" Sunny grinned and raised her other hand. From it hung a worn-soft, black leather keychain, jangling a half dozen keys.

Evie's eyes popped. "How did you get those?"

Sunny shrugged, still grinning. "I asked."

"Seriously? And he just gave them to you?"

"Not exactly," Sunny said, and threw her hair back with a laugh.

They crossed the school parking lot to a blue Buick parked under a big maple tree. It was pocked and battered with rust and dings. A total boat, with a trunk big enough to hide bodies in. It was called a Century, and it was about that old.

Evie stopped and stared. Réal Dufresne's car. She'd ridden in it dozens of times, but never shotgun and *never* with anyone but him at the wheel. It was always the boys who sat up front with Ré. It was always Shaun, Alex squished between her and Sunny in the back, his bony joints all jammed into her.

Sunny hopped in the driver's side like she'd done it a hundred times and leaned across, unlocking the other door with two fingers. Evie swallowed her nerves and slid into the passenger seat, where that familiar burnt-oil-and-sour-milk smell greeted her.

Sunny's brow arched wickedly as the engine roared to life. Evie was surprised at her confidence with the massive steel machine. The Buick was sacred ground. Réal and his car— they were like two parts of the same object, though it was a really shitty, old car.

As the girls nosed out of the parking lot, Evie's eyes darted sideways. A police cruiser was parked half up on the boulevard, and two officers were striding across the lawn toward the front doors of the school.

She remembered the principal saying police were investigating Shaun's death. What did that mean? "Do the police think Shaun was murdered?" she asked aloud.

Sunny glanced at her. "I don't know," she said quietly. "I guess so." They turned left and rolled out into traffic, heading away from those dark blue uniforms. "He was, like, really beat up, Ev. That doesn't happen by accident."

Alex's description floated through her head again. No shoes, no teeth. "Who would do that to him?"

Sunny *tsk*ed her tongue. She didn't say anything for a second, just reached across and squeezed Evie's hand.

Then she dropped it, taking up the wheel again. "Asshats, that's who, Evie," she said. "People with no respect for true grandiosity. Cock monkeys. Penis wrinkles." Sunny went on, throwing out every expletive she could think of, until Evie was almost laughing.

She rolled down her window, letting out the car stink, and splayed her fingers to the wind. A picture of Shaun's impossibly long golden hair wrapped around the headrest of the Buick, wind whipping it wildly around the cabin. Réal swatting it out of the way—*"Get a frickin' haircut, hippie!"* Shaun just grinning, sliding his fingers down behind the passenger seat and taking Evie's hand.

"Do you love Alex?" Evie asked.

"*What?*" Sunny's eyes flashed wide. "Where did that come from?"

"I'm just curious," Evie said, leaning back against the seat. "I just don't know what it's supposed to feel like."

"Oh." Sunny maneuvered the car onto the county highway, and soon they were flying past orchards and green cornfields. "I guess so," she said. "I mean, he's hilarious. And sweet. And a babe, even if he is a total mess."

"Does he love you?" Evie turned to look at her friend.

"Yeah, he does." A little smile played on Sunny's lips. "He's such a puppy. He totally worships Shaun, you know."

Evie laughed. "You think?"

Alex was like a thinner, sharper version of Shaun, with feathery reddish-brown hair to his shoulders and the same stretched-out T-shirts. He'd perfected all of Shaun's facial expressions, though on his angular bones they looked somehow meaner and more defensive.

"He's like Satan's Own royalty, you know." Sunny's smile had gone dark and sly. "His great-grandfather was an original member, way back."

Evie gaped at her. "Whoa. I knew his dad had a motorbike, but…"

Sunny cackled. "Yeah, it's a little more than just having a motorbike. His dad is full-patch. So are, like, a hundred of his cousins. But don't tell anyone I told you that."

"Who would I tell?"

"True. Ré already knows, obviously. And Shaun. I guess you're the last of us. But it goes no further, okay?"

Evie shrugged. She literally had no one else to tell. "Why is it such a big deal?"

"Just…reasons," Sunny said, laughing again.

"Does it bother you?" she asked. "That he's a biker?"

"Hells no!" Sunny cried. "It's, like, the only thing that's even cool about him."

"Seriously? But you guys have been together for a million years."

"Not quite three," Sunny corrected. "But yeah, long enough. And anyway, I'm kidding. There's other cool stuff. He's just so frickin' bombed all the time, it's hard to tell anymore."

Evie laughed. She pictured Alex, red slits in his face for eyes. He was the most stoned guy she'd ever met. And he never seemed to be without weed, though he didn't have a job of any kind. The others dabbled, but it was truly Alex who earned them all the "burnout" label that followed them at school.

The warm air whirling around the cabin of the Buick almost felt like summer—damp and heavy. Like right before she'd met Shaun the year before. Heat that promised sleepless nights. She pictured her stuffy attic bedroom, Shaun's ghost all over it still. Suddenly the thought of another night alone there seemed unbearable. "Do you want to go to the lake tonight?" she asked Sunny. "With the guys, I mean?"

Sunny pushed herself back against the cheap vinyl seat, contemplating. "That could be fun. I couldn't get there till later though. I have a thing tonight."

"A Korean Mafia thing?" Evie teased. Sunny was always disappearing to do secret stuff she never talked about.

"Don't mock me, *jjin dda!*" She swatted a long arm across the seat at Evie, laughing. "I'll sic my godfather on you! He's, like, ninety years old, but he's very fierce! Very fierce." She spoke these last words in the warbling old voice of her godfather and then cackled insanely.

Evie laughed and shook her head. She rolled her gaze back out the open window, across the empty fields, lifting her fingers to the wind again.

❖　❖　❖

R

Réal slapped the empty pockets of his jean jacket and thought, I am going to *murder* that girl. The leather clasp that normally clipped his keys to the inside pocket was missing, and when he ducked out to check the parking lot, sure enough, the Buick was gone.

He stood at the top of the stairs, jacket clenched in his fist, the crash of metal doors hitting their stops full force echoing across the pavement. No one drove the Buick. *No one.*

He flared his nostrils for one second more, neck tight, jaw tight, then turned, yanking the door open again.

Réal froze.

At the end of the first floor hallway stood two dark-blue uniforms.

They hovered outside the main office, talking to the principal, who was nodding a lot, looking serious.

Réal swallowed and opened his hand. As the door swung from his grip, the sun cast a white glare across the glass, and all he could see was his own reflection staring back at him, wide-eyed. His heart knocked against his ribs.

Ciboire! he swore. His books were still inside.

Behind him, the sound of a familiar engine rose up, and he turned to see the Buick bouncing back into the parking lot, Sunny smiling coolly from the driver's seat.

"Fuck, Sunny," he muttered, more relieved than he wanted to be at seeing her behind the wheel. He dove down the steps and yanked open the car door, getting in practically on top of her. "Move over, for Christ's sake," he ordered, tossing his jacket at the girls.

Sunny slid across the front seat, long legs and leather boots piling all over Evie. Réal swung around and pulled right back out of the lot again, the Buick roaring like a bull, Sunny whooping gloriously over the sound.

"*Ça va*, Réal?" she singsonged, leaning against him, her body warm and cool at the same time.

"Don't even talk to me," he said, eyes flicking at the rearview mirror.

"Aw, are you mad at me?"

"You stole my car! Yeah, I'm mad at you, dumbass."

Sunny shrugged. "I had to. Evie was having a meltdown. I had to take her home."

"Yeah, good work," he muttered. "She's still here."

"Well, I had to bring the car back. It was almost out of gas!"

Réal glanced at the gauge on the dash. "Fuck, Sunny!"

Sunny just laughed and leaned against him again. He pushed her off with his left hand. Fucking hurricane. It was always like this with her.

A minute later her fingers were under the edge of his T-shirt.

"Stop it," he muttered quietly, but he didn't push her away. He caught her maniac grin in the mirror and just shook his head.

They rolled down Division Street toward town, toward the river, in silence.

Sunny suddenly sat up and pointed at the big, rundown medical center on the east side of the street. "Drop me there."

When Réal pulled into the parking lot, both girls got out. Sunny brushed her hair back with both hands, twirling it into a knot before letting it fall across her shoulders again. All for show, he thought.

Sunny said to Evie, "Text me if you go to the lake." Then she spun off without saying goodbye—or thanks—to Réal.

He was left staring at the bright shape of the open door. Then he leaned across the front seat and said to Evie, "Come on, girl. I'll take you home."

5

Angry silence rolled off him in waves. Evie shrank in her seat.

Finally, Réal said, "You live on Shaun's street, right?"

"Yeah, but at the west end," she said. "Near the cemetery." Then she added quietly, "Sorry we took your car. She told me you gave her the keys."

He made a sound that wasn't quite a laugh. "Don't worry about it," he said.

Evie couldn't think of anything else to say, and he was intimidatingly quiet, as always.

The late afternoon was almost sticky, and a haze had fallen over the streets.

Evie turned to him again. "Do you want to go to the lake tonight?" she asked. "Feels like it'll be warm."

Réal didn't answer, didn't look her way.

"Not just us, obviously."

"Obviously," he said, and then, "Sure. Why not."

They turned onto Evie's street. Shaun's street. It was a long, single lane of rutted pavement and asphalt patches, buckled in the middle, with scrubby grass at the shoulders. One side had all the houses, and the other was just an empty field that had been for sale as long as anyone could remember.

"Did you know Shaun when you were little?" Evie asked.

Réal glanced at her. "Yeah," he said. "Since I was nine. We're in the same grade, but he's older."

"'Cause his birthday's in the summer," she said, watching the field go by.

"Yeah," he said.

Evie could feel him looking at her again. He asked, "How you getting to the lake?"

She looked away from the field, mouth slightly open. She didn't have a car. Shaun had always driven her in his beat-up, vintage green Challenger that, by miracle or more likely by bribe, was legally road-certified. She could still feel its cracked black vinyl biting her bare legs.

"Don't worry, I'll drive," Réal said, reading her mind.

A little ways down the road, Evie pointed out her house, and they slowed, pulling into the driveway. Réal ducked to look through the windshield at her shabby white bungalow, chipped, dark-green trim around windows all shaded with mismatched curtains. She'd have been embarrassed if she didn't know Ré's place was about the same.

He sat back and stretched his arm across the back of the seat, fixing her with the same look he'd had that day outside the gym. Worried. "Is anybody home?"

Evie shrugged. "My mom works nights."

"So you just hang out here all alone?"

"Yeah, except when Shaun—" she started. Her throat closed on the words, but Réal nodded like she'd said them anyway.

He said, "There's supper at my place. I gotta go home anyway. We can just head to the lake from there, if you want."

"Are you sure?" she asked, and he smiled.

"Beats coming all the way back here to get you," he said.

She screwed her mouth up, then nodded once, turning away.

Without another word, Réal threw the Buick in reverse, and they slid out onto the street again, going back the way they'd come. Neither of them mentioned it, but they both knew he was taking the long way home.

❖   ❖   ❖

The yard was a war zone. Toys exploded everywhere. Bikes, skateboards, tools, car parts, muddy boots. Réal swung out of his car and walked right through the middle of the minefield, while Evie picked her way along behind him.

A rusty loveseat swing hung from the porch beams, and more plastic toys were strewn across the deck. Réal held open the door for her. The smell of tomatoes and cooked garlic filled her nostrils, making her stomach kick.

"Come on in," he said, heading down a dim hallway to a large kitchen at the back of the house, where he tossed his jean jacket at a chair and dropped his keys on the table with a *thunk*. He lifted the lid off a slow cooker on the counter, poking around in it with a spoon. "You okay with chili?" he asked over his shoulder. "It's vegetarian."

She nodded, though she wasn't entirely sure she was okay with it, her stomach still uneasy. She stood in the doorway, looking around. There were knickknacks on every surface of his kitchen, painted handprints and photographs stuck on the fridge, a dog bowl in the corner with a radius of kibble spilled around it. Homey and chaotic, just like the yard.

"How old are your brothers?" she asked.

"Uh, Beni's sixteen," he said distractedly, shaking spice into the pot.

"Yeah, I had Geography with him last year," Evie said, remembering the back of Beni Dufresne's head. He had the same thick, dark hair as Réal, though Ré's was clipped military-short while Beni's was grown out, shaggy and wild.

"Oh, right." He nodded. Turning to face her, he leaned back against the counter and crossed his arms over his chest, his legs at the ankles. "So then Ivan. He's fourteen, and Luc and Mathis are eleven. They're twins."

If it weren't for his penchant for spitting *sacres*—those filthy Quebecois cuss words that always peppered his speech—it would be easy to miss that Réal's first language was French. But when he pronounced his brothers' names, *Ee-von*, *Luke* and *Ma-tisse*, his natural accent slipped through.

"My mom really wanted a girl," he was saying.

"So they just kept trying?"

He grinned. "Pretty much. Plus, we're sort of Catholic."

"Oh."

Evie blushed. His grin had made *Catholic* sound dark and mysterious, conjuring images of forbidden things. Mistakes. A picture of Shaun in her kitchen, knotting his fingers in her hair. His lips, his breath. Evie swallowed. She closed her eyes, and tears spilled again.

Réal did nothing for a second, and then he said, "Hey."

He crossed the kitchen, taking her arms lightly. "Hey now." She breathed, then opened her eyes. He gave her a long look before saying anything, then: "*He* was my brother too, Ev."

Behind them, the front door crashed open, and two boys exploded into the hall, shouting at each other. Evie backed away from Réal, into the wall.

She recognized Beni. The other boy was tall and lanky and had the same thick, black hair as the rest of them. Ivan, she guessed, as he ran up the stairs two at a time.

Beni came down the hall, giving them a look as he stepped past into the kitchen. "Sup," he said gruffly.

Evie looked at Réal, feeling like the wall was the only thing holding her up. "I don't think I can eat," she confessed.

"All right," he said, eyes as soft as his voice. "That's okay. You still want to go to the lake?" She nodded. "Okay. Just let me feed my brothers, and then we'll go."

❖   ❖   ❖

R

The lake usually meant Fun. Which usually meant Trouble. Réal was surprised Evie even wanted to go—she seemed way too miserable. But girls were confusing. They always said one thing and meant something else completely. He knew that about them, at least.

Back in the car, her dark hair spilled across her face. He couldn't see her eyes, and he couldn't tell what she was thinking. She just stared out the passenger window as the trees flew by.

"You mind if I grab some beer?" he asked. He wasn't sure if she'd be insulted, being knocked up and all.

"No, that's okay," she said, looking his way at last. She smiled weakly.

"Okay. Cool." He smiled back.

The lake was not far from town, along a tree-lined stretch of old county highway, but unless you were looking for it, you wouldn't know it was there. Locals only. It was shallow and cool, with a sandy beach and a fire pit that had seen its fair share of abuse.

In full summer, it would be packed with kids, but probably not tonight. School wasn't even out yet, exams still a couple of weeks away. But it was a warm night, promising warmer ones to come.

Réal pulled into the liquor-store parking lot. The trick to buying underage was to never hesitate, never look unsure. Also, to not buy like an amateur. Amateurs always bought stupid shit because they didn't know any better. Flavored schnapps or cheap hard liquor. Dead giveaway.

He went straight for the beer. Tall boys, same domestic brand every time, so when the girl rang him through, she treated him like an old regular and never guessed she should have been asking for ID for the last two years—and for the next six months, too, until he was actually legal.

When he got back to the car, Evie was on her cell phone, blue light shining up into her face as she tapped the screen with her thumbs. He got into the car and put the paper bag down between them.

"So is anyone else coming?" he asked.

"Uh-huh," she said absently. He heard the *whoosh* of a text being sent. She looked up from the phone. "Sunny says she has a thing, but she'll come later, with Alex."

"All right," he said, throwing the car into drive. "When's later?"

"I dunno, she didn't say."

Réal chewed his lip. It wasn't that he minded being alone with Evie. It was that Sunny operated on a schedule that took only one person into account. They could be out there for hours before she got there, and she might not even turn up at all. And he barely knew Evie. What the hell would they talk about until the circus finally arrived?

Réal leaned over and flicked on the radio. It scratched and whispered till he found a station. They took the same highway the girls had taken that afternoon. The horizon ahead glowed bright cobalt, darker in the east, with just the faintest starlight poking through. He sat back in his seat and whistled tunelessly with the radio.

Fifteen minutes up the road, he took a right off the highway onto a dirt track that wound through a thick wall of trees, high beams casting wild shadows into the dark. They bounced over familiar ruts and eventually came out onto a wide patch of sandy grass. There were two other cars parked there, but neither was Sunny's.

They got out of the Buick, and Réal put the bag with the beer on the roof of the car. He pulled a folded old blanket from the trunk and tossed it to Evie.

As they picked their way down to the beach, soft voices lifted in the dark. The fire pit was a rusted, burned-out cage of cast iron surrounded by lake rocks. It was full of ash and garbage. He went to it and kicked around. There didn't seem to be fuel, and they hadn't brought any. Probably the same reason no one else on the beach had lit it first. "Whatever," he said, turning away.

Evie shook the blanket out, and they sat on it, a few feet apart. He pulled a tall boy from the bag, crisp sound bouncing out over the water as he cracked it open.

She hugged her knees to her chest, resting her chin on them, and asked, "Do *you* think Shaun was murdered?"

Réal coughed into his beer.

He ran a sleeve over his mouth and looked at her, wide-eyed.

"If it's true, I mean," she continued, ignoring his look. "What Alex said about him being all messed up. Who would have done that? And *why*?"

"It's true," Réal said quietly, remembering the edge of blue light in the grass. "I saw him."

Evie finally turned to look at him. "So you think he was murdered?"

Réal didn't answer. He sat with his knees drawn up, elbows resting on them, beer dangling in his hands. He looked out at the water, though he couldn't see it in the dark. *Maybe tonight isn't gonna be so Fun after all.*

❖   ❖   ❖

E

"Can I have a beer?" Evie asked. He gave her a look. He didn't say it, but she heard it anyway—*what about the baby?* "Whatever," she snapped. "I'm not keeping it."

He shrugged and pushed the bag toward her. "Help yourself."

She lifted a wet can from the package and cracked it open. She'd been drunk once or twice before, but she didn't really *drink*. Not that she didn't have plenty of opportunity—it just didn't interest her all that much. Getting wasted was more Shaun's thing. Shaun's and Alex's.

But she wondered if maybe she just hadn't done it right before. Maybe their way was how you were supposed to enjoy drinking. She chugged back as much of the can as she could, like maybe she'd find something at the bottom that would fix the way she felt inside.

"Whoa," Réal said. "Take it easy."

She laughed, and he laughed too, nervously.

She thought about Alex, how all his close friends had known his big biker secret but her. It was like she didn't really know them at all. Only Shaun. She'd only ever paid attention to Shaun. But what happened to a moth when you turned out the lights?

"Tell me a secret," Evie said. "Something about you that no one else knows."

This time he didn't laugh. He squeezed the can in his fingers, making it crinkle, then drained it and reached for another. "Secrets, huh?" he said.

"I promise I won't tell anyone. It'll be just between us."

"Like your baby?" he asked. "Eye for an eye?"

"Yeah," she said. "Like that."

He was quiet a very long time, turning the fresh can in his fingers.

Then she said, "Oh, come on, you must have *one*."

"I do," he said. "I'm just trying to decide which one to tell you."

"I knew it!" she cried. "You're way too quiet not to have secrets."

He snorted. "Takes one to know one, Evie."

She sighed, disappointed. "Fine, you don't have to tell me," she said, "but I am taking another beer."

"Help yourself," he said again, sounding relieved that she'd dropped it.

This can she drank more slowly. Her skin tingled in the warm night air, and she felt like laughing, though nothing was funny at all. She kicked off her shoes and socks and lay back on the blanket, looking up at the stars.

"Life is so pointless," she said, "when you look at all that out there." She waved her arm across the shimmering sky. Endless, empty…she felt the weight of it all crushing her into the blanket.

"I don't know if it's pointless," he said. "Just…maybe not super important?"

"I thought you were *sort of Catholic*," she said, flopping her arm down on the blanket between them. "What does that even mean, anyway—*sort of Catholic*?"

"It means we're sort of Catholic," he said, defensive. Then he shrugged. "We're half Ojibwe too."

She turned to look at his shape in the dark. "Really?"

"Yeah," he said. "On my mom's side."

"I had no idea." She couldn't think of anything else to say, so she sipped her beer. Finally, she raised a finger and pointed at him. "That's a secret," she said.

He laughed. "No, it's not. I don't hide it."

"Well, how come I never knew?"

"I don't know. You never asked."

"Hello, Réal Dufresne," she said. "Are you by any chance Ojibwe?"

He hissed through his teeth. "Don't be dumb," he said, but he was laughing.

She rolled over and stood up, steadying herself, then walked down to the water's edge. Tipping her head back, she swallowed. The beer was almost warm now. She screwed the can into the sand at her feet and rolled up her jeans. She stepped into the water; it was the exact same temperature as the beer.

"Be careful," Réal called.

She waded in ankle deep, the cuffs of her jeans getting wet. The sandy bottom of the lake was smooth and hard and cold, worn into little ridges by the lapping waves.

"It's beautiful," she called back. She tipped her head to the stars again. The night was thick with them, surrounded at the horizon by a dark, uneven row of trees, their pointed tops biting at the sky. She kicked around in the water, then came back up onto the beach.

"I'm swimming," she told Réal. She pulled her shirt up over her head and shimmied out of her jeans, then swiped the can from the sand, taking it with her back into the water.

"Câlisse," Réal hissed, putting his beer down.

He stood and walked to the water's edge.

"Come in!" she called. "Swim with me." Her laugh echoed across the lake like loon song.

"Evie," he warned, "don't go too deep. Maybe you should get out now?"

"Oh, shut up, Ré," she said. "Just get in."

He hovered on the shore. "*Fuck*," he said.

6

R

Fucking skinny-dipping. Well, not *quite* skinny. He still had his underwear on, but he might as well be naked. The cold water shriveled his balls, and he spat more *sacres* than a priest on Sunday as he dunked into the black, all his muscles clenching.

He couldn't really see where she'd swum to, but he could hear her splashing around, breathing in gasps and bursts. Like a selkie, luring him out.

"Ev, this is crazy." He paddled toward her sounds. The lake wasn't very deep, but you could drown in a bathtub, so they say. Plus, she was drunk. Plus, he was supposed to be taking care of her—how had that gone so south, so fast?

He dove under the water and kicked toward her, breaching at her side. She was floating on her back with an empty beer can in one hand.

"Ev, let's go back," he said, treading water next to her. He didn't see that her ears were underwater. "Evie." He reached for her arm.

Instead of letting him pull her toward him, she did the opposite, pulling her arm toward herself and dragging him closer. She took his hand under the water and pressed his fingers to her belly. She didn't say anything, just kept kicking and looking at the sky. The little bump under his hand was harder than he expected it to be.

Then she tipped upright and suddenly they were face-to-face, skin-to-skin, in the water. He could feel the goose bumps trailing up her waist.

He sucked his breath. "Evie, what—"

She put her mouth on his, cold and wet and tasting of beer. Her breasts pressed against him, and blood-warmth flooded his groin—he couldn't help it. He gripped her slippery body, their legs kicking together.

"Evie," he said, pulling back. "Seriously. This is crazy. Let's at least get out of the water."

Her laugh was like a purr. It was like Sunny's laugh. Did all girls laugh like that? He tugged her gently, and she swam at his side without protest. At the shore, he saw she still had the empty can in her hand. She tipped the water out of it.

They grabbed their clothes from the sand and walked back up to the blanket, then just stood there, not touching, not talking. He had no idea what time it was. Alex and Sunny could arrive any minute, find them soaking wet and nearly naked—and then what? He bent and pulled his jeans on, yanking them over wet skin. She just stood there with her clothes in her hands, shivering.

He looked at her, groin twingeing. What the hell was that kiss? It still lingered on his lips when he licked them. She was so strange. Nothing like Sunny. The *opposite* of Sunny. She was small and soft-edged, and all her cards were covered up. And she was Shaun's, still.

He let his breath out at last. "Do you want to go somewhere?" he asked quietly. He swallowed. Swallowed again. Praying she wouldn't say yes. But she didn't say anything at all.

He stood frozen for another long second, then bent to the blanket, grabbing his phone as he gathered it all up. With one hand, he quickly typed **Lake sucks. Ghosting.**

He slid the phone into his back pocket and reached for her hand. "I'll take you home," he said.

The Buick coughed to a stop along the wooded track between the lake and the highway. *Fuck.* Gas. He'd forgotten about the gas. "Goddamn it, Sunny," he muttered.

He looked at Evie, bundled in the blanket next to him with her feet up on the seat, still not dressed, still not saying anything.

"Are you okay?" he asked. She nodded.

He looked out the windshield to the dark, lit up by headlights. The battery wouldn't last long. He killed the lights.

"I might have to walk somewhere for gas," he said. "Or call someone."

"Okay," she said. "Let me get warm, and I'll come with you."

He sat back and gripped the wheel in both hands. His phone vibrated in his back pocket, and he leaned to pull it out. Two words: **Screw you.** He *tsk*ed his tongue and threw the phone on the dash without replying.

He stared out at the darkness again, no lights at all.

He cleared his throat. Then he said, "I'll tell you a secret." She made no sound, didn't move. "I had an uncle. A great-uncle, like from a hundred years ago. And he...he was a cannibal."

He heard her shift under the blanket. She poked her head out to look at him, eyes big in the black.

He looked at his thumbs, resting at six o'clock on the wheel. "Uncle Chuck. Black Chuck, they called him, after. He was a trapper, way up north. This was seriously last century or something. Anyway, one really bad winter the Windigo got hold of him, and he ate his own daughter."

"Windigo?" she asked.

He took a deep breath. "It's like a demon," he said. "A suffering demon. Fills you with a hunger you can't satisfy. Makes you go crazy for human flesh."

"Seriously?" she said. "I thought you were Catholic."

"And Ojibwe." He laughed, looking at her.

"So you believe in God *and* demons?"

"Most Catholics do, Ev. Anyway, it's a true story. You don't have to believe it, but that's my secret." He shrugged.

She freed herself from the blanket and sat up. "I like it," she said. "Thanks."

He glanced at her. She was still almost naked but no longer shivering, and that squirrelly feeling returned to his belly, his legs. It made his hands tingle. He almost wanted to get out and run, but instead he let her slide across the front seat and put her mouth on his again. This time it was warm.

He reached for her, her ribs in his hands, muscle and bone sliding under the skin. She lifted herself, and he moved from under the steering wheel, pulling her to his lap, heart beating a million miles a minute.

She pushed him back against the seat, arching against him in her underwear, still damp from the lake.

And he was wrecked.

"Evie—" he whispered, shaking.

"Shhhh," she said into his mouth. "I am a suffering demon, making you crazy for flesh."

She leaned, pressing into him, and she was right.

❖   ❖   ❖

E vie thought of Shaun. She thought of his long bright hair curtaining around her, getting in her mouth. She thought of his low laugh, his murmur against her neck, the sweet things he'd say. The dirty things.

She thought of his shoulders working, flexing, pressing into her.

His golden skin.

Evie was crying before she knew she was.

"Hey," Réal said, cupping her cheek in his palm. "Hey, hey." Dark eyes catching her.

She took a shaky breath, pushing back against the dash.

"We can stop if you want," Ré said gently.

"No," she said. "I just need to cry."

He half laughed. "Okay," he said, "that's cool, I guess."

His fingers traced her throat and moved down her skin to her hips, making her shiver again.

What the hell are we doing? she thought. "This is crazy."

"Yup," he agreed, running his thumbs down her thighs, leaving a string of Braille in their wake. "I said that an hour ago."

"Yeah, you did."

She pressed her lips together, watching him as he traced her. She'd never really looked at him before. You just *didn't* look at your boyfriend's best friend. Not like this. Framed in the V of her legs, his plaid shirt open, flat belly crunched in little folds as he leaned back against the seat. Muscle tightly bound under his smooth, dark skin.

His eyes were nearly closed as he watched his fingers move, lashes spread like paintbrushes on his cheeks, full lips making a near-perfect archer's bow.

He was beautiful.

She leaned toward him again, her hand on the seat behind his head. He looked up and smiled a little, then pulled her in, and their mouths met, hers salty-wet with tears.

Then a sudden, bright beam of light raced around inside the car, and a sharp knock hit the glass.

Réal cursed, squinting at the light and ducking behind his lifted arm. Evie shrieked, grabbing for the blanket.

"Everything okay in there, Miss?" a man's voice asked.

Evie shrank under the blanket. When she realized it was a cop, she said through the window, "I'm fine. We just ran out of gas."

"Not what it looks like to me," the cop said, laughing. "Need me to call a tow truck?"

"Nah." Réal's voice was muffled under the blanket. "It's under control."

"All right, then," said the cop, flashing his beam around the car once more. "Better be gone before I come back around."

"Right," Ré said, tense. "I'm on it."

"Sure looks that way." The officer laughed as he walked back to his cruiser.

Evie pulled the blanket down. Ré looked so freaked out that she couldn't help but laugh at him too.

"Oh, that's nice," he said. "Spit all over my face."

"Sorry, it's just…" She shook her head, mystified. "This is not at all what I thought would happen tonight."

"Me neither, believe me," Ré said. "But we should get out of here before he comes back."

"Yeah," she said, reality crashing in as he shifted away from her.

She slid off his lap, and he got out of the car, buttoning his shirt with his back to her while she searched in the dark for her clothes.

They cut through the woods toward the Mohawk gas station on Highway 9, leaving the car and the dirt road behind. He was quiet, marching slightly ahead of her with a stick he fanned back and forth so they didn't walk into anything in the dark. He didn't hold his hand out for her to take, like Shaun would have done.

She said, "Tell me about the Windigo."

"What do you want to know?"

"Well…what does it look like?"

"They're super tall and thin," he said. "Like, skin and bones, with their lips all chewed to shit." He said nothing for a while, crunching onward. Then he added quietly, "Sometimes they have antlers, like stags."

"That's what your uncle looked like?" she asked, surprised.

"Nah," he said. "The spirit isn't the same as the demon. It's way worse."

"How come?" She picked her way along behind him, trying to see in the dark. He didn't seem to notice, or care, when she stumbled.

"'Cause," he said bluntly, "it can get anyone. In your sleep, in dreams. It catches you, and then you're infected. Then *you* become the demon."

"And that's what happened to your uncle? He ate his daughter because of a *dream*?"

"Pretty much," Ré said. "And I mean it that it's a secret, okay? It goes no further." He sounded defensive now. Distant and hard, like whatever spell they'd just been under had completely worn off.

She watched the shadow of his back as he moved, hunched, irritated, and she felt that invisible space rise up between them again. The same space there'd always been. And she knew they were back to who they'd been when Shaun was still between them—strangers.

She let go of whatever tether had been pulling her along behind him through the woods and fell back. He moved away fast, and the night rose up around her, dark shapes and shadows of trees. Her heart thumped in her ears, and she breathed like she had in the lake, staring up at the stars.

Floating just above drowning.

Empty and monstrous at the same time.

Thinking of Shaun.

Seeing him leap from that stupid fire escape a hundred and one times.

She slowed to a stop, letting Réal dissolve into the shadows ahead, the last point of light as Shaun pulled her under.

She fell to her knees, damp earth soaking her jeans. She dug her fingers into the dirt, sticks and leaves crackling under her weight. Tears wet her face. She thought of Shaun's rotten body. Smashed open and pulled apart, so much meat and bone. Not even human anymore.

Her skin crawled cold, the sweet memory of Réal's touch replaced by that picture of Shaun.

Just let me disappear, she thought. Or let the Windigo come get me. That would be better than this.

Feeling nothing would be so much better than this.

7

R

Réal looks down at the leg bones in his hands. They are too long. Not human. He waves them back and forth in the dark, and they tap against the trees, making hollow *tocks* like wooden pipes. He can't see which way to go—there is no light ahead, just the light that surrounds him, dim and gray.

He's lost her somewhere. Swallowed by the black.

He tries to call out, but no sound comes from his throat. At least, not a sound that makes sense. And then he knows. It is one of *those* dreams. The ones he's had since he was little—where he can't move fast enough, where the Bad Thing has already got him.

He looks up from the bones in his hands. The trees shake snow off their boughs with a soft *whoosh*, and then they aren't trees at all. They are deer standing upright, so that the greasy fur of their backs rounds up in matted spikes, their forelegs pointing together, with hooves like sharpened stones.

All the skin is worn off their long, white skulls, exposing tooth and vein, their long antlers reach up like pale fingers. The deer turn to him as one, eyes bulging, white and empty, no irises, their shine bleeding in whispers of light, blurring their pale faces. He tries to scream, but his throat catches, clicks, and he is choking.

Blood-warmth runs down his neck, across the wing of his collarbone, soaking his shirt. He looks down. The front of his clothes is stained dark and dripping. His feet are bloody and bare. He coughs, trying to get up whatever blocks his windpipe. He folds to his knees in the snow.

The deer don't move. They don't come closer, just watch his struggle with their pale eyes. He coughs again, heaving, and up it comes at last. In his hand hangs a lump of bloodied flesh. He stares at it, gasping for breath, bright red slipping through his fingers...

Réal sucked air as he woke, jerking back in the bed and knocking the lamp off the night table. Deer shadows fell over his walls. He gripped the sheet under him, white-knuckled, blinking and blinking until the room slid back into shape, and the demons melted away.

Fuck.

He breathed hard, trying to slow his heart, eyes bulging. He was home; he was okay. He sagged against the cold wall at his back. Relief washed through him.

And then anger.

Why the hell had she done that? Just sat down in the dirt in the dark, and let him go on without her for God knows how long.

He threw the covers aside and swung his legs off the bed. The red glow on the night table said he'd only been asleep a couple of hours.

Before that, he'd just lain on his back and stared into the dark, working his bottom lip between his teeth.

He hadn't even noticed she was gone. And when he had noticed, he had no idea how to find her again. He'd just swung his stick back and forth, calling her name, until he'd tripped right over her and they were both on the ground.

"What are you doing, Ev?" he'd spat, wet earth soaking the seat of his jeans, elbows pointing into the dirt. She hadn't replied. When he'd shaken her, she'd rocked back and forth like she was already dead.

"Evie!" He'd scrambled to his knees, grabbing at her, touching her to see her in the dark. She'd been lying on her side, head in the dirt, hair full of sticks, but she'd been warm, breathing. "Evie, say something!"

He'd gathered her up into his arms, all dead weight and flopping. He'd pinched the skin of her waist. Only then had she gasped and come alive, like a swordfish in his arms. "Don't touch me!" she'd shrieked, thrashing away. "Don't *ever* touch me!"

Far cry, he'd thought bitterly, feeling that sweet moment in the car slipping away.

He got out of bed now and padded downstairs quietly. In the kitchen he drew a glass of water and stood at the sink, looking out the window through the hanging crystal *doodem*—Ojibwe clan animals—that his mom liked to collect. Marten and bear and elk.

The backyard was blue, getting paler with dawn. He could see the shapes of all his brothers' toys scattered across the garden, returning to color. What was he supposed to do? If Evie was gonna be crazy, how was he supposed to take care of her? He swallowed the water, feeling it cool him from the inside.

Part of him wanted to just say, *Fuck it. Fend for yourself. Not my problem.*

But it *was* his problem. It was completely his problem. None of this would have happened if he hadn't fought with Shaun. Hadn't let himself get so damn mad.

He set the water down and raised his fingers to his lips, remembering her lips, remembering her weight on him, her skin and muscle and arch. His stomach tightened. Then he turned and went back upstairs. He dressed quickly and went out to his car, careful to close the door quietly behind him.

Réal took the long way. He hadn't driven past Nan's since the night he'd found Shaun. He came south along the cross street, then turned at the cemetery, coming up outside Evie's a minute later. He parked on the shoulder and sat staring up at her black windows from the driver's seat. The little gable in the attic stared back, empty-eyed.

When he'd finally got Evie home it was late.

They'd still had to walk out to the gas station, but on the second attempt he'd held her wrist so she wouldn't slow them down again. She didn't protest, so he'd fanned in the dark with his other hand, pulling her along like a dinghy.

When they'd emerged into the flickering fluorescents of the Mohawk, they were a disaster. Mud and twigs and little bloody scrapes, Evie dragging her feet behind him. But he hadn't cared what they looked like by that point—he'd just wanted to get home.

And she hadn't said another word. Had just loomed like a ghost while he'd thrown money down for the gas and hauled it, bumping against his leg, all the way back to the damn car. By the time they'd got to her place, he was beat. He'd pulled into the drive, dumped the car in Park and looked at her.

"Need me to come in?" he'd asked.

"For what?"

He'd rolled his eyes. "Not *that*."

She'd blinked, then looked through the windshield. "Thanks," she'd said. "Sorry."

He would have answered, *Don't worry about it*, or *I'm sorry too*, but she'd jumped out of the car before he could decide which.

Just before dawn, he shifted the driver's seat back and leaned into it, crossing his arms and tipping his chin to his chest. He'd gone home angry all over again and lain awake, and then that dream, that mouthful of flesh…

He shuddered.

He closed his eyes and breathed, trying to let it all slide away.

❖   ❖   ❖

E vie dreamed it. The sound of a car. That destroyed muffler. She rolled over, pulling the blankets and drifting back into sleep. Her hair smelled like lake against the pillow. Leafy and wild. Pictures shuffled past and disappeared. Darkness. Réal.

When she woke, the sun was bright and hot, her skin slick with sweat. She sat up, rubbing her eyes. Last night's clothes were flung across the floor, filthy and wrecked. When she saw them, the whole strange night came laughing back. She groaned, stomach fluttering.

She crawled out of bed and went to the window, pulling the lace curtain aside. The window always stuck, thick layers of paint expanding in the heat. She banged it with the heel of her hand and rattled it open to let in cooler air. Across the street, the empty field stretched off into sunshine, the smell of dirt rising with the dew.

Her mouth filled with saliva.

She barely made it to the wastebasket. There wasn't even much trying to get out—only those two cans of beer—but it was enough. She stared at the watery mess, saliva hanging from her lips. *God. When will this stop?* She crossed the short hallway to the attic bathroom and emptied the basket into the toilet, holding back another rotten, half empty heave.

Evie showered and went downstairs. Her mother would have gotten home just after dawn, crawling into bed long before Evie woke.

Evie padded quietly around the kitchen, used to the soft rhythm of the clock, the sleeping silence of the house. When her cell phone buzzed against the breakfast table, she nearly jumped out of her skin.

It was Sunny. **How was the lake?**

Evie stared at the text for a long time before answering, her thumb hovering over the screen. She could tell Sunny everything. Wasn't that what friends did? She could tell her about getting drunk and skinny-dipping and kissing Ré. She could tell her about the car, the gas. About wanting to die.

Fine, she answered back.

Ooh la la, Sunny replied. **Pepé Le Pew said it sucked.**

Evie's chest tightened. Had he already talked to Sunny? Had he told her all about how awful the whole thing was? She almost burst into tears on the spot.

She hesitated again before typing the next message.

Did you tell Sunny about last night?

There was no reply. She took the phone out to the front porch and set it next to her on the steps. She sipped her tea. She waited. The tea went cold.

When the phone did buzz again, she grabbed for it. **Taking the puppy for doggy treats. Should we come get you?**

Evie worried her thumbnail between her teeth. If Sunny knew anything about last night, she wasn't saying yet. **Sure,** Evie typed back.

She stood and went back into the house, dumping her cold tea in the sink. In the living room, she threw herself down on the sofa. She traced the fuzzy red pile with her fingers, watching patterns form under the weight of her hand, catching the light, brighter and darker. She traced a looping letter *E*, with a little *accent aigu* on top.

Then she scrubbed it out roughly with her palm. Pills of dust and sofa fuzz rolled up under her hand, and then one long bright-yellow hair caught the sun. She stretched it out between her fingers. It was perfect gold, like thread from a fairy tale.

It had been almost two weeks since they'd found Shaun's body. She pictured him lying here, legs thrown over the armrest, blond hair spilling across her lap. His blue eyes staring up at her, and that perfect smile, where his bottom lip touched his teeth.

She wound the golden thread around her fingers and tucked it into her pocket just as Sunny pulled into the drive.

8

E "Sup, Evie." Alex nodded from the front seat of Sunny's dad's sedan.

Evie moved to get in the back seat, but Sunny punched Alex hard on the shoulder. "Get in the back!" she shouted.

"Ow!" Alex shot back, rubbing his arm. "What's the matter with you?"

"Boys in the back, girls up front," she said.

"Since when?"

"Since now. Get in the back."

Sunny turned her face from his, discussion over, and he gave her a childish sneer but opened the door anyway. He wore a stretched-out black T-shirt that made him look paler than usual, and his hair fell in his face as he shuffled past Evie. "All yours," he grumbled.

Evie slid into the front seat. "I don't mind the back."

"I don't care," Sunny said. "I want you next to me."

Alex slammed the back door, and they pulled out of the drive.

"Are we going to the Olympia?" Evie asked.

"Where else is there?" Sunny shot back, laughing. She seemed anxious. Or, at least, more electric than normal. She sat too far forward in the driver's seat and tapped the steering wheel, energy barely contained.

Her fingers and arms were decked as always in silver rings and black leather bracelets. Dark-red triangles adorned her nails, making them look like bloody claws.

"You did your hair different," Evie said.

Sunny ran a jeweled talon over it lightly. "I'm trying a thing," she said. "Does it look stupid?"

Normally Sunny wore blunt-cut bangs that hung down into her kohl-black eyes like a mask, but she'd pinned it all back today, and the ends were slick with gel. It looked like a New Wave pompadour. "I saw it in Italian *Vogue*," she said.

"It doesn't look stupid," Evie told her. "Just...different."

"I'm thinking about dyeing it purple. Like, mauve, actually. Lavender."

"That would look really cool," Evie said.

"Yeah?" Sunny's hand went to her head again.

"Totally," Evie said, nodding.

"Cool. Maybe I'll do it. So the lake sucked, huh?"

Evie pricked awake. "What? No! It was fine."

"Yeah, that's what your text said. *Fine*. But what does *fine* mean?"

Evie blinked at her. "It means *okay*. It was fun."

Sunny glanced at her sideways. "Really? 'Cause that's not what Ré said."

"Oh." Evie's heart began to race, remembering it all. "I guess maybe it was a little weird, not having you two there. And then I didn't feel well, so we left."

"Huh," Sunny said. "And what was Ré like? Was he flirty?" She laughed again, a little too brightly.

Just as Evie started to squirm, her phone buzzed in her pocket. She pulled it out.

You okay?

Evie breathed. Ré, finally. She typed back, **Did you tell S??**

Why TF would I do that?

Come to the Olympia, we're there.

She put her phone away. "Ré says he'll meet us there," she said.

Sunny didn't reply.

Alex stuck his head between the two seats. "What?" he shouted. "I can't hear anything back here!"

"Oh, shut up, Alex," Sunny said, pushing his face away. "No one was talking to you."

He shrugged and slumped back into the cushions.

They pulled into the parking lot behind the Olympia and piled out of the sedan. Sunny marched ahead, saying nothing, and Evie started to feel like she was crashing a really awkward date. Alex, as usual, was oblivious.

Inside the café, Réal's brother Ivan sat with a group of skate punks in a booth near the back. If he recognized Evie from his kitchen the night before, he didn't show it.

The skaters all said "hey" to Alex as he went past, and Alex waved his lanky arm back.

"Hey, hey, Tiny Ré," he said to Ivan, who was taller than his big brother by several inches.

They slid into a booth near the front, Sunny and Alex on one side, Evie on the other.

A dark-haired waitress brought menus. "Sup, Holly," Alex said to her.

"Stop being so fucking friendly," Sunny snapped at him.

"What?" Alex reared back as though slapped.

"Just—you're getting on my nerves," she muttered, grabbing one of the menus.

Evie wanted to shrink into the vinyl.

"What time did Ré say he was coming?" Sunny asked her.

"Uh, he didn't say," Evie admitted. *Soon*, she begged.

Everything on the menu made her sick to think about. Frozen or fried or from a box, covered in salt and sauce. *Nothing's good here.* Evie's guts lurched again. She took a breath with her eyes closed, trying to tamp down the feeling.

"God, I'm not even hungry," Sunny said with a sigh. "Get out of my way. I have to pee." She poked Alex in the shoulder until he stood and let her out of the booth.

When she was out of earshot, Evie asked, "Are you okay?"

"Me? Why?" Alex grinned, looking confused. "Do I look fucked up or something?"

Evie smiled back, shaking her head. "No, you look fine. Sunny just seems a little harsh today."

Alex glanced past her shoulder toward the bathrooms and shrugged. "Yeah," he said. "She's kinda always like that."

Evie felt rotten for him anyway. Sunny was right—he was such a puppy. The way he loped around, all limbs, like a baby Great Dane that hadn't grown into his own body yet. He was goofy and cheerful, and maybe not the sharpest knife, but he chased Sunny's heels with total love. That had to count for something, right?

Sunny returned from the bathroom and slid back into the booth. For some reason she'd abandoned the hair experiment, and her blunt bangs were now back where they always were, falling into her dark, pretty eyes. But she didn't mention it, so Evie didn't either.

"Are we eating or what?" Alex finally said. "I'm frickin' starving."

❖   ❖   ❖

R

About the last thing Ré felt like doing was squeezing into a tiny vinyl booth with Sunny. Just like the lake, it used to be Fun. Her toes creeping up his leg under the table, resting where they shouldn't. But he didn't know how to feel now, after last night.

Which was stupid, because the only way he should have ever felt about it was Bad. Alex was his friend, one of his best friends. It had been Shaun and Alex first, and then Sunny, a distant fourth, and only because she was Alex's girlfriend. But you try stopping a hurricane.

So he'd let it happen. A lot.

So. Now what?

What was Evie thinking? What the hell had just happened? Ré licked his lips, remembering hers. He looked out his windshield and across the park behind the Olympia toward the empty band shell.

It felt like maybe only a year ago they'd all been little kids still. Hanging out at the park, doing skate tricks on the hollow planks of the band shell, the sound exploding like artillery through their brains. Shaun skating so close to the edge, not even looking, 'cause he never looked. If he went over, he'd land on his feet. He always did.

Ré looked down at his clenched fists, fighting the sharp feeling in his chest. His knuckles had pretty much healed. So had his face. Why had he even fought with Shaun in the first place? Let himself get that angry? It had been none of his business, and now it was *nothing but* his business. His and no one else's—he couldn't tell Alex about the baby, and he sure as hell wasn't telling Sunny. And anyway, he'd promised Evie he'd keep his mouth shut.

He shook his head. How had Shaun left such a big mess behind? The one guy who never looked, who always leaped, who, no matter what, always seemed dipped in gold—how did *that* guy leave such a mess of a life behind?

Ré felt his throat closing. That painful, humiliating desire to bawl like baby filled his chest. He squeezed his eyes shut and gritted his teeth.

The Olympia's back door flew open, and Ré's armor snapped shut with a bang.

His little brother and crew spilled out into the parking lot. Ré sniffled and wiped his eyes on his sleeve. Lucky Ivan, he thought, no idea whose messed-up life is out there, just waiting to take him down.

He opened the car door and shouted to his brother.

The taller Dufresne ambled over and put his hand on top of the Buick.

"What's up, Ré?"

"Your friend Mark—which one is he?"

Ivan looked surprised, but he turned and pointed at a black-haired kid who was skating away with the others. "In the Ramones shirt," he said.

Ré looked, took note. "You told me once his mom is a healer," he said. "Is that true?"

"Yeah, I guess so. That's what Mark said."

"And his sister too, that waitress?"

Ivan shrugged.

Ré said, "Next time Mark comes to the house, tell him I want to talk to him, okay?"

Ivan shrugged again. "Okay, Ré. See ya."

He threw down his skateboard and mongo-footed back to his friends, gangly limbs all flapping like some kind of freakish bird's.

The café's back door opened again, and it was Alex, at last.

"*Du-fresne!*" he woofed cheerfully when he saw Réal.

"Sup, Janes," Ré said. The boys clamped their hands together briefly.

The girls came out the door behind Alex, and Ré didn't know whose eyes to meet first, so he chose neither. He sat sideways in the driver's seat and waited for them to come to him.

"Where the hell were you?" Sunny asked. The edge was still in her voice, but she sounded tired.

"Not hungry," Ré said, not looking at her.

"No, I mean, *all day* where were you?" Sunny said. "I texted you a hundred times."

He lifted hard eyes to hers. "I said, *not hungry*. I had shit to do. What do you care?"

"Who doesn't have shit to do?" Sunny rolled her eyes.

Ré looked sideways at Alex, raising his brows, and Alex shrugged. *Hurricane.*

"So. What now?" Alex asked the girls. They offered no answers. Sunny just crossed her arms over her chest and looked away.

"Well, ain't this just a peachy way to spend a Saturday?" Alex drawled, leaning back against the Buick and putting his elbows on the roof.

After a pause Sunny said, "Let's go to the lake!"

Evie and Réal both answered at once.

"No!" said Ré.

"I can't," said Evie.

They flicked a look at each other, and Sunny looked at them, eyes wide and then narrow.

"Fine," she said. "If no one wants to do anything fun tonight, then I am going home. You all suck."

She went around to the other side of the Buick and yanked open the door. She leaned down, putting her hand on the seat, and hissed, "Is there something you two would like to share with us?"

Ré just stared at her, mute.

She retreated, lifting her hand, and then she looked down. She rubbed her fingers together, then looked at the passenger seat, eyes going wide again. Ré saw what she was looking at. A fine dusting of lake sand filled the creases in the vinyl.

A second later Sunny whirled away.

"Alex!" she barked. "Get in the car." She slammed the door of her dad's sedan and started the engine like she was kicking a horse.

Alex gave Réal a goofy smile, then loped over to the other car. Evie just stood there, looking abandoned.

Ré looked at her. "I think maybe you should get in," he said, nodding at his passenger seat. "I think we need to talk."

Evie's shoulders fell, but she nodded and went around to the far side of the Buick. She waved at Sunny, but Sunny just threw the sedan in reverse and tore out of the parking lot, grit flying.

"What was that all about?" Evie asked.

Réal shook his head and let out a breath. "You *really* don't want to know."

9

E

"Do you want to come in this time?"

They were parked across from Evie's drive, looking up at the house again.

"Is that okay? Is your mom home?"

Evie looked at her phone. Her mom would be up soon to get ready for work. "It's fine," she said.

She led him into the house and straight up the narrow, steep staircase to the attic.

"Take your shoes off," she said. "It's quieter."

The staircase bisected the attic. On one side was a bedroom with sloping ceilings, on the other a small bathroom. Evie went to the bedroom and sat on the bed. Ré stood in the doorway, looking around.

"Come in," she said. "Close the door."

He did that, then stood in the tallest part of the room, in the middle of a circular rug made of rags.

"So. You want to talk?" she asked.

"Yeah," he said. "We should. About last night, and about some other stuff."

Evie's stomach flopped. She gripped the edge of the bed beneath her and nodded.

"How you feeling today?" he asked, eyeing her. "A little crazy still?" He scratched behind his ear; she suspected he was more nervous than itchy.

She swallowed, looking down at the colorful rag rug beneath his feet. She'd had that rug forever. She used to lie on it and think about all the different pieces it had been made from, all the bigger parts that had been ripped up and twisted into that spiral. Where had they all come from? Did each one have a story, a whole life, before finally ending up as her rug?

"*Ev*," he said.

"I can't talk to you when you're standing over me," she blurted. The distance between them made her anxious, like she was under a spotlight. "Sit down. Please?"

He looked around for a chair, finding one at the desk behind him. But he stepped over and sat next to her on the bed instead.

"Better?" he asked.

"Yeah. Better." She heaved a breath, looking down at her knees.

It was stuffy in her room. It always got too hot in summer, too cold in winter.

"I'm sorry about last night," she said quietly, thinking of Sunny's words. *Pepé Le Pew said it sucked.*

"Are you?" he asked. "'Cause I'm not. Not really." He rested his elbows on his knees and folded his hands, pressing his thumbs together.

She looked at him, the side of his face. His tanned skin had a thin sheen of sweat.

"I mean, I'm not sorry I kissed you," he corrected. "The rest, I don't know."

"I think I kissed you, actually," she said.

He smiled, but still didn't look at her.

Then he said, "The thing is"—and although they shouldn't have, the words hurt before they'd even left his lips— "things are really complicated right now."

"I know," she said, and looked down at her knees again. There was a very fine white scar on her left leg, arcing around her kneecap. "Because of Shaun."

"Not just Shaun. That is fucking huge though." He took a deep breath. When he exhaled, she felt him shake. "Ev," he said, "there is a *whole bunch* of other stuff I gotta think about before I can think about last night."

She thought again of Sunny, how she'd been so angry with the boys earlier, with *all* of them. She thought about how she hardly knew Ré, how he'd always moved on the periphery. Shaun's dark, unknowable shadow. "Secrets?" she asked.

He smiled with just the corner of his lips. "Yeah, secrets," he said. "And, I mean, what about the baby? What are you going to do?" At last he turned to look at her. "I'm not judging in any way. I only want to know how to help you, what I should do."

Evie closed her eyes. *The baby.*

It wasn't even a real thing. Just an alien swimming through her, not connected to anything—not to Shaun, not even to herself. A tiny, distant star inside her that she couldn't even feel. The thought of it just made her sick all over again. She pictured her mom raising a kid alone, sixteen years on, no days off. She thought of Shaun's nan. Of Shaun, abandoned. Evie flopped down onto her side, into the pillows, and covered her face, trying hard not to cry.

Ré did nothing at first. Said nothing. Then he moved, tentative, bedsprings bowing under his weight as he lay down behind her. He wrapped his arm around her, knees up under hers, tucking her into the curve of him and holding her, breathing until they both fell asleep.

❖   ❖   ❖

R

Ré dreams he is wrapped around the rib cage of a large creature whose breath expands through him, pushing into him, pinning him down. It doesn't hurt, but he is unable to break free. He is carried by the creature as it moves across a snow-covered plain. Searching, hungry.

He can't see what lies ahead, only what circles behind— six howling wolves. They are fearless. They lope up through chest-deep snow and sniff the air, then discuss in yips and barks what they have found: a sinner, a killer. And the creature keeps moving forward, ferrying Ré along.

Between the trees, white eyes stare out at him, white antlers move. The creature is taking him to them.

Something takes his hand, curves into him, pulling him closer, and he feels his arm begin to stretch, thinning like gum until his hand falls off completely. Then his other hand goes. His teeth crumble. He collapses, boneless ash, into the snow.

❖   ❖   ❖

E

Evie woke to Ré's crying, the back of her neck damp with his breath. It was the same painful sound as in the car the day after Shaun was found. Sharp, wheezy breaths, a high, rasping whine. She rolled over in his arms to face him, tucking her head under his chin, cheek to his collarbone, fitting herself into him.

Her arm snaked out from under his to wrap around his body and pull him tight against her. She held him as he cried, and he held her, arms closing around her like a soft trap.

❖   ❖   ❖

R

When they woke again, it was dark.

He sucked a breath and rolled onto his back, rubbing his eyes with his fist.

"What time is it?" he asked, voice thick with sleep. She stayed curled up, not looking at the clock. "Ev, I gotta go."

She squeezed her eyes shut. "Okay," she mumbled.

He looked at her, fingers touching her hair. "I didn't mean to stay," he said. "I guess I didn't sleep much last night."

"It's okay," she said. "You're complicated right now."

He laughed softly. "So are you, Ev."

She smiled, tucking into him again for one last moment.

Then she rolled onto her back and stretched out, toes touching the brass rails of the footboard, hands stretching between the headboard rails to touch the wall.

He propped himself up on one elbow and lowered his other hand to her belly. The bump was almost nothing, just a slight rise, a firmness of flesh, but he imagined that what he felt was alive. That it kicked and swam against his palm, a selkie child.

Ré was the first of five sons. He'd touched the pregnant belly of a woman before. But it hadn't felt like this—like strange wonder leaping in his skin.

His heart began to *tap, tap, tap*. His breath became heavy. He knew he shouldn't—there were *so many reasons* why he shouldn't—but he did it anyway: he pushed up the hem of her thin shirt.

His fingers fell to her bare flesh, and the heat annihilated him.

"*Evie...*" he breathed, heart stomping through his throat and his hands and his legs so hard it shook him.

All the things he wanted to say. A tide of secrets ebbed against his tongue, pushing him to speak, to lean down and whisper against her throat. How good would it feel to just tell her everything? To confess it all. Be absolved...

He bit his lips together and closed his eyes.

Fuck.

He pushed away.

Scrambling onto his heels, he scrubbed his hands over his face to wake himself, to break her spell. He felt like he'd been sucking carbon dioxide, breathing her breath until they were both suffocating. The small, hot room was thick with dreams, loosening his grip on things. Like she'd done last night, in the water, in his car—luring him out from reality toward something that felt like *hope*.

"I gotta go," he said, not looking at her.

He crawled over her and opened the bedroom door, desperate for air. He stuffed his feet into the shoes he'd left on the landing, feeling her eyes, big and blue, pinned to his back. But he didn't want to look. Couldn't look. He couldn't stand to see the hurt in those eyes, if there was any—or feel his own if there wasn't. He just had to get away.

❖   ❖   ❖

E

After the roar of the Buick had faded down the road, Evie sat up in bed. She drew Shaun's long blond hair from her pocket and stretched it again between her fingers. In the dim light, it looked fragile white, not gold.

"Can you feel that?" Shaun had asked, low and sweet. Wrapped up here together, under the patchwork quilt, winter sunlight filtering through the curtain. His arm draped heavy around her, his heart beating slow against her ribs.

"Can you feel mine?" she'd asked him back. His laugh was no more than a murmur into her hair.

Can you feel my heart?

As close as she'd ever got to saying *I love you.*

Evie stood and took a journal from her desk drawer. Her mom had bought it for her as a place to keep all the things she'd stopped saying aloud, but she had never really used it.

At first she hadn't lived through anything interesting enough to put down on paper. And then later, when she had, it was nothing that should sit between such pretty covers.

She wound Shaun's hair into a small loop and tucked it inside the journal, replacing the book in the drawer. Nearly a year of her life in one tiny thread.

She went down to the kitchen, flicking lights on as she went. The ticking clock was joined by cricket song floating in through the open windows and, far off, the mournful call of the trains that passed by Nan's.

Her stomach growled fiercely. She'd slept the entire afternoon away and now felt raw and empty. It must have been days since she'd last eaten properly, without everything making her want to barf.

She grabbed a can of soup from the cupboard and dumped it into a pot.

It was Saturday night. Saturday nights used to be for all of them, together. Drinking and laughing in Nan's front room, Nan deaf and asleep upstairs. Or, when it was warmer, prowling along the train tracks, climbing fences. Racing cars at the edge of town.

Tonight, instead, they were scattered. Each one falling away from the next—all the ties that had once bound them growing thinner and thinner.

On the breakfast table was a note from her mom.

Hi, Ev—Car out front. Boy in the attic. Do we need to talk??

Evie folded the page in half and put it back on the table. A pointed thing turned in her gut. She still hadn't really talked to her mom yet. Of course, her mother knew that Shaun was dead. The whole town knew. But even when he was alive, Evie had kept him to herself. She'd never had the right words to explain him to her mother. That was exactly why her mom had bought the journal—to keep her from bottling everything up.

Her mom was always going on about letting in the light, getting some fresh air, seeing the bright side. But what exactly was so bright and fresh about Evie's life? Every chance it got, all it did was hurt—even with Shaun, who was supposedly perfect. And what was the point in talking about that? In writing it down so she'd never, ever forget how much it all sucked?

How could she talk to her mom about a thing like Shaun? Her mom hadn't even known she had a boyfriend when he'd slept two nights out of three in that brass bed upstairs. And now he was dead. Writing it down was never going to change that, and there was no point in talking about it now.

Besides, her mom trusted her—she couldn't work nights if she didn't. And she worked nights 'cause they needed the money. They *always* needed the money. So the sneaking out, the drinking, hopping fences, Shaun...confessing it all now would only break that trust, and that was something Evie knew they couldn't afford.

She slumped down at the table and put her hands over her face. They filled instantly with tears. But she didn't know if it was really Shaun she was crying for.

10

R

Réal avoided the hill on Monday morning. He pulled into the parking lot late and ducked into the school by the side door, racing to class just under the bell. As he slid into his seat, a nagging feeling bit at his gut. He tried to lose himself in the algebra under his elbows, but his gaze kept sneaking out the window, almost like he knew that cop car was going to pull up when it did, right where his eyes had been waiting for it.

Seeing it, though, he swallowed. He inched toward the window, watching the officers stride across the lawn and disappear from view. And when the old black phone on the classroom wall rattled its bell, he just knew it was for him.

The teacher spoke into it briskly, then turned and pointed at him, like the Grim Reaper digging a bony finger through Ré's chest. "Dufresne," he said. "Downstairs. Pronto."

And then everything just lifted right off his head.

He stood up like he was on strings, not saying a word, and marched out of the room.

His ears buzzed and his chest felt like water, like even his organs were abandoning him. But he felt weirdly okay about it all. The sleepless nights, the terrible dreams, the memory of blood and violence. It was all over now. He could breathe again. It was done.

As his feet numbly touched each step down to the main floor, his mind itched to rebel against the strange calm his body felt. He eyed the side door. He could still run. But no. If they were asking for him by name, they already knew everything. It was time, he thought, to face the fucking piper, or whatever it was they say.

His dirty Vans squeaked against the polished hall tiles, announcing him. They were still flecked with Shaun's blood, with his own. Through each little classroom window, he saw faces turned toward blackboards, heads ducked to notes. Exams started next week. And then he would have graduated, been done with this place. If only.

He put his hand on the door to the main office, took a breath and pushed.

Inside was the usual Monday morning chaos. Three kids already lined up on death row—the hard wooden bench that faced the high counter where detentions and suspensions were doled out. He knew the bench well, but not the faces. Just puppies. Fresh meat. They all stared at him with big eyes, the famous Ré Dufresne, tough old dog.

He stepped up to the receptionist's desk, knowing he'd likely be fourth on that bench by the end of this conversation.

She held a finger up as she spoke into the phone in an already exhausted voice. He slid his hands into his back pockets. The room smelled like hot printer ink and cheap coffee. Chemical and poisonous. There was paper everywhere, bright sticky notes, plastic folders, shitty carpet, artificial light. What a place to work.

To his left, past the high counter, he could see the frosted-glass door of the principal's office. Behind it, dark shapes moved like things in murky water. Like the wolves in his dreams, licking their teeth. He closed his eyes. He imagined that he could hear what they were saying about him right now.

Same things everybody said.

Psycho. Sick. Dangerous.

Beni would have to take over being big brother, feeding the kids, making sure they didn't turn out like him. Would he disappear? Would his parents even acknowledge that he'd once existed? Would Sunny, or Alex, or Evie, once they knew? *Fuck.*

The receptionist cradled the phone between her shoulder and ear, swiveling in her chair to reach for something on the floor beside her. When she sat back up again, she had a stack of books in her hands. She held the bundle out to him across her desk, nodding for him to take them. He blinked. His hands reached of their own accord, taking them but not understanding. They were his own.

The receptionist put her hand over the receiver. "You left these in Ms. Markell's class on Friday."

He looked at her, then back down at the books. Was this a joke? What good were these now? He didn't thank her, just tucked them under his arm and kept on standing in front of her desk, waiting.

A second later the principal's door creaked open, and Ré's heart skittered off at a gallop. One blue uniform hovered in the doorway, still in conversation with the others in the room. Réal raised his chin, squared his shoulders, ready for it.

"Réal!" the receptionist snapped, putting the phone back in its cradle. "What are you doing? Get back to class."

Startled, he looked at her again.

"Go," she said, waving him away. "I've got enough to do today without you hanging around."

She took a plastic folder from her desk and went to the high counter. He looked from her to the blue uniform and stepped backward, squeezing the books to his side.

The door behind him opened, bumping him, and someone scuttled out of his way. "Oh, sorry, Ré!" said another round-eyed puppy. Réal barely heard him. He stumbled backward out the open door, into the hallway, breathing hard.

What the hell just happened? Why hadn't they seen him? He looked down at his hands, his books, to be sure this wasn't just another strange dream.

He could hear voices through the office door, and as it opened, he bolted, squeaking around a corner into the closest stairwell and up to the next landing two steps at a time. The officers walked past the foot of the stairs, turning left and away, clicks of their boots getting smaller as they headed for the exit.

Ré crouched against the wall on the landing, heart racing, watching them go.

❖   ❖   ❖

E

"You seen Sunny today?" Alex sat down across from Evie in the cafeteria. He'd turned the chair backward and was leaning over the backrest, stuffing potato chips into his mouth.

"No," said Evie. "You seen Réal?"

"Nah," he said past a mouthful. They both looked down at the open textbook in front of her. "Studying?"

"Exams," she said, shrugging. He nodded, but she could tell he wasn't the slightest bit interested.

He tossed the empty chip bag down on the table, licking his fingers and wiping them on his filthy, sleeveless jean jacket. "Where the hell is everyone?" he asked.

Evie looked up at him again, then around at the lunch crowd. "I don't know," she said. "Last I saw anyone was Saturday. Everyone is being strange."

"Yeah, no kidding," he said quietly.

He was pensive for a moment, like he didn't want to say what he was about to say. Then he muttered, "I miss Shaun."

Evie swallowed and put down her pen. "Yeah. Me too."

"Things are so messed around here without him," Alex said, grasping the chairback and leaning his elbows on the table, arms crossed in an X. "Everyone's acting like such a freak since he died."

"I know," Evie agreed, thinking only of herself.

"I can't talk to Sunny anymore without her yelling at me," he said. "I don't even know what I'm doing wrong. She's just pissed all the time. But what the fuck did I do? I didn't kill the guy. I didn't want him dead."

Evie cocked her head a little as she looked at him. He was talking down into his arms, long hair falling forward. He had a fine dusting of orange cheese powder at the edge of his lips. She said, "Nobody wanted him to be dead, Alex."

"Yeah, I know," he said. "But Sunny's acting like I did it myself or something. Like I had anything to do with it. That guy was my bro, y'know? He was..." His voice trailed off, choked.

"Maybe Sunny's just mad generally? Not at you, but, like, at *everything*?"

"I don't see her yelling at anybody else."

Evie almost laughed. "Really? She seemed pretty pissed at Ré the other day."

He screwed up his lips but said nothing. She could see by his eyes that he was thinking about that, but he didn't look up. Instead he said, "*So* many other people deserve to die way more than Shaun did." His voice was small and hard.

Then he said, "He was only eighteen. That's way too young." He took a deep breath. When he blew it out, Evie could smell his chip breath. Then he laughed, a short, hard laugh, and shook his head. "Know what I'm getting for my eighteenth birthday?"

She didn't know. She didn't say anything.

He looked up at her then, hair falling back from his angular bones, thin smile looking darkly amused. "The family business," he said. Then he laughed like that was the craziest thing he'd ever heard.

Evie stared at him. Could that be true? Did he mean *biker* business? And what even was that besides riding around on motorcycles looking cool, like Charlie Hunnam?

Then Alex leaned forward, patting his chest pocket. "I got some shit that'll bomb you till Tuesday, if you're interested."

Evie coughed and glanced around. "At school?" she hissed.

He just laughed again. Then he shrugged and shoved back, off his chair. "I'm going to the hill. Come if you want," he said.

She stared after him for a second, then stood and gathered up her books, following his bony legs out of the room.

Outside, she blinked in the bright sun, feeling like a total poser. It was not *her* following Alex Janes out to the hill. This was some other Evie. That wild one. Floating in the lake, staring at the stars, waiting for something, *anything*, to come pull her out from the mess of her life.

Alex threw himself down in the grass, shoulders propped against his backpack, and started rolling a joint between nimble fingers, using his T-shirt as a table.

Evie sat next to him, cross-legged, looking down the grassy hill. It was a beautiful day. Summer, officially. She leaned back with butterflies in her belly—what were they doing, getting high on school property in the middle of the day? It was nothing new for him, she was sure. She tried to feel as relaxed about it as he looked.

Alex flicked open a silver Zippo and lit up. Around a mouthful of blue smoke, he said, "D'you know what he was like?"

He licked his finger and spread orange chip-spit along an edge that burned too fast, then handed the joint to her.

"Who?" she asked. She put the thing to her lips and inhaled, choking on the awful taste. She coughed, waving a hand in front of her face like it would help, her eyes instantly full of water. She handed the joint back to Alex, feeling like a complete amateur.

"Shaun," he said, sucking hard and holding his breath for an impossibly long time. Finally, a massive cloud unfurled into the breeze. "Shaun was like Chuck frickin' Yeager, man."

"*Who?*" She coughed again.

"Some guy in a movie about astronauts," he said. He took another haul and passed it back to her.

"Everyone else in that movie got dealt a better hand," Alex explained, lying back and looking at the sky. "But Chuck was the damn best. He shoulda gone to the moon."

Evie just stared, no idea what he was talking about. She passed the joint back.

Alex took it and raised it into the air, making rocket noises, ferrying the burning end across blue sky. Then losing altitude, plummeting to earth as Alex whistled through his teeth. His other hand burst open in an explosion, then fell back to his chest.

He sucked the joint again and passed it back to her. She shook her head no.

"Suit yourself," he said, stubbing it out.

Evie lay back, stretching her legs out in the prickly grass, thinking about Chuck Yeager. She pictured a blond-haired guy doing skate tricks in the sky, laughing down at all of them. Going to the moon, stardust and strands of gold all trailing behind. She closed her eyes, lulled by the sun and the sound of Alex breathing steadily beside her, and she slipped away.

❖   ❖   ❖

"Dude, wake up."

Somebody shook her, pulling her back through the clouds. She groaned, fighting it. When she opened her eyes, she saw Alex leaning over her with a huge grin.

"We slept right through third period!" He laughed.

She sat up slowly, swallowing at the wreck of her mouth. Her whole body felt overcooked. She blinked and squinted in the sunlight. "What time is it?" she croaked. Her throat had never been so dry.

"After two," he said thoughtfully, clasping his hands together around his bent knees. "No point in going to class now."

"I guess not," she agreed.

She couldn't tell if she was still high or just sunbaked. Heat seemed to buzz under the surface of her skin, inside the shell of her ears. Then a bright, sharp pain slid through her skull, and suddenly she was afraid she might vomit.

"Hey, you okay?" Alex asked, peering at her closely.

Evie held her breath, unable to answer.

She stood, wobbling a little, and walked down the uneven hill, blades of grass stuck to the backs of her bare legs, her dress damp and sweaty and clinging to her skin. She stumbled over her boots back down the hill to the parking lot, praying, *Don't puke, don't puke...*

Sleep trailed after her, teasing, wanting her back. She fought to keep her eyes open.

In the parking lot, she found the rusty blue Buick, its chrome shining in the bright afternoon sun. She yanked the door handles, but they were all locked.

"Hey, Ev..." Alex appeared behind her, holding her backpack. "Are you sure you're okay?"

She crumpled against the passenger side of Ré's car, knees folding, butt hitting the pavement.

"Oh shit," Alex said, wide-eyed. "Okay. Stay here. I'll be back. Don't move."

He dropped her backpack at her feet and bolted, leaving her alone on the ground beside the car. She gathered up the bag, hugging it close and resting her head on the bundle. Sleep won the battle swiftly, dragging her back the second her eyes were closed.

11

E

"*Ostie d'crisse!*" It was Ré's voice, low and gruff. Evie's brain swam around the words, trying to make sense of them in her sleep. She felt a gentle hand on her cheek, turning her flushed face up, and another pushing back her damp hair.

"Evelyn," Ré said. "Wake up."

She lifted her hand to cover his and pressed it to her cheek as she leaned into his touch, still dreaming.

"Ev," he said again, pulling his hand away. "You gotta get up, girl."

As he tugged her to her feet, her backpack tumbled from her lap, and they danced over it, her weight falling into him. He propped her up as he opened the passenger door and maneuvered her into the seat.

"Jesus, Alex," he muttered over his shoulder. "The hell did you give her?"

"I didn't do anything, I swear," Alex chirped, hands up. "She must be sick or something."

Réal hissed through his teeth. He closed the passenger door and turned to Alex, raising a finger to his chest. Evie could hear the muffled shape of his voice through the glass, sharp, threatening, but he spoke too low for her to make out the words.

She had never felt so tired in her life. But it wasn't Alex's fault. She wanted to say that, to speak through the glass. She reached for the window button, but the car wasn't running, and the button was dead.

It was even hotter inside the Buick, baking in the sun all afternoon like a kiln. Its sour-milk-and-oil smell knitted itself into her eye sockets. Sweat ran down her ribs, her scalp. Her bare legs burned on the hot seats.

She scratched at the door handle, shoving it open and hitting Ré in the butt. He stepped away, surprised, and both boys turned to look at her.

"I have heat stroke," she said, guessing. "It's not his fault."

She struggled to get out of the car, but Ré was on her in an instant, grabbing her arms again. "Stay where you are, Evie," he said. "I'm taking you home."

"Ré, it's a million degrees in here. And it *stinks*."

Alex snickered, and Ré threw him a look of pure death.

"Fine," Ré said, jaw clenched. "Let's go." He pointed for Alex to get in the back.

"What about Sunny?" Alex asked. "Should we wait for her?"

"I'm not a fucking limo service, Janes," Ré snapped over his shoulder, throwing himself into the driver's seat. He started the car and blasted the AC, but all it did was blow stale, warm air in her face. Evie pressed the window button down and fell back against the hot seat. Glancing at her, Ré snapped the AC off again with a flick of his wrist.

❖ ❖ ❖

Twenty minutes later they pulled into Evie's drive. No one had said a word the whole way. She felt better after the cool wind had blasted through the car, and she was especially glad it had made it too loud to talk. She didn't want the lecture she felt Ré had in him right now. His hands on the steering wheel were tense and white, his glances brimming with irritation.

She shot out of the car without a word, and Ré followed after her, leaving Alex in the back seat. She didn't look at either of them, just went up the steps and keyed open the front door. Ré invited himself in right behind her, and she turned, surprised. "What are you doing?" she asked.

He didn't speak, just stepped past her into the living room and looked around. He seemed to appraise the old rug, the pictures on the wall, the red fuzzy couch, stepping out of himself, out of his anger, just for an instant.

Then he swung it all back on her again.

"What are *you* doing?" he said. "Seriously, Evie. Getting high? With *Alex*? In the *middle of the day*?"

"You're not my dad," she scoffed, chucking her backpack at the foot of the stairs. "Don't tell me what to do."

He shook his head, sliding his hands into his back pockets. "I'm not trying to be your dad, Ev, I'm trying to be your *friend*. You still haven't told me what you're doing about the—"

"Stop asking me!" she shouted over him, not wanting to hear the word. "I'll figure it out on my own. I don't need your pity party."

His mouth closed and his eyes rounded.

"I mean it, Ré," she continued, though she knew she shouldn't. "You barely even looked at me before. And now all of a sudden you're *in* my life, in my head. Making me feel crazy." She choked on the words, throat closing. "I should be thinking about Shaun, because he's dead and he loved me, but instead I can't stop thinking about *you*. So just stop, okay?" She shook her head, tears spilling down her face. "*Please.*"

And there was a moment, a breathless one—just after the words had left her lungs, just before she breathed again. They both felt it, she knew, like a surge of lava welling up around them, squeezing them together, crushing. Réal stood there staring at her, but she could see it burning in his eyes too. Their dark brown glimmered and twitched all over her, filled with the words he wasn't saying.

He pressed his lips closed, his jaw tight.

Her heart punched against her ribs. She wanted to take the words back, but instead she just stared at him, swallowing hard.

Then he breathed, finally, and his shoulders dropped. His eyes fell away to the floor. "I'm sorry," he said quietly. "If you want me to leave you alone, I will."

Her voice wavered. "I don't know what I want," she admitted. "I'm so confused."

He laughed, low and gruff, like he knew exactly what she meant.

She watched him run his bottom lip between his teeth. He shook his head, and she followed his gaze out the front window. Alex had moved from the back seat. He was leaning against the Buick, waiting, hands stuffed in his pockets.

"I'm sorry," Ré said again.

He stepped toward her, and her breath caught. He pushed past her in the narrow doorway; she could smell the soap of him, the skin, the salt, his jean jacket sliding across her bare arm, his body heat. All her senses pulled in his direction, a tide to the moon. He threw open the screen door and took the steps two at a time.

Alex jumped to attention when he saw Ré coming. The boys said nothing to each other as they moved to get in the car, but Alex glanced back at Evie once, his face a question mark.

She watched them pull out of the driveway too fast and disappear in a blink at the end of the road. The sun was still high, but the afternoon had cooled a little, and shadows stretched across the empty field. She felt like she could smell the dirt hiding under its yellow grass, but it was probably just her imagination, senses already running too high.

She walked out onto the porch, locking the door behind her, and went down the steps. She turned in the direction the boys had gone, but at the end of the road she went north, toward the cemetery's scalloped white gates.

As she walked past all the old gray headstones, a breeze followed, high up in the trees, making yellow sunlight dance in the grass under her feet. At the end of a row of flat plaques set in the ground, she found his, fresh and tidy, a wreath of plastic flowers standing sentinel on wire legs.

The police had scraped Shaun's body from that field, even though, according to the boys, there was hardly anything left to call a corpse. Evie didn't even know if he'd had a funeral. None of them had had the courage to go back to Nan's house yet, and so no one had asked when—or *if*—one might even happen.

And if there had been a funeral, Evie wondered, had his mother come? Had she been sober enough to know, or selfless enough to care, that her own and only son was dead?

She ran her fingers over the stone. *Shaun Phillip Henry-Deacon, Beloved Grandson.* Just shy of nineteen. Evie couldn't imagine that he was just dirt now. All that light, all that spark and shine. It seemed impossible.

The small plot was covered with a strip of fresh sod, like a fuzzy green blanket tucked over him. She peeled the edge back and dug her fingers into the soft, wet earth below, squeezing it between her fingers.

She remembered all of them, last Halloween, climbing the fire escape at the Grains. Shaun boosting her till she'd caught hold of the rough, rusty bars that had flaked under her grip as she dangled and kicked. She'd followed the ladder up into the dark sky, the abandoned building's eerie black windows spurring her upward.

Halloween in Cold Water meant a dance and a bonfire in the park by the river, a DJ in the band shell and fireworks that lit the night sky. From the top of the Grains, you could just see their colors glow. Brilliant, bright sparks and smoke rising, faintly screaming and fading away.

Sunny, Ré and Alex had lined the roof already, feet dangling over the side, all looking west toward the fireworks. Far below them, Evie saw long, parallel lines of moonlight on train tracks curving off in both directions. The drop had made her shiver.

She'd lowered herself onto the ledge next to Ré. His backpack was full of beer, and as he handed her one, his fingers had brushed hers. It was the first time she could remember actually touching him. His skin was warm, and his eyes had flicked up to hers, surprised but unreadable. They'd both looked away quick.

Then Shaun had thrown himself down on her other side, charging her shoulder, teasing her balance. He'd pulled the beer from her and pressed her hand to his thigh. It had become habit by then, the feel of him under her fingers. His crash at her side. That fear of falling. On the roof of the Grains, on top of the world, he'd said low to her, "I'll never ever let you go."

Remembering those words, and the feel of his living body, she squeezed the dirt in her hands till it crushed between her fingers. Is it still true? she wondered. Are you still here? Up on that roof or in my bed still? Or are you just *here*, in this dirt, and gone?

She hadn't meant to get drunk that night, but the cold air and the fireworks, that rusty old rooftop, Shaun and Alex cracking dirty jokes. The surprise in Ré's eyes. It had made her drunk already. Drunk on them—Sunny and the boys.

After the fireworks, they'd all thrown pebbles into the sky, trying to hit the rail containers. Ré had won. *Bang.*

"What would you do?" she asked Shaun now, lying back and looking up through the trees over his grave. Puffy, white clouds floated through a jagged patch of sky. Her hand was wet and filthy, black half moons under her nails. She rested it on her belly, trying to feel whatever it was Ré had felt two nights ago, right before he ran out of her room, scrambling to get away.

"What would happen," she asked again, "if I chose Réal now?"

She thought of Shaun's mother, choosing herself over her son, weakness over blood. Would she be doing the same thing—abandoning Shaun?

That night on the roof, she'd been spilling with love for all of them. She'd gotten drunk on them, climbing that rusty fire escape to the highest point of their whole lives. Opening herself to the endless, exploding sky.

"Don't get much better than this," Alex had said, holding Sunny's hand.

And maybe he was right.

Because getting back down had been a lot harder than getting up. Getting down had been climbing over the edge and seeing just how far there really was to fall. Trusting that the bolts would hold. That you'd make it back to earth in one piece.

And even when you'd safely reached the end of the escape, you still had to jump the last ten feet into glass and garbage and cracked concrete.

Shaun had been the first to go over. And when he got to the end and the ladder ran out, he'd just let go, trusting. Maybe, she thought, instead of climbing down, they should have all just jumped that night, right off the roof into the black.

12

R

"What the hell were you thinking?" Ré snapped. All his feelings bubbled over as soon as he slammed the car door. If he couldn't get mad at Evie, Alex would take the brunt.

"Aw, come on, Ré," Alex sighed, shaking his head. "Nobody twisted her arm."

"Yeah—but that super-loud hydro shit you smoke? That would knock a fucking elephant on its ass!" Ré knew Alex was right, but he couldn't let it go. He was almost shouting, foot heavy on the gas like the car would do all the fighting he felt like doing right now.

Alex smirked out the window. "Dude," he said quietly, "did you just call Evie an elephant? That's harsh."

Réal hissed a string of *sacres*, but as he turned his face away, he couldn't help but grin.

"Seriously, Ré," Alex continued. "Why are you so pissed off? She knew what it was. So she got hella stoned. It's not the end of the world."

Ré sucked his tongue against his teeth and said nothing. What could he say—that he was worried about the baby? Worried about the choices she was making? Half the time, he felt like Evie was screaming out to be taken care of, and the other half, she was screaming at him for actually doing it. He didn't have a clue what she really wanted.

He squeezed the wheel in his fists, trying to keep her words from turning the car around and pulling him right back to her driveway. *All of a sudden you're in my life, in my head. Making me feel crazy...I can't stop thinking about you...*

He felt the same: crazy. He should be thinking about a thousand other things, a hundred thousand, but all he could think about was her.

That moment right after she'd said those words. Staring at each other, half scared. Heart beating sticks around his ribs. He'd wanted to just step forward, slide his fingers into her hair, pull her mouth to his, taste her tongue against his own.

What the hell is happening to me?

He thought, Am I cursed to only fall for my best friends' girls?

He ran a hand over his face, pulling these thoughts away.

"Hey, Alex," he said, glancing sideways.

Alex shifted to look at Ré, cheekbone propped on his fist, elbow resting on the door. "What's up, man?"

Réal swallowed hard. "I, uh, gotta tell you something." He squeezed the wheel again, biting his lip. His eyes darted over the road, looking for a way to *not* say what he was about to say and not finding one.

When he spoke again, his voice was thin.

"I was with Shaun the night he died."

The silence that hung between them transformed. It became full and heavy and curious. Alex said nothing, but his mouth opened a little, his eyes narrowed.

"I beat the living crap out of him," Ré continued. "And he near busted my nose." He glanced at Alex again to see if the image would register—those Irish sunglasses, his nose all scabbed and bloody. It did.

"Why?" Alex's voice was just a breath.

"That's a long story I can't tell you," he said wearily. "But the thing is, he was alive when I left him at Nan's. Beat up, but no worse than I was."

"So what happened?"

Réal's chest crushed. Alex's face was as hurt and confused as a dog's smacked by its master. Réal swallowed and shook his head, choking the words out. "I don't remember. I left him, I drove around, and then—"

He gripped the wheel tighter to keep his hands from shaking. All the nightmares. The creatures. The lump of flesh in his throat…His mouth filled with spit, like he might puke, but he swallowed it back. "And then nothing," he said.

Alex slowly pushed his long legs straight, spine pressing back into the vinyl seat. As Ré's words took hold, Alex's hands curled into fists. His voice, when it came, was reedy and desperate. "Are you fucking telling me *you* killed Shaun?"

"No, man!" Ré said, though it wasn't very convincing. "I'm telling you I don't know what happened. I can't remember anything past midnight."

"*JesusFuckingChristRéal!*" Alex cried. "When were you going to share all this?"

"I'm doing it now, aren't I?" Ré snapped.

Alex breathed out hard, looking away. Silence. And then, "That is messed, bro. That is—"

"You think I don't know that?" Ré shouted. "You think I haven't been *killing* myself the last couple weeks? Like I'm not sitting here just waiting for red lights in my mirrors?"

He glanced again at Alex, his voice almost pleading now. "I really, *really* wish I could, man, but I can't remember a goddamn thing."

Alex shook his head, letting a long breath out between tight, thin lips. His skinny body, normally so loose and relaxed, was suddenly a sharp shape, digging in everywhere it touched the car. In an instant, his puppyness had gone. Next to Ré now was a knife.

Réal's mind spun with images of sharpened hooves. Of deer skulls moving through trees, empty eyes spilling sightless white light.

The chunk of chewed flesh in his hand.

The Windigo.

Réal stomped on the brakes and yanked the car to the side of the road.

He threw open the door and leaned out, puking his guts into the dust. He heaved and clenched, all his muscles convulsing, trying to force up every single thing he'd ever eaten in his life, trying to get it all out, trying to cleanse.

Alex slammed his door behind him and walked away from the car, fists clenched in his coppery hair.

Ré breathed hard, ragged breaths, eyes bulging at the dirt. Tears streaked his cheeks, and silver threads of snot hung from his nose. He leaned his forehead to his arm on the car door and wept.

He hadn't meant to lose it in front of Alex like this. Of all of them, Ré had it the most together—he was *never* the bombed-out mess or the reckless idiot his two best friends were. He was always in control. Or, at least, he used to be. Now he wasn't sure what he was. Just some blubbering, vomit-covered loser whose life was totally falling apart...

For a moment, he just sat there, trying to get hold of himself.

Then he ran his sleeve over his face, wiping the tears and snot away. His breath still shook, but it had slowed. He sat back, leaning his head against the headrest, and stared out the windshield. Alex stood a few feet in front of the car, his long fingers clasped together behind his head. Wobbly, hand-painted letters stretched between the shoulders of his dirty denim vest. *Buried Alive*, it said. *Fuck.*

Ré banged his fist on the horn once, then signaled for Alex to get back in the car.

"Come on, man," he said, voice thick and weary. "There's something I gotta do."

❖   ❖   ❖

Cold Water wasn't that big. Two main streets that met in a T, with the Ohneganohs River cut right through the middle, dividing east from west. Shops and some apartments lined those streets, feathering out into tall Victorian-era houses and pre-fab sprawl the farther it all got from the river.

There was a ridge along the western edge, with a private woodland and a fancy boys' school. Stretching off to the east were mostly farms and factories. There just wasn't a lot of ground to cover, not that many places to hide.

How hard can it be to find one little kid?

There were some pretty fancy houses on the west side of town—people there had *money*—but a friend of Ivan's likely wasn't one of them, so Ré stuck to the east end. The tracks, the park behind the Olympia. All the places he and Shaun used to hide before they'd scrounged up the money for cars and the world had opened wide.

Not much had been said between him and Alex after he'd barfed all over the road. Ré had dropped him at Sunny's house and didn't wait for her to open the front door.

Finally, just as the sun dipped to the western ridge, throwing gold and black all over the patched pavement, Ré spotted him. That kid Ivan had pointed out. *Mark*. He was skating the parking lot at the boarded-up Dairy Lakes under the bridge with six or seven other kids Ivan's age.

Ré swung the car around and pulled into the lot, suspension bouncing like a show pony, kids leaping out of the way like bowling pins.

Even though some of them had known Ivan for years—and by association, his older brother, Réal—they still looked a little scared when he leaned out the driver's window.

"You," he said, pointing to the kid he was after.

Mark looked up through his thick, black waves of hair. "What's up, Ré?"

"Get in the car. I gotta talk to you."

He glanced at his friends. "Why?"

Ré said, "Come on. I won't bite."

Mark threw another look at his friends, who shrugged or stared, eyes round. He kicked up his skateboard, grasping it by the trucks. In a pinch, Ré knew, it was a pretty solid weapon, but Mark wouldn't need it. It wasn't going to be *that* kind of conversation with Ré Dufresne.

Ré backed out of the lot the second the passenger door slammed, wheeling around onto the street again and back down toward the docks.

"What's up, man?" Mark repeated, flicking the hair out of his eyes. He gripped the "oh shit" handle in one hand, the other wrapped around the nose of his skateboard. As always, Ré drove a little too fast.

"I got a problem," Ré said. "And I think you can help. But I need to know if I can trust you."

"Okay." Mark sounded surprised, nervous. "You can trust me," he said.

They swerved to avoid a pothole, jostling Mark in his seat. Ré saw him squeeze everything a little tighter. "I mean it, man," he warned. "What I'm going to tell you, it cannot get out."

"I swear, Ré." Mark's voice was soft. "I swear on my life."

Réal just shook his head. *Kid doesn't even know what that means yet.* He looked back at the road and sighed, shoulders sagging a little.

Then he spoke. "Ivan told me your mom is a healer, a *Midewikwe*. Is that true?"

Mark just shrugged.

"And your sister, Holly?"

"Yeah, I guess so," Mark said. "Why?"

They'd reached the end of Mill Street, and Ré nosed the Buick through the rusty gates and out onto the dockyards, going slower now, dust kicking up all around them, stones pinging off the belly of the car. He squeezed the wheel in both hands. "So what about you?" he asked. "Are you a healer too?"

Mark opened his mouth, but nothing came out. He blinked at the road ahead.

"'Cause I got a problem," Ré went on. "I need a *Midewikwe*, but I can't talk to your mom. And I can't tell your sister. And *you* can't either." The ropy muscle standing out on Ré's bare arms suggested what might happen if Mark told anybody at all.

Mark was silent for a minute, and then he shook the hair from his face again, half glancing at Ré. When he spoke, his voice was low. "Yeah, man. I can do it. What do you need?"

The road ran out beneath them and Ré slowed to a stop, throwing the car into Park and turning it off in one well-worn action. He got out and walked around to the front of the car, leaning back against the hood. After a second, Mark mirrored him, leaving the skateboard on the seat.

Réal glanced at the younger boy, folding his arms across his chest. He still didn't feel ready to say it out loud. To make it real.

"If I tell you this," he said very quietly, "and you tell a single soul, I swear to God I'll fucking kill you, man. I'm not even joking." Mark stiffened at the words, and Ré continued. "And I will know it's you, 'cause you will be the only person on this good earth who knows what I'm about to say."

Mark held up his right hand. "I swear, Ré. Not a word."

Réal took a deep breath. He looked out over the black river toward the empty pier on the other side, sunlight sliding away into evening. The boy's oath didn't feel nearly rock-solid enough. But then again, he wasn't sure anyone's would, and he was clean out of options. He couldn't just keep waiting for the clock to run out. For the police to puzzle it all together. For the thing inside his soul he knew was coming for him.

"Okay," he said at last, voice dropping, eyes falling to his blood-dirty shoes. "Tell me what you know about killing demons."

13

Early summer heat pressed heavy in Evie's attic room. The smell of dry wood pricked her lungs like a sauna. It was way too hot to study. At least, that was her excuse. Exams were just days away, but she pushed her books across the desk and leaned back in her chair, sweat sticking the whole room to her skin.

She stared at her phone. It hadn't buzzed in days.

She hadn't seen anyone at school. Well, she'd *seen* them, of course, but they had seemed somehow to dot a faraway horizon, disappearing as soon as she approached. Their absence stuck in her mind like grit in a shoe, small but impossible to ignore.

She picked up the phone and clicked open her contact list. Ré's number, of course, was at the top. *Dufresne.* She stared at it miserably. If she called him now, would he even answer? They hadn't spoken since she'd yelled at him in her living room, days ago. He'd made himself just as invisible as the rest.

And that was what she'd asked him for, wasn't it?

She scrolled through the numbers, *Henry-Deacon, Janes* and finally *Seong*. She hit *Call*. Sunny answered on the second ring.

"Whoa," she said. "Actual phone call. Must be serious."

Evie laughed. "No, not serious. Just bored. What are you doing tonight?"

"I have a thing until eight," Sunny said, sounding disinterested. Evie pictured her examining her perfectly painted-black fingernails as she spoke. "But I could come get you after, if you want."

Evie glanced at the clock beside the bed. That still gave her two hours to kill, but it was better than cooking in the attic all night with nothing but homework to do. "Perfect," she said. "See you then."

Evie hung up, but she kept staring at the phone. Her heart turned slowly, a dark feeling seeping out around the edges. She thumbed through the numbers again, back up to the top. She swallowed at the lump in her throat, then dialed.

This time there was no ring at all, just a voice. Rough and sweet and familiar. Her heart skipped at the sound.

"Hey, you've reached Shaun. Leave a message."

Her breath caught. It hadn't occurred to her before that the number would still work. That it might trap his voice like a bug in a bell jar. No one used phones anymore—at least, not as phones. She couldn't remember the last time she'd actually called him, even when he was alive. Phone calls, like Sunny had said, were only for serious things.

She'd forgotten the sound of his voice, the way he drawled a bit, stretching *hey* and *Shaun* out from the back of his mouth, giving the words a lazy, friendly tone. It was mostly affection. None of the others spoke the way he did, the way she imagined surfers talked in California, mixed with a little backwoods Brad Pitt. But no one questioned it either. It was just Shaun. Just the way he was.

The voice mail beeped in her ear, snapping her back to the attic. She pressed *End* and dropped the phone to her lap. Nothing left of him is real, she thought. Just pictures on Facebook and voice mail that no one will ever check again.

She pushed her chair back and went to the window, pulling the curtain aside. If she leaned her cheek to the frame, she could just see the patch of uncleared land at the edge of the yellow field. Nan's place was beyond it, hidden from view at the far end of the road. Was his phone still there? Did Nan even know how to use a cell phone? The idea made Evie strangely sad.

A picture of his room, the disaster of it. Pale-beige water stain blooming across a corner of the ceiling, clothes on the floor, peeling posters, broken skateboard decks. And at its center, Shaun turning to grin at her, embarrassed, pulling his earlobe, his other thumb hooked to his jeans. His toast-and-honey drawl: "It's kind of a mess."

He'd once told his story about Nan walking in on him in bed with a girl. It had sounded so implausible, just an excuse to talk about sex. But after she'd seen his room, she wasn't surprised that Nan hadn't noticed the girl in the ruins. The place was like the crater of a blitz bomb. Evie's own little attic might have been small and cold all winter, and too hot come spring, but it was sure better than Shaun's room.

But still, some of the best nights of her life had been at Nan's. In the front room, all of them together. Sunny lounging her long bones in Alex's lap, swinging her hair and laughing her bright, pointy laugh. Ré as slouched as the faded chair he sat in, looking dark and moody as always. And King Shaun, of course, holding court.

To think of Nan's place now, empty and still, was just too painful. Like swallowing something jagged that scratched all the way down.

❖   ❖   ❖

Three hours later Sunny pulled up to the house. She leaned on the horn for an obnoxiously long time, forcing Evie to leap down her front stairs so the neighbors didn't shout out their windows.

She threw herself into the car, breathless. "God, I didn't think you were coming!" she said. "What took you so long?"

Sunny threw the car into reverse and backed out of the drive with the same mighty confidence she'd had with Ré's car. "I told you," she said. "I had a thing."

"You always have a *thing*," Evie said, clinging to the passenger door and her irritation.

Sunny shrugged. "I'm a busy person. Besides, what else were you doing tonight?" She whipped a cold smile at Evie that pushed her down in her seat.

Evie wondered what bug had crawled up Sunny's butt and died, but she said nothing, just counted streetlights as they went by.

"Earth to Evie!" Sunny snapped impatiently. "God, you're so spacey, Ev. Seriously, if you don't want to talk, why did you call me?"

"Sorry," she said. "It's just been kind of a weird week."

"Yeah," Sunny agreed. "Tell me about it." But neither of them said anything more.

Sunny drove toward town just a little over the speed limit. It was a bad habit every local shared—knowing the roads too well. Letting their shapes unfurl beneath the wheels, curves and dips and hidden stops as familiar as old gloves. Evie pitied the rare tourist who found himself a car length ahead of Cold Water drivers like Sunny, her high beams up his tail, insistent, annoyed, shouting, *Go faster.*

On the south side of the highway, just before town, a flat-roofed strip mall stretched out. Its faded fluorescent-lit signs twitched and flickered, though the shop windows were mostly dark. The parking lot was empty, just a handful of cars catching red lights off the Chinese restaurant at the far end of the strip. Sunny pulled in, parking in front of the late-night pharmacy.

"I gotta pick up a prescription," she said. "You coming in?"

Evie shrugged. "Sure."

There was a nicer pharmacy on Hope Street, just across from the Olympia. It was homey and well stocked, with leaded windows lit by string lights. Its aisles were filled with the plastic-vanilla scent of decorative candles, more like a gift shop for the unwell than an actual drugstore.

This place was its opposite. Dingy and medicinal, with cold fluorescent lighting. Dust bunnies huddled under the shelves, awaiting extermination. Evie followed Sunny inside, but the other girl took off toward the back with a speed that said she didn't actually want the company.

Instead of chasing her, Evie wandered the aisles, poking through bins of cheap chocolate and tubes of sunscreen, the bright lights making her feel as faded as an old photograph. It was nearly closing time. She and Sunny were the only customers, maybe the only ones in hours, but the girl at the cash didn't once look up from her magazine.

Evie ran her fingers over plastic pots of eye shadow, lip pencils and rows of nail polish that looked like bright, bottled candies. A whole wall devoted to making women more enticing, lips and eyes like fishing lures twisting in river water. Masks to hide behind. Evie flicked a glance in the shop girl's direction, then slid a twenty-dollar lipstick into her shirt pocket.

"Christ, let's get out of here," Sunny said, stuffing a small paper bag into her fringed purse and pulling Evie along with her momentum. "This place is like a fucking zombie movie."

Evie smiled at the girl behind the cash as they sailed past her. "Thanks," she said.

14

Sunny parked behind the Olympia. A single streetlamp threw faded yellow across the parking lot and into the trees. It was barely enough light to see by as the girls picked their way down the cement steps into the park.

At the band shell, Sunny jumped up, swinging herself easily onto the stage. Evie was too short for that route and went around to the stairs at the side. She crossed the wooden planks and sat next to Sunny, her fingers gripping the edge of the stage.

Sunny had been tight-lipped all evening, which was not like her. She was never short on words like Evie was. But unlike Evie's long silences, Sunny's appeared to work furiously below the surface. Words seemed to boil under her tongue. Evie could almost hear them lining up to be said.

When Sunny did speak, her voice was as hard-edged as her limbs.

"What's going on with you and Ré?"

Evie's mouth turned to glue. "What do you mean?"

"I don't know," Sunny said, sounding like maybe she did know. "Seems like you guys are all super tight or something now."

"Oh." Evie looked down at her bare legs. She could smell the sweetness of the stolen lipstick on her mouth—it tasted like cake.

Sunny kicked her feet impatiently, boot heels smacking the wooden facing of the stage. She jutted her chin toward the park. "I don't think you know him as well as you think you do," she said. "That's all."

That dark feeling seeped into Evie's chest again. She wanted to ask Sunny how well *she* thought Evie knew him. But she didn't speak. Sunny had been friends with Réal a lot longer than she had, and maybe she was right. Maybe Evie didn't know him at all.

Sunny's long hair shook as she spoke, hiding her eyes. "He was with Shaun the night he died. Did you know *that*?" Her words were full of defiance and challenge, but they showed surprise too.

Evie looked at the side of Sunny's face, trying to pick out the meaning behind her challenge. "I knew," she said.

Sunny looked at her, lips pressed tight. Her eyes seemed to flick all over Evie's face and arms, making Evie shrink behind the lipstick. Then she turned away, long hair hiding her face again. "See what I mean?" Sunny muttered. "You're all tight now."

Evie expected Sunny's voice to throw the knife it always carried, but instead it was a strangled, hurt sound, laced with envy. Totally un-Sunny.

Evie sighed, looking away from her.

Inky trees blurred the edges of the star-pricked sky; dull purple light shone in the streets beyond the river. It was a warm night, and they weren't alone in the park, but Evie didn't know the other voices floating in the grass, and they didn't call out to be known. "Sunny," she said, "Shaun is dead. My boyfriend, Ré's best friend, is *dead*. Ré and I kind of have a lot in common right now."

"So what happened at the lake?" Sunny asked, with just the edge of the knife. "He's been weird ever since then."

"Weird how?" Evie asked. Ré had never fallen asleep in her bed before. She'd never held him while he cried. Evie didn't know what to compare that to.

"I don't know, like he's avoiding us or something. He never answers my texts anymore." Sunny shook her head and looked down at her jeans. They were dyed ombré, fading from black to pale gray the farther down her long legs they got before disappearing into her beat-to-shit biker boots. Evie pictured her on the back of a motorcycle, a Valkyrie in black leather.

"Do you love Alex?" Evie asked.

"Why do you keep asking me that?" Sunny snapped. "What does it have to do with anything?"

"I just—" Evie hesitated. She pressed her lips together. "I never told Shaun I loved him."

Sunny stared at her, saying nothing. Then she looked away and said, "You don't have to feel guilty for that, Ev."

"That's the thing," Evie told her. "I don't. Not for that."

Sunny looked at her again, waiting.

"I never told him," she said, "because I never really felt it." She thought of Ré's hand on her belly, of the look in his eyes before he'd run from her bedroom that night. "I didn't know what it was supposed to feel like," she said. "And I didn't want to get it wrong."

"Well, Shaun loved *you*. He wasn't worried about getting it wrong." There was a sneer in Sunny's voice, like Evie should be more grateful.

Had he really loved her though? It might have been close to love, a cousin of love. It was huge and bright, and it had burned away the person she was before he came along. But was that *love*? Or was that just Shaun being the white-hot center of everything, like he always was? It had never been Us Against the World, Love Conquers All, blah, blah. The truth was, everyone close to Shaun was just a bit player on *his* stage, and they all knew it.

And that's why she'd never said *I love you*. Because Shaun had never *really* loved her. He'd never stepped outside his own spotlight long enough to love anyone but himself. He'd simply cast her in a role. He'd *chosen* her.

Evie squeezed the wooden planks beneath her legs. "No, he wasn't worried," she said quietly. "But he *was* wrong."

Sunny scrambled to her feet and stalked away from her, stomping her boots. She stopped and whirled back. "What are you trying to say, Evie? That your whole thing with him was just *bullshit*?"

The curve of the band shell grabbed her voice and threw it across the open park. There was laughter in the dark from where it landed, and other voices threw it back, mocking her: *"Yeah, Evie, is that what you're trying to say?"*

Evie sighed. Of course, she knew how they all felt about him. How they looked up to him, and how much it must hurt to hear that she didn't feel the same way. It was like admitting that she was a fake. That she'd never really been part of their tribe.

She lay back against the boards and folded her fingers over her belly, legs dangling over the side of the stage. The inside arc of the band shell was painted sky blue with wobbly gold stars spattered across it, but in the dark it was all just gray. "I hate this town," she said, staring up at it.

Sunny shifted but said nothing.

"I *hate* being poor," Evie continued. "My mom works all the time, and we still have nothing. And my dad barely stuck around to help her out. But you know what? They were in love too once. And maybe they didn't think they were getting it wrong, but they sure as hell were."

Tears slid from the corners of Evie's eyes down into her hair. She blinked them away, keeping a steady gaze on the painted sky. It wasn't exactly self-pity she was feeling, though she couldn't quite name it anything else.

"I don't want to get stuck here my whole life," she said. "Living in a shitty house at the ass end of town, just like my mom did when Dad ran out." Evie closed her eyes and breathed deep a few times, letting the air press her body outward from the inside. Then she sat up and rubbed her eyes, sniffling.

Sunny crossed her arms over her chest. She looked away, into the dark. Neither of them said anything for a long time. And then, very quietly, Sunny said, "I have to go home now."

❖   ❖   ❖

Evie remembered them all up at the lake, not so long ago. The last time they'd all been there together. Too late to be winter, but not yet really spring.

If they were honest, it was still too chilly to be there, and despite the huge fire they'd built, the sand was cold and damp, and they'd all given up trying to sit in it.

Evie had huddled in a too-big jean jacket and red flannel shirt, babysitting a bottle she wasn't actually drinking from. She didn't know which of them had started it, but Shaun and Alex were taking turns leaping over the flames, spraying sand and pebbles in all directions when their feet hit the beach.

It was always like that when those two drank together. One would poke the other's rib, crack a joke, and some silly dare would snowball out. This time, it was fire walking. Seeing whose long legs could fly highest over the flames. Screams of fearless joy bounding out across flat water.

Alex loved Shaun. Loved him *ferociously*. He was Shaun's coppery double, his adoring kid brother. Evie liked watching them together, the way Alex fought for dominance but was just as happy to lose it. The way they slapped each other's arms and laughed and put each other down. The ape language of boys, all gesture, grunt and grin.

She'd hovered at the edge of the fire, trying to stay warm, but the shrapnel of sand and pebbles kept pushing her farther back into the dark.

Shaun landed a jump and fell into her, stumbling, laughing, arms windmilling. He snatched her up by the waist and kissed her hard, still smiling, so his teeth smashed into her lips, sparks flying out across her mouth. Then he pulled the bottle from her hand and whooped into the night sky.

King Shaun, the invincible. Evie stepped back and walked away.

The dark closed in pretty quick just outside the firelight. The smell of newly thawed earth filled her nose, sharp, cold and alive. She lifted her fingers to her lip and felt where Shaun's teeth had crashed into it, hot with blood under the skin. He got like that when he was drunk. Careless. Reckless. Other bruises whispered under her clothes. He never really meant them, but he'd never tried to stop them either.

The sandy, twiggy earth under her feet slid and cracked as she found her footing in the dark. When she blinked, she could still see yellow flames printed inside her eyes. She made her way back toward the cars, Shaun's and Ré's, trying to pick them out against the trees. She came upon them faster than expected.

To her left, several feet into the darkness, Evie heard a small sound. It was hardly anything. The boys' shouts from the fire were bouncing all over the beach and scattering in the sand, louder than anything else even at a distance. She sucked her lip, running her tongue over the angry part, trying to soothe it, trying to keep her eyes from filling with tears.

And she heard it again. A whispered *ahh* and a soft laugh. A purr. Evie stopped and looked toward it, still sucking her lip. Her tears were flowing now. It wasn't just the sting of her lip. It was that Shaun was indestructible. Always falling into her like a freight train, like whatever was in his way couldn't hold him, couldn't stop him. She couldn't even try.

She heard Sunny's voice. A low murmur, not her voice, and then Sunny's again, dismissive, laughing: "He's fucking drunk."

Evie could picture Sunny tipping her dark hair back, her long white throat releasing the sharp notes into the air. Evie walked toward the sounds.

Sunny and Réal were strangely tangled against the trunk of the Buick. Evie blinked at the picture—*were they...?* She blinked again, but the picture had changed. Ré was walking away, toward the fire. Sunny looked over her shoulder at Evie, eyes gleaming in the black, the smile on her lips like a switchblade.

Pictures from that night shuffled back to her now, like cards in a bad hand. The boys gone all *Lord of the Flies*—well, just Shaun and Alex. Ré had barely said a word that night. But of all of them, Ré was most like a stone, an anchor in the water. He was always quiet, so she hadn't thought anything of it. Hadn't even noticed. Her smashed lip and her irritation had got all her attention that night.

But now? As she eyed Sunny across the tan leather seats, she could see the hint of that soft *ahh* on her lips. Her and Ré pressed to the back of the Buick, dark clothes and dark hair camouflaging the real shape they had made in the shadows.

Sunny's Valkyrie swung low over Evie's shoulder, switch-blade in her hand. How could she have been so blind? She tried to think of other moments, other clues. Ré's low voice telling Sunny to *stop it* that day they'd taken his car. Sunny so stressed about what had happened at the lake without her. *Was he flirty?* It ate a hole through Evie's gut right down to the leather seats.

"Sunny," she said, feeling sick. "Let me out here. I'm going to walk."

❖   ❖   ❖

The moon was high and thin and lifeless, barely lighting her path. If she followed the highway, it would take an hour to get home from where Sunny had dropped her, so Evie aimed for the cemetery, the remains of that night at the lake playing on as she cut through the quiet streets.

Shaun had been wasted. Not as bad as Alex, but bad enough. They had settled down as the fire began to die, Alex staring blankly into the embers, not noticing his ass getting wet in the sand. The last of the bottle hung in his hand, catching firelight between his knees.

Shaun had come to find her again, to wrap himself around her. His low laugh into her hair, rough chin across her cheek.

"You're too drunk to drive," Evie had said, still mad about her lip.

But he'd only laughed and pushed her away. "I'm fine. Stop being such a suck."

She'd known it was stupid, that it might have killed her, but she'd let Shaun drive her home that night anyway. And he'd been careful, he'd gone slow. They all knew the roads so well, every curve, every turn—God, even the potholes were familiar. She'd always known just when to brace herself.

In the car, he'd reached over and taken her hand, pressing it flat against his thigh, laying his own down over top to keep her there. She could hear the grin in his voice without even looking at him.

"Hey, if we crash, at least we'll die together, right, babe?"

She'd only laughed at him. "So, live fast, die young. Is that your big plan?"

And he'd turned to her, grin hanging ear to ear like a string of Christmas lights, just one finger on the wheel. Letting the road go on below them without even looking at it. "Beats havin' to grow up, I guess."

15

R

Black Chuck was Ré's mother's family. Great-uncle to his mother's grandmother or something. He was young in the only photo Ré'd ever seen of him, wearing a funny, old suit made for a different man, a taller one, so that the high, old-fashioned collar rubbed the underside of his chin, and the cuffs fell nearly to his knuckles in the dim, gray light of a grainy old black-and-white.

His hair was parted above his left brow and combed to the side, though it looked too thick to stay that way. It made an unruly wedge of black on top of his head, and Ré's would do the same if he ever grew it long enough to get a comb through it. The hairstyle of a white man. It didn't suit Chuck, and it wouldn't suit Réal.

When he was little, his mother's sisters had told him the story. How, in the dead of winter, Black Chuck had eaten his only daughter. The knives he'd used to carve her up. Soft parts boiling in a black pot. Fire simmering fat and flesh. Mouth sucking at the old clay bowl.

His aunties' words had dug under his skin like little ticks. Made him afraid to fall asleep. Sleep only brought dreams, like a door left ajar.

And when sleep did catch him, he always woke screaming, clawing anyone who tried to comfort him, fearing Chuck's hands on his skinny arms, making a meal of him next.

He'd grown up ashamed of himself, pissing the bed over some stupid story that probably wasn't even true. Just some old boogeyman his silly aunties had made up to scare him.

But still.

There was something real in Chuck's black-and-white eyes. Something wild and scared, just the same as Ré's after waking.

He should have known. You can't outrun the things you dream for.

Ré sat in his car, seat pushed nearly flat back, arms crossed over his chest. He looked out at the dark, empty field, the wedge of night sky above, with eyes that only opened halfway. He'd thought those dreams had ended a long time ago, when he'd decided to just be a man about it. When he'd buried all those fears deep inside.

But ever since Shaun, since their fight, they'd come again.

He knew well what it was. He didn't need a *Midewikwe* to tell him that. It had been coming for him all his life. He was almost glad it was finally here. He just prayed that Mark could tell him how to stop it before anyone else got hurt.

❖   ❖   ❖

A ticking clock. No, that wasn't it. A tapping. Ré opened his
eyes one at a time and blinked through the darkened window.
Evie stood beside his car, brown hair tipped toward the glass,
shading her face. Ré groaned at the sight of her. More dreams,
he thought. He pressed his eyes closed again, squeezing his
arms tighter against his chest.

"Ré!" she said.

And he was awake.

"*Câlisse*," he muttered, sucking air and sitting up. "What
are you doing out here?"

"Uh, really?" she said, stepping back and rolling her eyes.
"I live here, obviously. What are *you* doing out here?"

"I saw the lights off," he said. "I thought you were asleep."

He snapped the driver's seat upright. He nearly reached
for the keys dangling from the ignition, but then he stopped.
He was already opening the car door before the words were
out of his mouth. "Evie, what happened to you?"

The Buick's interior light shone a pale little pool over her.
She looked down, turning her leg to see the thin red lines
snaking down to her ankle.

"It's nothing," she said. "I cut myself climbing."

"The fuck were you climbing, girl? A pile of glass?"

"No, just that stone wall at the cemetery." She gestured
behind her vaguely.

He lifted a foot out of the car and raised his hand as if he
meant to grab her, but she took another step away.

"Come on, let me look at it," he said.

She stared at him for a second, then stepped into his reach. He tucked his fingers lightly into the cove behind her knee and rubbed his thumb over her skin. It was a dry and jagged cut, at least an hour old, and her shoes were filthy with mud.

"*Ostie*," he hissed. "Where have you been, Evie?"

She shrugged. "I was out with Sunny, and then I went to see Shaun."

He lifted his fingers without a word. His brain was reaching for the keys, but his body wouldn't move, half in, half out of the car.

"Seriously, Ré, what are you doing here?"

He stared at her filthy shoes. He had a hundred million things to say, but none that he could speak out loud. "I couldn't sleep," he finally said, because it was true. "I thought maybe it would be easier here."

"Okay," she said slowly. "Do you want to come in?"

"No!" he answered, a little too fast. And then, "I mean, I don't think that's a good idea."

He glanced up, catching the look in her eye—curious, confused.

Then she started walking backward again, and he thought for one second, *No, not yet!* as all his insides reached for her. But she was only going around the back end of the Buick to climb in on the passenger side, which was maybe just as bad as leaving.

She sat and stared at him for a long time, big blue eyes, blood-red mouth. He couldn't think of anything to say, so he just said, "Nice lipstick," and she smiled.

"It tastes like cake," she said.

Fuck.

He looked away, out the windshield, teeth working on his bottom lip, breath caught at the very top of his lungs.

Then he looked back at her and, despite all the sense God gave him, said, "Cake, huh?"

And she just smiled some more.

He wanted to fold himself up into origami. He wanted to press his thumbs to her bleeding skin. He wanted to slide across the damn seat and shake her into little pieces.

His breath burst from his lungs. "Goddammit, Evie Hawley, you *are* a suffering demon."

She just laughed, pleased with herself, no doubt, and looked away at last.

After a while she said, "Réal?"

"Yeah, Ev?"

"Is something going on with you and Sunny?"

And the floor fell right out of the Buick, Ré's ass hitting gravel. He gaped at her, but she was still out in that empty field somewhere.

A zillion answers to her question flew through his head, but none both good and true. He looked down at where his thumbs hooked onto the steering wheel and said, "I can't answer that right now, Evie."

She said nothing. He looked at the crescent moon her turned cheek made in the dim light. Willing her to look at him so he could see what kind of man he was in those eyes now. But she stayed out of reach, out in that field. A fist full of claws dug through him.

He sighed, looking away. "Could you—I mean, someday, when things are not so messed up—could you maybe ask me that again?"

He expected her to laugh at him, or shout, or get out of the car and slam the door on him in a hail of curses, but she did nothing. Just kept staring out the window at the dark.

And then her fingers slid right through his ribs and took everything they found in there. "Okay," she said.

He stared at her.

Her voice was light. Not angry. Not judging. Not jealous. Just *Okay*.

And then at last she turned to look at him, blue eyes big and round, red lips curving in a Mona Lisa, knocking his lungs out.

"Good night, Ré," she said. "I hope you get some sleep."

She opened the door of the Buick and got out, careful not to slam it behind her. She didn't glance back as she crossed the road and went in her front door, but Ré watched her the entire way in case she did.

❖   ❖   ❖

E

Evie leaned against the front door as soon as she was on the other side, and she breathed for what felt like the first time in her life. She closed her eyes and felt Ré's fingers on the back of her knee, soft and light, though they were so often clenched into fists. This could not be happening. Him, outside her house, in the middle of the night. Not throwing stones to be let in, not twisting her arm into staying out.

Not asking for anything at all.

Just trying to get some sleep.

She opened her eyes and smiled.

It was the very last thing she *should* do, but she couldn't stop it. A strange, bright, bursting feeling exploded inside her. A million colored lights at once. And she couldn't stop it. She couldn't *not* feel it if she tried.

No, this could not be happening.

She pushed off the door and climbed upstairs to the attic, kicking her filthy shoes aside. Everything had changed, somehow, the moment that Buick had come into view. Her step had slowed when she saw that car, but her heart—it had stopped.

Ré. Parked outside her door. Asleep.

All the things she'd just confessed to Sunny. The gross truth about Shaun. Everything she'd tried so hard not to feel, smashed lips and small bruises, they were all gone. She was free.

I don't think you know him as well as you think you do, Sunny had said. She was right. He was so much more than the toughest boy Evie knew.

She crossed the bedroom to the gable window, pulling the curtain aside.

The Buick was still there, dark and rusty blue in dull moonlight, the driver's side window half down. Ré had put the seat flat again. She could just see his bare arm, the sleeve of the black T-shirt he wore, the dark shape of his tilted head. He was still. Maybe already asleep. She smiled again, lifting her fingers to the glass, touching from a distance.

An anchor in the water.

Not going anywhere.

R

Ré dreams. Wet cake pressed against the roof of his mouth, juice slipping from the seam of his lips, tart and sweet and boozy. Like cherry liqueur. Like the stuff his aunties drink at Christmas. It makes a warm spot at the bottom of his belly, makes his lips and fingers tingle.

The cake is rich and heavy, so good it can't be real. It's devil's food. It makes him so happy, he feels like a little kid again, stealing his *mamie's tarte au sucre* and stuffing his face behind the kitchen door till he's sugar-sick.

He chews and chews, but the cake doesn't get any smaller. He can feel pebbles of cooked flour and egg sticking between his cheeks and gums, under his tongue. It begins to fill his whole mouth. Each time he bites down, there's a little more.

He opens his eyes, confused, and sees the woods around him, the snow that buries his feet. He is naked but for his jeans, and shivering.

And then he knows.

The bridge of his nose begins to sting, his eyes to burn. Salt water blurs his vision. He starts to cry, because he can't stand it anymore. Because he knows from one instant to the next that this dream is the same as all the others, even though it's sweet: he is choking.

When he opens his mouth to spit the cake, it's blood. It spills salty and hot across his chin, across his collar. It pools in his shoulder bones, pours down his arms, bare chest, his jeans and bare feet. Snakes of blood, squeezing tight. His lungs scream for air.

He reaches into his mouth, scraping cake and blood from his airway. He falls to his knees, one hand clawing his mouth, the other disappearing to the elbow in red snow.

And he sees the deer at the edge of the woods, watching. Their antlers rattle and knock, soft sounds as though they're speaking. His eyes are wild, pleading, but the animals don't come any closer and they don't help him.

And he thinks, Goddammit. If this demon is coming, let it come now. I've had enough. Let it come. I won't fight it anymore.

At the back of his throat, his fingers catch in a mess of fibers. He pulls, and it comes up from his gut with a sliding-backwards feeling, like he is pulling his own insides out, flipping himself like a sock. He pulls and pulls, and more of it comes. It is black and sticky, wound in a bundle. It tangles in his fingers, and he pulls.

When it finally slides free of his throat, when he can at last suck the breath his lungs scream for, he opens his hand to see what he's caught.

He blinks and stares. He thinks of Evie's face tipped toward his car window, blue eyes, dark mouth, and he thinks, *No, not you…*

It is hair. Long and dark and sticky, like bloody black rope.

The breath he's just sucked rushes from him. He folds over into the snow and sobs, the tail of hair clutched tightly in his fist.

16

E

Alex was all loose energy, elbows bobbing as he talked, hands shoved deep in the pockets of his denim vest. Sunny looked away with a bored expression on her face. Evie smiled when she reached their perch on the hill.

"Last day, bitches!" Alex chirped when he saw Evie.

"Don't call us bitches, you tool," Sunny snapped at him.

He started. "I didn't mean, like, *bitches*."

"Then why'd you say it? What the fuck do you think it means?"

Evie groaned silently, her smile fading. These two bickering was exactly the opposite of how she wanted the last day of school to start.

"Sup, Ev," Alex mumbled, taken down a few notches.

"Hey," she said back. "Hey, Sunny."

Of course, Ré wasn't with them. He'd been gone when she got up, the strange night washed away without a trace.

Not that she was surprised. She glanced back toward the parking lot, but he wasn't there either. She'd already checked.

Sunny said nothing, but flicked her eyes to the parking lot too. She crossed her arms over a loose black tank top printed with a pale rib cage that could've been a photo of her own bony body. She looked beautifully scary, as always, and skinny as a clothes hanger. She could probably wear a bunch of plastic bags and still look ridiculously cool.

Evie felt short and sloppy by comparison, in cutoffs and a loose plaid shirt, dark hair hanging lifeless and uncombed at her shoulders. She'd been avoiding the mirror that hung from her bathroom door, not wanting to see her shape in it, the skin between her hip bones gone tight over the thing inside her.

"So guess what?" Alex said. "My dad is letting me have a grad party."

"Really?" said Evie. "That's cool."

"Totally." Alex's feathery hair swung with his nodding head. "It's too perfect. It'll be just like a bush party, only you won't have to piss in the woods!" He nudged Sunny, smiling hopefully. It was a strong selling point—poison oak and peeing on your own shoes were two big reasons bush parties always kind of sucked. "And the best part is, no chance the cops will bust it up."

"Really? Why not?" Evie asked.

Sunny smirked at her, making her feel stupid, and Alex just laughed, shrugging his shoulders. "It's kind of a no-cop zone, that's all," he said, not actually explaining.

"Sounds like fun," Evie replied lamely.

She'd never been to Alex's house. Never even seen it. She'd only sat in a car outside Sunny's—a big Victorian on the nice side of the river—a handful of times. And she'd been inside Ré's just that once, before the lake. Evie felt again like she barely knew her own so-called friends. Shaun had asked for all her attention, and she had just given and given.

At the bottom of the hill the first bell rang, but still no Buick.

"Last day of school for-*evah*!" Alex announced. He stood and stretched out his long arm theatrically. "After you, ladies."

Evie couldn't help but smile at his chivalry, even if Sunny was unimpressed.

❖   ❖   ❖

Sometime during third period, Evie noticed the Buick in the parking lot, but still no Ré in the halls. It was a pretty huge school—the only public high school for miles—but still, if you wanted to find someone, it was usually pretty easy.

Then again, if you didn't want to be found, that was easy too.

❖   ❖   ❖

Evie stood before her empty locker, half feeling like she wanted to just step inside and close the door. Maybe spend the summer there. But then there were hands on her shoulders, shaking her lightly, and a long arm draped around her.

Alex beamed. "E-*vie*! Sup. We did it! It's fucking *over*, dude."

She smiled at him—he looked so happy she could practically feel his mood pushing her own out of the way. He really was a lot like Shaun.

"You coming to the Olympia?" he asked.

She shrugged. "Is that where everyone's going?" *Ré,* she wanted to say.

"Yeah, of course," he said. And then, "I don't know. It's over, man! Who cares?"

Alex seemed to have forgotten that they still had exams to write, but she wasn't going to point it out. Instead, she let him drag her out to the parking lot, her bag heavy over her shoulder.

They burst out into the bright sun, and chaos exploded. The parking lot was jammed with kids and cars, engines running, music blasting, bumpers edging through the crowd. People were shouting and laughing, horns honking, sunlight smashing into everything, making her squint. Alex threw himself into the fray like it was his natural habitat, and Evie picked her way along behind him, letting him break the waves.

Ré, at last.

Leaning against the front panel of the Buick, arms crossed over his black T-shirt—the same one he'd had on last night? she wondered. His dark figure seemed to swallow all the brightness from the parking lot. The air around him was still. He didn't smile when he saw them. And if Evie had hoped for any acknowledgment, any look that said *remember,* she was disappointed.

The boys greeted each other with a quick clasp of hands.

"Yo, you coming to my party next week?" Alex asked.

Réal looked surprised, but he nodded.

Alex punched him on the shoulder. "Good," he said, then started headbanging to a silent beat, his hair flying. "School's out for-*evah!*" he sang.

Sunny arrived, and Alex attacked her like a puppy trying to play with a cat—grabbing, shouting, shaking, grinning. She let him do it, though she looked about as pleased as any cat would.

Ré turned and got in the car, and they all fell into formation—boys up front, the girls in the back. Alex stretched his long legs out in the extra space of the front seat and twisted on the stereo. Black Sabbath poured out of the shitty speakers, rattling the dash and making Evie's hair shake.

"Yeah!" Alex whooped, nodding in time to the heavy bass. He threw a glance at Réal, who didn't say a word.

"Ugh!" Sunny shouted over the blast. "Dinosaur music! Turn it off!"

Alex just turned, flashing bright eyes and a wicked grin, and sang the wrong lyrics over his shoulder at her, *"Satan's Own around the bend..."*

Sunny rolled her eyes and looked out the window. He turned back, ignoring her, and clasped his hands behind his head, grin cutting ear to ear, just like Shaun's used to do.

Evie blinked at the back of his gingery-brown hair. King Alex? she thought. When did *that* happen?

❖   ❖   ❖

The Olympia was packed. A wall of noise hit them as soon as they opened the door. Evie didn't know if it was Ré's reputation or just good timing, but when he glanced at a booth full of younger kids, they all quickly paid and left, giving them the last good seats in the room. Sunny and Alex took one side, Ré the other. Evie took the seat next to him.

No one said anything.

Evie cleared her throat. "So what about this party?" she asked.

Alex grinned. "Next Friday, after exams. I'm gettin' a keg. And, yeah, invite whoever. I want it to be epic."

Evie didn't know who else she was supposed to ask. Everyone she might have invited was already sitting right here.

"Cool," she said quietly. She glanced at Réal, who was staring down into the menu like he'd never seen it before. "If June comes back, can someone order me fries?" She got up from the table and didn't wait for anyone to say yes.

Evie went down the hallway that led past the kitchen. The bathrooms were there, the ladies' room mercifully empty. She pushed open a stall door and locked it behind her, leaning back against the scratched paint.

She couldn't help it. The tears just came, like she'd been hauling ten tons on her back all day and only just noticed it now. It wasn't just Ré. Fuck him. If he didn't want to see her, talk to her, *look* at her in the light of day—fine.

It was *everything* else.

She looked to her shoes, at the almost obvious way her body now pushed against her clothes. She put her hand on her belly, trying to feel something other than flesh, but her mind just filled with horror movies. Aliens. Creatures. Parasites.

Evie heard the bathroom door swing open behind her. She took a shaky breath and wiped her face on her sleeve, then flushed the toilet needlessly with the toe of her shoe and opened the stall door.

Sunny stood by the sinks, arms crossed. "What's wrong with you?" she asked, one eye squinted as though Evie were hard to see.

Evie bent to slap cold water on her face.

Sunny's hand was suddenly on her shoulder, pulling her upright with more force than necessary. "I asked you a question," she said, and panic punched through Evie's chest.

"I'm fine," she said, shrugging Sunny's hand away. "I'm just tired." At least that wasn't a lie. She was tired all the time now, it seemed.

Sunny stared at her in obvious disbelief. Then she cocked her hip and said what she had probably really wanted to say last night, at the band shell.

"You know, Ev, while you and Shaun were off in la-la land this year, the real world was kinda happening back here without you." Her hand flew up in Evie's face like a frightened bird. "You can't just walk right in like you've been here the whole time and act like you're one of us now. You don't have a clue what's really going on around here, so maybe just back off a little, huh?"

"What?" Evie almost laughed. "What am I doing?"

And Sunny did laugh, harsh and cold. "I see you two, you know. Your little glances at each other. I know something is going on with you and Réal. I mean, WTF, Ev. Shaun is dead. Ré was *there*. And you *knew*. And now you two are—what? A *thing*?" She shook her head in disbelief. "Do you even know how fucked up that is?"

Evie twitched at the words. Sunny had hidden it well, but Evie could see it now beyond a doubt. And Ré had as much as confessed it last night, when she'd asked. Sunny and

Réal were involved somehow, and no matter how "fucked up" things might really be, Sunny was plainly jealous.

She was also fearless—she might actually fight her for this, even though she had no right to in the world.

But that didn't seem to matter to her.

"I—I," Evie stammered out, "don't know what you're talking about. Seriously. I'm just not feeling well."

She wanted to say, *There is sooo much you don't know, Sunny.* She wanted to say, *At least I waited till my boyfriend was dead!* But she didn't. She wasn't going to blurt it all out in this dingy bathroom, with half the school on the other side of the door. She didn't want the higher ground. She didn't want Sunny's sympathy or her hurt or surprise.

Let her have her rage instead.

Evie brushed past her and hurried back to their table, where Alex sat alone in front of three plates. "What the hell?" he bleated when he saw her. "Where did everyone go?"

Evie slumped down into the seat opposite him and stared at her fries. The urge to toss them all on the floor was almost too strong to ignore.

A minute later Sunny returned. Neither of the girls said anything, and Alex just looked back and forth between them as if a tennis match were playing out across the table. He *tsk*ed his tongue. "Everyone is so damn moody these days."

And then Réal slid down next to her, shifting the vinyl and old springs in his direction, his leg touching Evie's under the table.

"Where were you?" Sunny snapped.

Ré gave her a look that sewed her lips shut. "You my parole officer or something?" he muttered. The first words Evie had heard him say since last night.

He grabbed a fork and started jabbing French fries, elbows on the tabletop. The muscles of his arm stood out with each jab, as if the fries needed fighting.

Alex quickly picked up his fork and followed suit. Sunny, as usual, was the only one without food in front of her. That X-ray skeleton on her tank top probably ate better meals than Sunny ever did, Evie thought bitterly. Then she stared down at her own plate, feeling defeated before she'd even begun.

17

R

Ré pushed his empty plate away. Under the table, his heel tapped the floor. Restless. Itching to get out of this booth and away from everyone. He turned his wrist on the table, checking his watch. He glanced around the dining room.

Where the fuck is Mark?

The room was jammed with kids, but no sign of the one he needed, or of Ivan, or any of their friends. Ré pulled his phone from his pocket, checking his messages for the millionth time. Nothing.

His foot began to tap again.

This wasn't exactly how today was supposed to go, but he hadn't had the balls to say no to Alex for longer than he liked to admit. Guilt is a powerful negotiator. And anyway, he was surprised that Alex had even asked him to come. They'd pretty much avoided each other since he'd told him about the night Shaun died.

Maybe Alex just needed the ride downtown—but even if that's all the invitation really was, Ré owed him that much at least.

He wasn't following the conversation, which seemed mostly to consist of Sunny's voice, peppered with the occasional Alex. His eyes danced around the room, anxious. He chewed his bottom lip.

It was too weird, this new configuration. Ré was used to being on the edges of the group, not smack in the middle like this was some kind of messed-up double date. If it were just Sunny here, he could handle that. Even Sunny and Alex. He'd handled that for months. But there was something else now. There was Evie. And he didn't even know what that was yet, except that it felt an awful lot like sitting two inches from a house on fire.

The springs in the seat below him squeaked in time with his bouncing leg.

Then a hand pressed down on his thigh, and the whole world fell off a cliff. For a split second he was scared the hand was Sunny's, even though he could see hers on the table in front of him.

He looked down to his lap, then at Evie. Her eyes were red, like she'd been awake all night, or crying. Or both. She looked so bruised, he was suddenly ashamed that he'd tried so hard not to look at her before now.

"Please stop," she said quietly.

He lowered his heel to the floor, flexing like it took all his strength to do it. A crush of words jumbled up in his throat. A thousand apologies for last night. A thousand more for today. He swallowed them all back. "Sorry," he muttered.

She lifted her fingers, and it took everything, everything, to keep his own hand from darting under the table to make her stay. To thread their fingers together, to let her in.

And then Mark's sister, Holly, walked through the front door, and Ré sprang up, tripping away from the flames.

"Hey!" he said.

Holly looked up in surprise. She was a small girl, with black, bobbed hair and dark eyeliner winged out at the corners of her eyes. He'd seen her around school and waiting tables at the Olympia, but she was two grades behind him, and they weren't friends.

"Hey," she said back. "Réal, right?"

"Yeah," he said, hands slipping into his back pockets. She kept walking toward the back of the restaurant, and he sidestepped along beside her. "I'm looking for your brother, Mark?" he said. "I was supposed to meet him after school, but I got kinda sidetracked, and now he's not answering my texts."

She looked at him again, shrugging. "I haven't seen him, but he usually comes by after six, if you feel like waiting." She was tying a short black apron around her waist as she walked, obviously just starting her shift. "Or you could ask my mom," she said, nodding at the other waitress.

"June's your *mom*?" Ré asked, eyes wide.

Holly laughed. "Yeah, of course!" she said. "You didn't know that?"

Réal looked at the older woman sliding plates from the pass-through window and loading up her arms like a pro. She did not look like a *Midewikwe*. Or at least, not what Ré had pictured a medicine woman to look like. She just looked like a middle-aged lady working in a diner. He wasn't sure if that was good news or bad.

"Do you want me to pass on a message, if I see him?" Holly asked, drawing his attention back to her.

"Yeah," he said. "Tell him to text me. I gotta head home for a bit, but if he could wait right here for me, I'll be back. I really gotta see him tonight."

Holly eyed him for a moment, then put her hand on his bare arm and gave it a squeeze. Nobody he didn't already know real well ever touched him like that. For a small person, she was awfully bold.

"Okay, Réal," she said, nodding once. "If I see him, I'll tell him he's got to wait." Her tone was so serious, he almost laughed, but really he was glad.

"Thanks," he said. He turned to go back to his table.

"Réal," she said. "Be strong, whatever it is."

He turned again, but she had already disappeared into the kitchen.

18

E

The walk to Nan's took exactly ten minutes from Evie's front yard, and the house looked just the same as it always had: two stories of chipped white paint behind a slanted, faded front porch. The snarled remains of a garden. It had been pretty once, Evie guessed, but had run down, chip by creak, until Nan just couldn't take care of it anymore.

Shaun's Challenger was still parked in the driveway, and she half expected to see him in the driver's seat, grinning. *Hey girl, where you been?*

She put her hand to the glass, peering into the car. When Shaun was alive, it had been as messy as his bedroom was, schoolwork, skateboards, old crumpled-up clothes piled in the cramped back seat. He'd patched the cracked upholstery with duct tape, and it had peeled up in places, sticky, black and filthy.

Now it was spotless. The upholstery was still ruined, but the garbage was all gone, the carpets vacuumed clean.

Did Nan do this? she wondered. And then she saw the For Sale sign stuck in the window. *Call Sherrie*, it said. His mom. Of course.

Even though it made perfect sense—there was no way Nan would ever drive this thing—it still felt like a punch in the gut. As rusted out and used up and broken as it was, this ridiculous lime-green car was Shaun's spirit animal. His pride. How could she think of selling it?

Evie looked at the house again. They'd all avoided Shaun's place for weeks. His best friend hadn't even been brave enough to drive past. And it was easy to avoid—planted at the tail end of a long, bumpy road, past empty fields and factories and train tracks stretching away. A forgotten place, tucked under the rug at the empty edge of town with a bunch of other houses just like it.

Evie climbed the front steps and pulled open the rusty screen door.

She was surprised to hear a crowd of voices shouting and laughing inside, canned music playing in the background. She looked back at the green car gleaming in the sun. It was the only one in the drive. Whoever was inside must have walked over, like she had. Maybe the neighbors were here?

She rang the bell and waited.

As the door swung open, Evie was hit with the familiar smell of this house—wilted gardenias and cough medicine. Shaun's nan stood before her, looking smaller than ever, translucent white skin hanging slack from her little round face. Her watery eyes fixed on Evie.

Evie smiled. "Hello, Nan. Do you remember me?"

Nan's eyes worked, and Evie could see her trying to answer the question, but in the end she only smiled.

Evie said gently, "I was a friend of your grandson's." Still no recognition. Evie wondered if Nan could even hear her, deaf as she was. Almost shouting, she said, "I knew Shaun!"

And then Nan's whole face lit up. "Oh!" she gasped. "Yes, I remember. Please, come in." Her bony fingers closed around Evie's arm, and the tiny woman pulled her through the doorway, into the house.

It was dim inside, after the bright sun, and Evie's eyes took a moment to adjust.

When they did, her heart fell.

The front room was a disaster. A chair was knocked over, pictures had fallen off the wall, dirt from a potted plant was spread across the carpet. Someone, probably Nan herself, had walked through it, trailing footprints back and forth to the front window. Evie thought of Ré, his two black eyes. Him and Shaun grabbing and clawing through this room like animals. That fight had been weeks ago—had no one cleaned this room since then?

A stab of guilt twisted through her. They'd spent so many nights here, partying in this front room while Nan slept upstairs, deaf to it all. They had completely taken advantage of this house. And then they'd all just walked away. Including Sherrie—Evie guessed the only reason she'd bothered to clean Shaun's car was because it was worth something.

Nan shuffled down a short hallway to the kitchen, and Evie stepped along behind her. On the kitchen counter, a radio blared some kind of religious show at ear-splitting volume—the crowd of voices she'd heard from outside. Nan was very much alone.

Evie looked around the faded kitchen as if for the first time. Stacks of plates and cups and bowls had all been taken from the cupboards and placed on the counter, on top of the microwave, even on chairs. There were half drunk cups of tea everywhere, their surfaces going hairy. Boxes of paper spilled onto the floor.

It was like Shaun's disaster of a bedroom had infected the rest of the house, and now the whole thing was sick with mess.

A scorch mark ringed the burner on the stove, and a soot-black kettle perched there. Evie remembered Shaun telling her how much he worried about Nan, how she wasn't safe alone. He'd missed so much school to take care of her that he wouldn't have even graduated this year. It made her sick to think of Nan here without him.

"Nan," Evie said over the radio's blare, "does anyone come to see you? Does Shaun's mom ever come here?"

But Nan didn't answer. She was doddering at the counter, making small noises to herself, and Evie began to wonder if she'd forgotten that Evie was there.

"Nan," she tried again, going to the old woman's side. Nan turned a sweet smile on her, but said nothing. She was busy stacking envelopes and junk mail, weeks-old flyers, making it all orderly amid the mess. "Does your daughter ever come here?" Evie tried again.

"Oh, do you know Sherrie?" Nan asked, sounding pleased. "She's all grown up now. She had a baby, you know." For a second, Evie thought Nan meant another baby, that Shaun had a sibling, but then she realized Nan was just talking about Shaun.

Nan tutted to herself, shaking her head and clacking the edge of the papers on the counter. "It was hard for her, being so young. She moved away a long time ago, I think." The look on Nan's face told Evie that she was trying to put together a puzzle, but for whatever reason, the pieces wouldn't stick.

"When was the last time you saw her?" Evie asked.

"It was a long time ago," Nan repeated. "When the men came to look at Shaun's room—" Nan stopped short and looked up from the papers, blinking at the cupboards in front of her.

"What men?" Evie asked.

"Oh, policemen, I think," she said.

"And they looked in Shaun's room?" Evie felt a sudden urge to run up the stairs, to somehow protect his privacy from the strangers who'd already been here weeks earlier.

"They looked in Shaun's room," Nan agreed, but she sounded as if she were assuring herself, not Evie.

"And Sherrie never came back after that?"

"Oh no! Sherrie moved away a long time ago." Nan smiled again.

They were going in circles. She'd never talked to Nan this much in the entire time she'd known Shaun. Was this what every conversation with her was like?

Shaun was a totally different person with Nan at his side. Not the invincible, not the king, but just a boy, fussing affectionately over the unsteady old woman who'd raised him. Guilt stabbed at her again. For not being here for Nan after he'd died, for not loving Shaun when she'd had the chance.

"Nan," she said, "do you mind if I look in Shaun's room too?"

"Oh, I'm sure he won't mind," she said, eyes twinkling with water.

Evie left Nan in the kitchen and climbed the stairs to his room.

It still smelled like him. Familiar and warm and boyish. It was as messy as ever, clothes all over the floor, broken skateboards, posters curling. She stepped gingerly over it all, looking around.

His dresser was littered with loose change, deodorant, a pair of pliers with a broken tip, a sealed package of white sport socks, elastics for his long yellow hair. His last movements preserved in patterns of clutter, things resting just where he'd dropped them, peaceful as a museum.

His cell phone sat in a sealed plastic bag amid it all. She lifted the edge of the bag and saw a receipt from the police marking it *Released To Family*.

Had it been sitting right here the night she'd called his voice mail?

For some reason, that made her think of a book she'd read once, about a submarine crew searching for the source of a distant radio signal after a nuclear war. Even after everyone on earth was dead, technology would whisper mysteriously on.

Evie took the bag and dropped it into her backpack, then slumped at the edge of Shaun's bed, looking around at the mess.

On the floor between the night table and bed frame, a box of condoms spilled an accordion line of shiny blue packages. She and Shaun had mostly used these. Obviously, not every time. She didn't know why she'd never expected the worst to happen, except that it was Shaun, and the worst *never* happened with him.

Evie sighed. She couldn't pretend much longer that this thing wasn't inside her. This looming future. It was growing every day and eating everything she had—literally. All her strength and energy and will, all the food she put in her mouth. Every second of rest she stole was never enough for it. It was Shaun's kid, sure enough.

She'd been sleepwalking with it for nearly four months, drifting on its tide, pretending it wasn't really happening. And soon it would be too late to do anything but exactly what Shaun's mom had done—ditch and run.

She lay down on the bed, curled up and cried.

❖   ❖   ❖

A gentle voice broke through her dreams, a hand on Evie's shoulder.

Evie opened her eyes, confused. She blinked at the room, trying to piece it into something familiar. *Oh God*, she thought, and bolted up.

"I'm so sorry, Nan!" she gasped. "I didn't mean to fall asleep." She rubbed her eyes, swollen and sticky with dried tears.

Nan sat down next to her. "You're a friend of Shaun's, aren't you?" she asked, folding her hands in her lap.

"Yes, Nan," she said. "I'm Shaun's girlfriend. We met before." But Nan said nothing. Evie took a shaky breath. "Nan, I have to tell you something. About Shaun." Nan just kept on smiling. Evie looked down at Nan's old hands, so fragile and bony and blue. "I—I mean, Shaun, that is, we—" Oh, just say it, she thought, kicking herself. "I'm pregnant," she said. "And, um, it's Shaun's."

The words felt heavy as weights. The only other person she'd ever spoken them to wasn't even alive anymore, and she felt like she'd just confessed to his murder. She collapsed into tears all over again. "I'm sorry, Nan. So, so sorry…"

Nan reached for her hand, squeezing it in her own more firmly than Evie expected. "Oh dear," she said, "it can't possibly be as bad as all that."

"But it is, Nan. It's really, really bad," Evie practically wailed.

Everything she'd been pretending not to feel, everything she'd buried and ignored and covered up—it all rose up and crashed over her, sucking her out to sea. "I don't know what to do," she confessed. "I'm so scared. And I can't tell my mom."

"Well," Nan said, "I think you probably can. She'll still love you, you'll see."

Evie blinked at her tears. The wise words hardly seemed to match the person who'd been randomly stacking things in the kitchen, who'd seemed confused about who Evie even was. "Do you still love Sherrie?" she asked. *Even though she dumped Shaun on you? Even though she ran away to be crazy and drunk?*

"Of course I do!" Nan said. "Sherrie is a good girl. She does her best."

God, Evie thought, some best.

"And I got my grandson from her," Nan added. "My bright star. I can't be angry about that now, can I?" She beamed proudly now.

She patted Evie's hands and then stood up, shuffling toward the door. When she got there she turned and smiled sweetly. "If you see Shaun," she said, "will you please tell him to come home?"

Evie ached as she watched the lucidity drain out of the tiny, fragile woman, watched her slide right back into lonely confusion. Should I tell her? she wondered. Should I break the awful news again until it sticks? *Shaun is dead, Shaun is dead, Shaun is dead…*

Evie blinked back fresh tears. "Okay, Nan," she said. "I'll let him know."

19

E

Baxter Grains had once been a pretty big employer in Cold Water, but it had mostly closed when the economy had collapsed, leaving this whole end of town limping and destroyed. The Grains still operated, but not like it used to. Most of its buildings were empty now, most of its workers long gone.

But that's what made it interesting.

With its lattice of crumbling fire escapes, and storehouses full of rust and echoes, the Grains was a fantastic secret fortress. One big, broken playground.

Freight trains still ran through it, but they didn't stop anymore. Just blew on past like they couldn't get away fast enough. Evie had learned how to listen before running across six lanes of tracks, how to feel for the rumble in the steel. Everything with Shaun had been a slide of adrenaline, from her brain to her fingertips, from her heart right down to her toes. Even just walking across a field.

She came up alongside that dirty industrial yard, bright sun picking out bits of broken glass, making it sparkle and wink in the breeze. If she squinted, she could just see him kicking around in the scrub, hair the color of dry wheat against a light-blue sky.

She asked, *Do you remember, Shaun Henry-Deacon? Do you know what happened to you?*

And then she was climbing. Sliding the toes of her sneakers into the too-small holes of the fence, her weight cutting into her fingers where they curled around the wire.

Before Shaun, Evie had never climbed a fence in her life. She wasn't sure she'd ever climbed *anything*, to be honest. But if you wanted to hang with the boys, you had to learn to keep up. She'd climbed her first fence after watching Sunny go gracefully over this one, and since then she'd seen most of the town from fence-tops just like it.

On the other side, she jumped the last few feet to the ground, tumbling onto her rear end—gravity had changed a little since she'd got knocked up. "Crap," she muttered. The cut on her knee had reopened. She wiped a dot of blood away, then stood and brushed herself off, picking bits of stone from her hands.

Shaun's body had been found on the other side of the empty storage building, close to the corrugated fence that blocked the parking lot from the tracks. There was a little hill there, where a thin trail skirted the bottom of the fence.

Evie had never used the trail. The tracks there went from six to eight lanes, two of them peeling off onto Grains property, and if she were honest, she was too chicken to go near them, even though they looked rusty and probably hadn't been used in years.

Besides, if you walked just a little farther west, the ground went flat, the tracks thinned out, and you could see in both directions for a good long way.

But Shaun had been found by the trail, so she headed in that direction.

The grass was already brittle and dry, though it was barely summer yet. It looked like a mangy hide, long in some places, scratched bald in others, flea-bitten skin poking through. For years, people had used this field as a trash heap, throwing litter over the fence and letting the rats and coyotes sort it out. The ground was strewn with faded takeout containers, bent soda cans, rusty nails, glass. She stepped through it toward the fence.

As she rounded the side of the storage building, she saw remnants of yellow police tape lifting in the breeze. Three whole weeks had passed since they found him here— was there *still* no verdict yet on what had happened to him?

Maybe nobody really cared, she thought. Shaun was just a punk-ass burnout flunking out of high school. Kids at school had *laughed* at his memorial. His own mother didn't want him, and his nan didn't even know he was gone.

She stepped over the twirling end of tape and started up toward the trail. The ground was uneven, covered in loose gravel with bits of grass shooting through to keep it all from sliding back down onto the tracks. There was less garbage over here. Fewer people came through this way. Or maybe the police had gathered it all up as evidence and hadn't bothered to bring it back.

At the top of the hill, she continued east, eyes scanning back and forth across the trail, searching for anything that might have been his, might have been missed.

She reached the arc light and stopped. There was nothing here. Either the police had already taken it all, or there had been nothing here to begin with.

That same surreal feeling—that it was all a fake, that Shaun was going to jump out, laughing, any minute—rose up inside her. How can a guy like that just blink out of existence? One second he wants *forever* from you, and the next he's just...*gone*.

Of course, she knew his body had been found. He wasn't missing—he was dead. But it just felt so impossible to believe. Was it really so crazy that Nan still waited for him to come home?

Evie saw a glint of metal at the edge of the little hill. She crouched down. It was a shiny silver bead about a centimeter wide, and as she rolled it between her fingers, the ground began to rumble. "Shit!" she hissed, stuffing the bead into her shirt pocket.

The gravel shook, and she stumbled to her knees and rolled, trying to skitter back up over the lip of the hill before the train reached her, but it was too late.

It wasn't on the closest track, or even the next one over, but still. The thunder of it pinned her to the ground, and as it passed, the first engine let out a succession of short, staccato wails, as if it was coming right at her.

She threw her hands over her ears and huddled into a ball. It was one thing to love this sound from her bedroom window, to hear it drifting from far away and think of it as lonesome. It was another thing entirely to be almost underneath it. Tons of steel and iron, howl and fire, hurtling by like hell on wheels.

She squeezed her eyes shut as the train's two massive engines screamed past. But as the rest of the cars flew by, the sound leveled out to a steady, clacking roar, and she was able to shuffle back from the edge of the incline, kicking in the dirt till her shoulders hit the corrugated fence. She plugged her ears and watched the cars rattle by.

Why was he found way over here? This trail was nothing—it didn't go anywhere. It ran out after a few hundred feet, and then you had to cut through the only part of the Grains that was still used anymore to get out to the road beyond.

A hundred yards back the way she'd come stood the old storage building. Inside were smooth, flat, wide-open concrete floors perfect for skateboarding, and getting in was stupid easy. After the train had passed, Evie stood and walked back toward the storehouse.

Partway down the west side of the building was a boarded-up window she knew wasn't really boarded. She pulled the rotten wood aside and lifted herself through the gap.

The main floor was dark, and full of rats and other things Evie tried not to think about. The windows were covered to keep people from smashing them, so it was damp and moldy inside. But as she climbed the steel staircase to the second floor, sunlight poured in from above.

There were floor-to-ceiling windows on the second floor, and the sun had baked the smooth concrete, warming the whole place like an oven. Old, dusty ceiling fans stood motionless along the rafters. Paint peeled in grotesque bulges all over the ceiling. She could hear the coo of pigeons roosting, the sudden flutter of wings.

The first time she'd ever come here it had been sweet with the thrill of breaking in and the chance of getting caught. It was nighttime, black and cavernous. But Shaun had held her close, held her hand, hadn't let her get scared. The moon and arc lights shining through the windows had lit his grin, calming her a little in the darkness.

When she'd finally seen this place in daylight, she realized how silly her fear had been. It was actually beautiful. Sunbeams marked the dusty air, and there wasn't half as much garbage inside as there was out in the field. Shaun had cleaned it up himself. He'd wanted to build a ramp in here, maybe one day a half pipe. In the dust on the floor she could still see the faint tracks of his wheels, carving huge ellipses around the pillars. In tighter corners, his fingers had touched down too. Shaun had come here a lot.

She kept climbing all the way to the third floor, where it was dirtier, not as pretty as downstairs, and the ceiling was lower. On the side facing the tracks, a busted-out doorway punched a huge hole in the wall. A section of broken fire escape clung to the outside of the building, but its landing had long ago been kicked in, leaving a dizzying drop to the landing below.

Despite this, she'd seen Shaun use this doorway a hundred times, monkeying hand-over-hand down the rusty bars to the second floor, making the old metal sing like a tuneless guitar.

She walked to the hole in the wall and looked out over the field, the tracks. It was late afternoon now, the sun leaning long shadows through the grass. Empty beer cans littered the floor up here, gathering dust. There were fist-sized holes in the moldy walls. It was possible other kids came here too, but Evie'd never seen any. This whole building was like Shaun's private playground.

She reached into her backpack and pulled out his cell phone. She didn't know his passcode, and the battery was probably dead anyway, so she didn't bother taking it out of the plastic bag.

Instead she got her own phone out and keyed in his number. She leaned against the frame of the busted-out doorway and put the phone to her ear, waiting for that phony surfer-drawl that widened out the words and bounced them against his perfect, white teeth.

"Hey, you've reached Shaun..."

She took a deep breath. The voice mail beeped.

"I saw your nan today," she said. "I told her, y'know, about the baby and all. She wasn't even mad. She told me about your mom, how she was young too. That made me feel a bit better, I guess." Evie sighed, all her words weighing heavy on her chest. "She really misses you. We all do..."

Evie gazed over the dirty field, past Réal's place and the cemetery, past Sunny's, past town, out past everything beyond. She squeezed Shaun's phone in her fist, feeling like the very worst person on earth. "I just...I want you to know how sorry I am for everything, and I—"

But she choked.

And the voice mail beeped before she could tell him why she'd really called: *I think I might have this baby after all.*

20

R

Five kids meant a lot of food. A lot of clothes and toys and things to spend money on. It meant bills and a mortgage on a big house. It meant that both his parents had to work, which had left Ré in charge since he was barely old enough to handle it.

His main job was feeding the kids, and he was home at the same time every day to do it, whether he himself ate or not. And lately he had not.

At least, not the meat parts. Not since Shaun.

Not since seeing his best friend's insides scratched in the dirt of that field, sand and grass and trash all stuck to it like it was old pink bubble gum.

Every time he was faced with a plate of meat, he just wanted to puke his living guts out. He had become a bona fide vegetarian.

So when Mark slid the brown paper bag across the table, its contents struck Ré with a horror that seemed designed just for him.

"What the fuck is this?" he yelped, shoving it away.

Mark hissed, glancing around the dining room. The Olympia crowd had thinned since three o'clock, but there were still more people hanging around than either of them would have liked. "It's the cure," he said, leaning in. "Do you know how hard it was to get this?" He touched the bag protectively.

"*Ostie d'câlisse de sacrament!*"

Even if you didn't know French, it sounded pretty vicious.

Réal pressed himself back against the booth, leveraging his hands on the table edge and staring at the bag like it might lunge at him. That familiar green sickness washed through his gut. He swallowed it back with effort. "What kind of fucking cure is *that?*"

Mark shook his head. "Look, you asked me to help you, and this is what I got. I mean, cut me some slack—I don't even know northern medicine. My family's Cayuga."

Ré took a long, deep breath and blew it out slow. "I know," he said. "I'm sorry. It just doesn't seem like this is what it should be. A cure, I mean. For *this.*"

"I swear, I read through everything my mom had, dude." Mark shrugged, but it wasn't dismissive, just a little disbelieving. "All the stories said you need to eat meat. Lots of greasy, red"—he lowered his voice to a hush—"*nonhuman* meat."

Ré shuddered. His fingers went to the mouth of the bag again, tipping it open. He peered in. His bottom lip pulled down, like he was afraid to know, but he asked anyway. "What's in the jar?"

Nestled in beside the biggest, bloodiest slab of meat he'd ever seen was a large mason jar, half full of a waxy, yellow substance that slid down the glass and pooled in gelatinous lumps.

"Bear fat," Mark said. "You have to drink it."

"Oh *fuck*," Ré moaned. "You gotta be kidding me!"

"I'm not," Mark said, but not without sympathy. "You have to heat it up and drink it."

The horror was all over Ré's face. "All at once?" he asked.

"Shit. I don't know," Mark said. "Yes?"

Ré went blank, the thought just too awful to process. Then he said, "So it's bear too, obviously."

"Yeah," Mark said, wrinkling his nose. "Sorry."

The thing must have weighed ten pounds, oozing red into the wrinkles of the cling film it was wrapped in. Réal couldn't help picturing the poor creature it had been taken from. The thought of eating it made him feel utterly worthless. "Well," he said. "Thanks, I guess."

Mark held out his hand for Ré to take—not in a handshake, more like they might arm-wrestle. Ré took it, gripping hard. "Hey, man," Mark said. "Good luck."

❖   ❖   ❖

Black Chuck ate his only daughter.

When she was just small, they said. *The size that you are now.*

It was deep in winter, there was no meat but hers.

Just snow and snow for miles. Eyes, scared and wild.

He knew this story well, but there were others just like it. Fathers feeding on blood when the food ran out. Burying starved-to-death children under frozen lakes to kill the temptation to suck their little bones. Windigo spirit passed down from one on to the next until it got to him, *Black Ré.*

He thought of Evie's eyes today, red and glassy. He wasn't just no good like this—he was dangerous. How was he supposed to be there for her, for the baby, with his dreams so full of teeth?

The cure sat on the Buick's passenger seat, staring up from its brown paper bag. Ten pounds of bear meat and a liter of fat. How in hell was *that* gonna kill a demon?

Mark had said something about tricking his mind, leading it away from dark desires. But seriously. The last time meat had passed Ré's lips, it had been going in the wrong direction. He had no idea how *this* horror show was supposed to stay down.

Just as he turned the key in the ignition, his passenger door flew open.

His heart jumped out the window and ran away.

"Hi, Réal," Sunny said. She ducked in the open door, giving him a look that blinded like bright lights.

"What do you want?" he asked, angry, panic rising. He reached for the bag.

"I want to talk," she said, "and I don't want your bullshit answers." She shoved the bag over and got in the car, slamming the door behind her.

"Where's Alex?" He looked past her out the window.

"Home," she told him. "His dad picked him up."

"Does he know you're with me?" She rolled her eyes and flashed him a look that said, *Don't be stupid.* He shook his head. "Okay. So talk."

"Not *here*, Ré," she snapped. "The entire school is watching." She gestured toward the park with a bangled arm, but she was exaggerating. No one seemed to have even noticed them.

"Okay, Sunny," he said, giving up. "Where do you think we should talk?"

"My parents are out tonight," she said. "My place is empty."

"Fine."

That familiar, crowded feeling he got when she was too close started to bloom inside his chest. Like she couldn't be reasoned with or resisted, and it was easier to just let the storm blow him down than to fight it. It was exactly what had got him into this mess with her in the first place.

He threw the Buick into reverse and stomped on the gas, jarring her so she had to brace herself against the dash. It was childish, he knew, but she didn't exactly bring out the best in him.

Sunny's place was a little north of downtown, on the west side of the river, in a pretty nice neighborhood. Réal didn't know what her parents did for a living, but they had a big house and a car with a pearly gold paint job and real leather seats. Sunny had an older brother Ré had never met, who went to university down in the States somewhere. *Fucking golden boy* was all Ré had ever heard about him.

When they got to her street, she said, "Don't park in the driveway. The neighbors will get weird."

He parked farther down, hidden from her house by a boxwood hedge. He turned the key. "Sunny, can't we just talk right here?" But she got out of the car and threw the door closed without answering.

He shook his head and looked at the bag on the seat beside him. How in hell was a guy supposed to eat ten pounds of meat and not drop dead of a heart attack on the spot? His chest hurt just thinking about it.

"Ré!" she snapped, banging her hand on the trunk. "Come *on!*"

21

R

The inside of Sunny's house was all soft edges and beige.
The furniture matched the knickknacks, and the carpet
went right to the walls in a color that wouldn't have lasted
ten seconds at Ré's house. And it was quiet, the low hum of
central AC the only sound. He had a hard time believing that
the hurricane had swirled up out of a place as calm as this.

She went up the stairs ahead of him, leading him to
the third floor. Her bedroom was at the front of the house.
Like Evie's, it had a gable facing the lawn, but unlike Evie's,
it had a door onto a small balcony, and the paint wasn't all
chipped to shit.

Sunny sat on the bed. Ré walked past her to the balcony
door, looking out instead of at her. "So what's up?" he asked,
sliding his hands into his back pockets.

"What's up?" she echoed indignantly. "Why don't you
tell me?"

He flinched. "I don't know what you're talking about."

"Yes you do, Ré."

He took a deep breath, still staring out at the trees. "Okay," he said. "What's up is that you're my buddy's girlfriend."

"Oh, whatever, Réal," she snapped. "You and I both know how much that means to you."

He turned to look at her. "It means a hell of a lot more than you think it does, Sunny."

"Oh yeah?" She raised her voice. "That's funny. 'Cause it didn't seem to at all until Evie came along." Seeing his reaction, she said, "Yeah, that's right. I know something is going on with you two. I'm not blind."

He stared at her with his lips pressed thin. "There's nothing going on," he told her quietly.

She said, "You're a shitty liar, Ré."

He'd known Sunny for three years, and they'd been almost instant friends, but not in a buddy-buddy way. More like fire and gasoline. Hornets and honey. So when had things got so fucked up between them? He thought back to September, to Shaun getting a real girlfriend instead of just laying his good looks down and catching whatever walked by.

That's it, I guess, Ré thought.

Before Evie, he and Shaun had spent most of their time together. But girlfriends have a way of taking time, and so Ré had spun loose, found a new constellation. He and Sunny couldn't be more different from each other, but somehow that had only made them like each other more. He acted like he hated her, but the truth was a lot more complicated.

He shook his head and said, "Sunny, I can't do this anymore."

She didn't answer right away. And then she whispered, "I knew it." Tears had welled in her eyes, pulling his heart out through his bones.

He crossed the room and sat next to her on the bed. He put his hand on her back lightly, but didn't know what else to say. He'd never broken up with anyone before. And she wasn't even *his* girlfriend. It was all just such a mess.

She took a shaky breath and wiped her eye with the back of her wrist, smearing black makeup across her cheekbone. Then she put her hand down on his thigh.

"*Sunny…*" he warned softly, looking at it.

"I know," she said, her voice a breathy whisper. He closed his eyes.

She turned into him and touched her mouth to the curve of his neck, where it met the collarbone. He gasped, eyes fluttering open, then closed again. *I can't*, he wanted to say. *Please, stop.* But the words never made it out of his brain. Her lips opened, her tongue warm and wet against him, and her hand moved slowly up his leg.

Fuck, fuck, fuck.

His breath caught in his chest. He wanted to put his hand over hers, to stop her, but he couldn't move. Instead, he leaned into her, his whole body wrapped up in the warmth of her mouth, dangerous and perfect and bewildering all at once, like it always was with her.

Her long fingers went under the edge of his T-shirt, tickling his bare skin, gathering up the shirt and pulling it over his head so it flipped inside out. She threw it on the floor.

"Sunny," he said again, his voice a quiet whine. "I—"

But she kissed him, stopping the words before he could say them. And he kissed her back, hard, their mouths tangled up together, his hand going to the back of her neck. Silky black hair sliding through his fingers.

She'd lured him here for this. And he'd let her. He knew that now. In all the months they'd been careening at the very edge of it, they had never let actual sex become a possibility. And that fact had been the one and only thing convincing him that he wasn't a total asshole.

He'd told himself over and over that it was under control, that it would never in hell get as crazy as this.

But like she said, he was a shitty liar.

They'd never been this alone before. And now they had this whole house to themselves, and he was half naked, and her hands were on his belt buckle. His mouth was on her throat, his hand up under her tank top, her bone-white skin so soft and hot and alive.

She wore a bandeau top, but no bra. He tugged at the stretchy fabric and it slid down, and her naked breast was in his palm, small and warm.

This is insane, he thought. This is *stupid-fucked-up-crazy*.

Last night, in his car, he'd wanted to be with Evie so bad it had made his stomach hurt. Not just be with her *physically*, like this, but to be there when she needed him. To care for her. Maybe even love her. He'd wanted to do the right thing, for once. To be brave.

And he'd thought that it would change all this. That he wouldn't want *this* anymore—this melting, sliding, too-hot feeling Sunny always gave him. But instead, he wanted it worse than ever.

Maybe I *can't* fall for someone new, he thought. Maybe I'm too far gone.

Maybe I don't deserve more than this.

Well, if I don't, he thought, then I'll take what I've earned.

Sunny pulled away from him. Her face was flushed pink and dazed, and she put her hand on his bare chest. She pushed him down onto the bedspread, and he let her. She straddled his hips with her knees, ripped up cutoffs riding high on her thin legs, making him want to tear them to pieces. Damn, he thought. Her fingers worked at the fly of his jeans.

He dropped his head back, closing his eyes, arms sprawled across the duvet. His heart was beating so fast his breath couldn't keep up, and he shivered all over.

He thought of Evie at the lake. The V of her bare legs on his lap, goose bumps across her damp skin. The way she'd held him when he dreamed. He thought of her smile, her lipstick. He thought he might die and never taste it.

Sunny got his zipper open.

He grabbed her wrist.

"Sunny," he rasped, eyes open. She gazed down on him with a look like she was dreaming. A smile teased her lips but never fully got there. "I gotta tell you something."

He swallowed hard, his dry throat sticking. He closed his eyes, not wanting to see her face when he said the words. "I've never done this before."

She went perfectly still. He swallowed again, all his nerve fleeing through his chest and legs under her slight weight. And then she laughed.

His eyes flew open. Her head was tipped back, and her shoulders shook, and she laughed that awful cackle. A cold spike rammed through him, like she was swinging a sledgehammer.

"What's so funny?" he snapped.

"Oh my god, Ré," she said too loudly, shattering the mood. "You are totally joking, right?"

Anger, humiliation welled up. He pushed himself up on his elbows. "I am not fucking joking," he said. "So I've never done it. What's the big deal?"

"Oh!" She gasped with laughter, eyes huge. "I don't believe it! You are so full of shit."

She stings like a damn hornet too, he thought. *Shoulda known.* "Screw you, Sunny," he muttered, but she only laughed harder.

"Well, that was the plan, wasn't it?" she shrieked gleefully.

"You're such a bitch," he spat, pushing her off his lap. She fell to her side on the bed and shook with giggles.

He leaped up, fists clenched at his sides.

"Aw, come on, Ré," she said in a cruel, condescending voice. "It's okay. I just thought you were more of a man, that's all." She giggled again. "Hey, you're a pretty good liar after all!"

"*Picrelle*," he spat. "*Trou de passage!*" They were harsh, nasty, terrible words his mother would have smacked his mouth right off his head for saying to a woman, and he was half glad Sunny didn't know their meaning.

"Seriously, though," she said, a little sweeter now, but still smiling too much. "It's totally cool, Ré. I'll be your first."

"You think I want that now?" He was twitching with rage. She said nothing, just stared up at him wide-eyed, her pretty mouth pinned shut.

"Y'know, you're right, Sunny," he said, shoving the blade in. "Things *are* different because of Evie. Because she makes me want to act like a decent human being." He waved a dismissive hand at her. "All *you* ever make me feel is fucking ashamed of myself."

She jumped up from the bed. "You son of a bitch!" she spat back, shoving a finger into his chest. "You wanted it too. Don't act like you didn't. If you feel bad about it now, don't blame me! I never twisted your arm."

He shut his mouth and just glared at her—because no matter how much he hated her right now, she was right. He'd never been helpless. He'd never actually *tried* to stop the hurricane.

Just then a roar like thunder rose up through the trees, so loud it rattled the windows.

They both looked toward the balcony. The roar had stopped in front of the house, and a second later there were footsteps banging up her front porch.

Réal and Sunny looked at each other, wide-eyed. They both heard the front door open.

"Hey, Sun!" Alex called. "You'll never guess what my dad just gave me!" His feet were already bounding up the stairs two at a time.

Ré went white. "What the fuck!" he whispered.

Sunny looked around frantically. "The balcony!" she rasped, pointing. They both dove for it, getting the door open, and she shoved him outside. "Get down. I'll keep him away."

The tiny balcony was only big enough for a small table and a folding sun chair, offering little shelter from the street. There was a large window on either side of the door and six small panes of glass in the door itself. It was the shittiest hiding spot of all time. He might as well have stood beside her bed with a lampshade on his head.

It was dusk, almost dark now, and that gave Ré a little cover, but not enough to slow his heart. He crouched, leaning his bare shoulder against the door, below the windows, praying Alex would not come near it.

He heard Alex burst into the room, cheerful, excited, talking a mile a minute. Sunny's voice, low and anxious, muffled by the wall of glass between them.

He heard the floor creak on the other side of the door as Alex chirped, "Come on—you gotta see it!" The doorknob turned. He tried to breathe, but his chest was so tight he thought it might crush his lungs, so he stopped.

He squeezed his eyes shut. Could he make himself disappear if he prayed hard enough? Could he fight Alex if he had to? It wasn't his strength he doubted, but his conviction. He could easily take Alex out if it came to that, but he didn't know if he would. *He* was the not righteous one, hiding half naked behind a bedroom door.

And then he thought, Is she really worth all this? Fighting and hiding and sneaking around for a girl who took every chance she got to make him feel like he'd never, ever be good enough for her, never be exactly who she wanted...

His eyes flew open with a revelation—that he did the exact same thing to her.

He was never kind to her, never gentle. And no matter how much he liked her, he had never touched her with anything but lust and want and emptiness. Because even if she wasn't with Alex, and they were free to be together, the only chance in hell they had of ever lasting was if they were both completely different people.

Fire and gasoline was a mix meant to burn itself out.

All at once, he felt the fire drain right out of him, the puff of smoke rise up from the ash. It was over. Really over. At last.

And then their voices were gone, and it was only his own heart slamming in his ears. Relief washed through him, and he relaxed a tiny bit, adrenaline still pumping so hard he could taste it, bitter, at the back of his throat.

Moments later Alex's voice rose from the street below. Ré edged toward the wooden railing of the balcony, jeans still half hanging off his hips. As he leaned, his knee nudged the sun chair, making it scrape against the gritty floor. The sound echoed off the arch of the balcony, amplifying, and he froze, clenching his eyes shut.

When he opened them again, he saw a motorcycle parked in front of the house. Slick, low profile, chopped drag bars, suspended seat, decked in leather and black paint and gleaming chrome, with short silver pipes jutting up on either side of the back wheel. It was as beautiful as it was sinister, like a massive black mud wasp.

Silver letters on the gas tank spelled out *Triumph*, and Ré knew exactly what it was: Alex's grandfather's Café Racer. One of the nicest bikes Ré had ever seen. Looking at it, Ré wondered if Alex ever thought about where his family's money really came from. Not that Ré'd be too proud to accept such a gift—he'd just never in a million years be offered one.

But despite everything, Ré was actually happy for him.

And then Alex stepped into view, his back to Réal. That filthy denim vest he always wore was now layered over a beat-up black leather jacket. A bike helmet hung from his left hand, Sunny from his right.

Ré stared. Alex had been riding since long before he was legal, and Réal had seen him many times on the back of one bike or another. But there was something different about this one. Standing next to it, Alex looked nothing like the goofy, wiry kid brother he'd always been to Ré and Shaun. He stood so sure of himself. Proud and unfamiliar.

Sunny turned slowly, and her eyes met Ré's over Alex's shoulder, whites showing around the black, even from a distance. She, too, looked different. Not herself. She looked...*scared*.

Ré scuttled backward, grasping for the doorknob, and threw himself into her bedroom ass first.

Inside, he leaped to his feet, swiping his T-shirt from the floor. He dressed as he ran downstairs to the kitchen, to the sunroom and out the back door to the garden, where he jumped over the back fence and took off at a run as fast as he could.

2 2

R

Réal lay in bed, head cradled in his clasped hands, waiting to feel different.

Last night, he'd walked for an hour or more through the hushed, dark streets of Sunny's old-trees-and-iron-fences neighborhood, listening the whole while for a motorcycle coming up behind him.

But it had never come. And when it got full dark, he'd doubled back, sneaking past Sunny's like a thief. Alex's bike had been gone. Her bedroom light had glowed at the top of the house, but he'd just kept going till he reached the Buick.

It had felt like days, not hours, since he'd sat across from Mark at the Olympia, since Evie'd put her hand down on his leg, since his last-ever day of high school. He'd driven home exhausted and stashed the paper bag in the basement fridge, praying no one would find it there. Then he'd fallen asleep like a dead man.

The second he woke, though, his brain started replaying the whole long day on a jagged loop. Evie's hand. Last day of school. Sunny. The sun was barely even up yet, but his mind was already miles away at a gallop, like he'd left the gate open in the night.

He lay in bed thinking about the whole mess while the sun curved over the house. It was a rare thing to have this place to himself, but his smallest brothers had hockey on Saturdays, and the other two would stay in bed till sundown if you let them. As soon as he heard his dad's truck heading for the arena, Réal rolled out of bed.

He pulled on yesterday's jeans and took the stairs double time to the basement.

He lifted the mason jar from the paper bag, then bundled the bag back up and stuffed it behind a box of peaches on the bottom shelf of the fridge.

In the kitchen, he got a spoon from the drawer and scooped the yellow contents into a dented double boiler. His tongue stuck in his throat. Not that he was super health-conscious or anything, but it still seemed like the wrongest thing in the world to knock back a jar full of hot fat.

He put the pot on the stove and stirred till the fat went soft. The thick smell of gamey meat filled the kitchen, clinging to his skin, his hair. This is so fucked, he thought, staring into it. Was it supposed to taste good, or was it straight-up punishment? Mark had not offered any insight; he'd simply handed him the bag. Shoulda just asked his mom, Ré thought. She'd have known what to do.

Réal had cooked hundreds of meals, thousands maybe. He was always thinking about food, making sure his brothers had enough. But he'd never thought twice before about what it meant to eat it. He'd never considered the trade-off the animal had made, its life for his. Right now, it felt like a pretty crappy bargain for the bear.

He closed his eyes and tried to remember the words he'd heard his aunties say so many times. *"Gitchi-Manidoo,"* he started, the name of the Creator coming awkwardly off his tongue. Of his three languages, this one was most like a newborn animal standing on skinny legs. *"Gigagwejimin ji-zhawendaman maanda miijim, zhawenimishin gaye niin noongo."* Each syllable tick-tocked out in a slow beat—*I ask you to bless this food and to bless me today.*

"Miigwech," he said. "Thank you. To this good thing that gave up its life here upon the earth, so that I can live. *Miigwech, Gitchi-Manidoo, miigwech."*

He opened his eyes and stared into the liquid fat, but he didn't feel any better, despite the prayer. He lifted the inner pot from the hot water and poured the grease back into the jar, raising it to the sunlight from the kitchen window. Viscous, amber yellow, sliding against the glass in long fingers. *"Miigwech,"* he said again, frowning, and tipped the jar to his lips.

It had been weeks since he'd last eaten anything that could think and feel. That might miss its time on earth. He held his nose and squeezed his eyes shut and tried not to breathe the animal stench. He tried not to see the eyes and snout of the bear, the bloody paws, the open belly, organs all pulled out. The butchery of such a mighty thing.

He tried not to see Shaun, lying in the glow of the arc light.

The grease hit his tongue—hot and slimy, coating his teeth and numbing his gums. His throat closed reflexively, gagging fat back up into the jar, but he tipped his head again and forced it down, gulping even as his body fought to reject it.

Fat leaked from the corners of his mouth, running warm down his chin and neck, spattering the counter. His toes curled against the tiles, his fingers into a fist, as he slugged it back, remembering Shaun's busted face, his jaw ripped apart, blond hair matted with blood. Shirt torn, belly torn, tubes of entrails pulled out, soft, sweet organs chewed away.

The taste of blood in his teeth.

He was a sinner. A killer. Deep down, he knew exactly what he'd done, even if he couldn't remember doing it. There was no other explanation for Shaun being as fucked up as that. If Ré hadn't seen it with his own eyes, he might never have believed a human body could look like that, twisted, butchered, broken open and just *wrong*.

It was all Black Chuck. He'd known his whole life this was coming.

The thing you feared the most *always* heard your call.

Réal dropped the empty jar and doubled over the sink, nearly puking it all back up the second he'd got it down.

Salt and slime coated his esophagus, acid sawing through him on a rusty edge. His stomach tightened, pressing everything up into the basket of his ribs. The veins of his neck and arms stood out. His muscles shivered and flexed. Ropes of spit spilled into the sink. He coughed for air, tongue hanging so far out it was like it was trying to grow legs and run away.

Tears stung his eyes. He knew he deserved all this and much, much worse, but he cried for himself anyway.

He swayed and his knees gave, and he slid to the floor in front of the sink, reedy sobs scraping through his chest. Please, God, he begged. Please, *Gitchi-Manidoo*, let this be over, just let this be the end.

I never meant to hurt anyone.

I'm so sorry, Shaun. I'm so, so fucking sorry.

He pressed the heels of his hands into his eyes till white sparks shot through the black, his chin dripping fat and spit and tears.

Despite his belly full of grease, he felt emptier than ever.

He knew this was nowhere near enough for what he'd done. He knew he'd never truly be absolved. But if this held the demon at bay—if it kept everyone else he loved safe from *him*—then at least he stood on the road to forgiveness.

Now all that was left was to walk it.

23

E

The doctor prodded Evie's belly, making soft noises of concern. "Have you been to see anyone else yet?" she asked. "Your family doctor maybe?"

"No," Evie replied.

"I see." Something fluttered across the doctor's face, but she didn't ask Evie why she hadn't seen her own doctor, and she didn't chew her out for not coming to this clinic sooner. "And what are your plans here? Are you going to follow through with this pregnancy?"

"Um," Evie whispered, squeezing the examination table under her. "Yes?"

"Okay," the doctor said gently. Everything about her was soft and nonthreatening, Evie noticed, even her voice. That was good. Evie wasn't sure she could handle it if the doctors at this clinic were anything but fairy godmothers. "And do you plan to keep this child, or would you like to talk about other options, such as adoption?"

"I, uh, I really don't know yet," Evie said, swallowing. "I haven't really told anyone about this. I'm sorta on my own."

The doctor smiled sympathetically. "So the father is..."

Evie almost said, *Dead, ma'am. The father is dead.* Instead she mumbled, "He's not around."

"Right," said the doctor, rolling her chair away from Evie. Her manner had gone brittle in an instant, though Evie felt it was directed more at the absent father than at her. If she only knew. Shaun had so wanted this. Tied together forever. He would have loved it.

"Well, from what I can tell, you are pretty far along, kiddo." The doctor wrote something on a large pad of pink paper. She signed the bottom and tore it off. "This is a requisition for an ultrasound," she said, handing it to Evie. "I want you to take this downstairs to the lab, and tell them you need this done today, okay? You've waited an awfully long time, and we just need to make sure everything is hunky-dory."

Evie took the paper, staring at its puzzle of words and body parts. "Okay," she said quietly.

"This is the suite number." The doctor put her finger at the top of the page. "You go down there now, and then you come right back up here, okay?"

Evie swallowed again, feeling so, so guilty—not just for everything, but for the baby now too. What if something was wrong with it? God, she thought, I'll die if there is.

Then the doctor put her hands on Evie's shoulders and gave her a squeeze. "You're not on your own anymore, sweetie. I'm with you now, and everything is going to be just fine."

Evie only wished she could believe that.

She left the doctor's office and walked back toward the stairs, head bent to the pink page. Did the doctor really think there was something wrong with her baby? Evie thought back to being drunk at Nan's, or stoned with Alex, the sunstroke and the skinny-dipping and the beer, all the while knowing exactly what was inside her.

She felt like a troll. What kind of person does that to an unborn thing? Her chest was so tight she could hardly breathe.

As she reached the stairs at the clinic's second-floor mezzanine, she noticed a group of girls her own age coming out of an office down the hall, and her eyes went round with surprise. Sunny was with them.

The group came toward her in a cloud of chatter. If Evie didn't hide fast, Sunny would surely see her, and then she'd have to explain why she was here, what the pink paper was for. She slipped past a pillar to the left of the staircase.

Sunny's group was nearing the stairs. If Evie was lucky, Sunny wouldn't notice her running the other way.

By the time Evie reached the opposite side of the mezzanine, Sunny was already at the bottom of the stairs. She didn't see Ev. She was too busy smiling at that bunch of strangers. Happy smiles. Not the fake, mean, bitter smiles she usually wore.

Evie tried to pick out a familiar face among the girls, but saw none.

Even though she was still pissed at Sunny for cornering her at the Olympia yesterday, Evie felt a little stab of jealousy—who were those other girls? How did Sunny have friends she'd never seen before, friends from some *clinic?* Sunny's whole life was a noisy, brash, screeching open book. She had no secrets.

But then, there was Réal...

She looked at the requisition in her hands and felt like running right out the front door. Like putting her head back in the sand until it all magically disappeared. Instead, she kept going around the mezzanine, circling back to the stairs as Sunny's voice faded below. As she passed the door the girls had all come out of, Evie glanced at the plaque pasted to the wall: *The Cold Water Center for Mental Health.*

What?

Evie peered through the window. Inside was a pale-yellow doctor's office like the one she'd just left, with the same potted plants and ugly, tweedy chairs.

"Can I help you?" said a voice behind her.

Evie turned to see a man trying to get past her through the door. The tag pinned to his blazer said *Dr. Sharma.* "No, sorry," she muttered, and stepped back from the window.

Holy shit, she thought. Sunny's crazy?

She backed toward the stairs, heart knocking in her chest. Did the others know about this? Was this, like all their other secrets, something everyone knew but her? If Sunny was crazy, that explained a few things, Evie thought, without a trace of sympathy.

She turned and ran for the stairs. She took them quickly, feeling lighter than she had since the Olympia. No—since the band shell. Whenever it was that Sunny had started picking at her armor, trying to figure out what was happening with her and Réal.

At the bottom of the stairs, she wheeled to the right, heading to the lab at the back of the building.

Sunny stepped out from behind a wilted palm.

Evie slid to a stop in front of her, almost falling to the floor.

"What are you doing here?" Sunny asked, dark eyes slicing at her.

"I, uh—" She raised the pink form to her chest like a flimsy shield, stepping back. "N-nothing," she stammered. "What are *you* doing here?"

Sunny's jaw tightened. "I had a thing."

Evie sneered. *She always has a thing.* So were those things all *here*? At a *mental clinic?*

The girls stared at each other silently, neither giving an inch. Then Sunny snatched the pink paper from Evie's hand.

Evie dove for it, but Sunny turned, blocking her. As Sunny's eyes flew over the paper, Evie saw her face change, like water soaking through sand. Everything teetering, tipping, threatening to fall. *No, no, no, no,* she begged as her insides dissolved.

"What the fuck?" Sunny said, her edge gone soft with genuine surprise. "What is this?" Her eyes ran over the page twice.

"Never mind," Evie said. She snatched the page back, face on fire, tears threatening. "It's none of your business." Her voice pleaded for a mercy she wasn't sure Sunny had in her to give.

"Like hell," Sunny said. "A *fetal ultrasound*, Evie? You're *pregnant?*"

And there it was. Out loud.

The floor began to wobble beneath her. Her ears filled with white noise, her heart all talon and scratch inside her ribs. Was there any point in begging Sunny not to tell the world? She could already feel the weight of opinion and advice and good intention bearing down from all corners, like whatever she chose to do about this was suddenly everyone's business but her own.

A picture of Shaun, crashing over her. A picture of him leaping from the Grains.

Blood rushed from Evie's head. If she didn't sit down, she would surely fall down. Sunny's voice sounded muffled, like her mouth was full of stuffing, and Evie backed away. She could see Sunny's lips moving, her liquid-dark eyes almost hidden by her thick, black hair.

Evie turned away from Sunny, and away from the lab. She started walking fast toward the front of the building, and then she was running—right out the front door, before Sunny could see the tears streaming down her face.

24

R

Réal gathered up the pages of the second-last exam he'd ever write in his life, God willing. As he carried them to the front of the classroom, a familiar shape passed by the open door. He shook the pages at the teacher. "Come on, man. Take 'em," he muttered. The teacher raised a brow, but took the pages without a word. "Thanks," Ré said, halfway out the door.

Evie's black sneakers squeaked with each quick step away from him.

"Hey!" He ran to catch up with her.

She turned. Her eyes darted over his shoulder before they settled on his, as if she'd seen something looming up behind him. "Hey," she replied.

"How are you?" he asked. He shoved his fists into his jean jacket. "Feels like I haven't seen you in days."

She shrugged. "You haven't."

"Yeah, right. Exams, I guess," he said. She just nodded. "So how you been?"

She looked at him funny again, blue eyes darting all over before she answered. "I don't know."

Réal ran his lip through his teeth. *I'm sorry*, he wanted to say. Instead he said, "Hey, you need a lift home or something?"

She shook her head like she was saying no, but then she said, "Yeah, okay."

Ré smiled, but something fluttered behind his ribs. Every single time he'd been near Evie in the last month, he'd been half waiting for Sunny to jump out at him. Not like she had any right to be jealous, but she would be. She was. But that was over now, so she couldn't care one way or another. Right?

They walked to his car. Réal opened the passenger door, then went around and hopped in the driver's side. He brought the big engine to life with a flick of his wrist. Neither of them said anything as he eased out of the parking lot and headed east, through town.

Finally, she said, "They're selling Shaun's car."

He glanced at her. "Really? How do you know?"

"I went to Nan's."

Ré's brows shot up. "Whoa," he said quietly. "How is she?"

She gave him a look like, *how do you think?* But she didn't say that. She looked down at her lap. "She asked me to tell him to come home."

"Fuck," he said, breathing out. He checked his mirrors. He hadn't seen the cops lurking around the school in a while. Maybe the worst was over? Maybe that thing with the bear grease had actually worked? "Ev," he said, "can I ask you something kinda weird?"

She looked at him, curious.

"I was wondering if I could cook something at your house," he said. "It's meat. Please don't ask why."

She didn't laugh, like he'd thought she might. She just nodded like she was thinking it over, then said, "When?"

"I was thinking maybe Saturday?"

Again, silence. He glanced at her, fully expecting a no.

She leaned against the headrest and looked out the window. "Is it a secret thing?" she asked.

"Uh, kind of," he admitted. "It's also just a roast, but I can't do it at home or my folks will think it's dinner."

She wrinkled her nose. "Will it be disgusting?"

"Nah," he said. He hoped. "It's pretty normal, I guess." *If gorging on bear meat to kill a demon is normal.*

She shrugged. "Okay."

He smiled, relieved. "Thanks, Ev."

After a while she said, "Can we go to your place right now? I don't feel like seeing my mom today."

He looked at her, puzzled. She stared back, big blues, her dark hair sliding across her cheek in the breeze. He checked his watch and calculated how many brothers might be home at this time of day. Two at most. Maybe none. "Sure," he said, heart fluttering again.

He pulled a U-ie at the next lights, and five minutes later they were in his driveway.

2 5

R

Réal led her into the front room, then stood in the doorway, not sure what to do next. He scratched behind his ear. "You thirsty?"

She shrugged. "Not really."

He tried to see his living room the way she was seeing it now, for the first time. All the toys and shoes and laundry in baskets that would probably just get picked through and worn again before it was ever folded. He might have once been embarrassed by the mess, but that was pointless. This room never looked any better than it did now.

"Where's your dog?" She nudged a leash on the floor with her sneaker.

"Upstairs, probably. He's super old. The twins'll walk him when they get home."

She nodded. She stood with her hands balled in the pockets of her cutoffs.

"How come you don't want to see your mom?" he asked.

She glanced at him and took a deep breath, letting it out before saying, "You keep asking me what I'm doing about the baby." Before he could protest that he'd laid off, she continued. "And I didn't tell you 'cause I didn't know. I didn't want to think about it. But when I saw Nan the other day...I don't know. Something happened."

Réal kept quiet, waiting.

She cupped her hand around the little bundle of her belly. You'd hardly even notice it unless you were looking for it. "It's not just an alien," she said. "It's Nan, and it's Shaun, and it's his mom. And it's me, even though I don't love it yet." She shook her head, her voice sad and hollow. "And I might never love it, but...I've decided to keep it, for now."

"For now?" he asked.

"Yeah. I mean, I've decided to have it. I'm thinking about adoption."

Ré breathed out in a rush. "Wow," he said. "That's huge."

"Yeah." She glanced at him. She looked scared as hell. "So I gotta tell my mom, I guess. But just not today."

"Shit, Ev, that's great. I mean, that you figured it out and all. That's awesome. *Right*?" From the look on her face, he couldn't tell how she felt about it, and maybe that was because she still didn't know. He hesitated, then stepped over and put his arms around her. She didn't resist, but she kept her hands in her pockets.

"Sunny knows," she said into his shoulder.

Ré stiffened. There she was. Good ol' Sunny, jumping out whenever Evie was around. He pulled back a little, looking into her eyes. "Does that matter?"

Evie shrugged, looking miserable. "I guess not."

Ré stepped back and ducked a little to see her eye to eye. "Evie," he said, "it does *not* matter. *She* does not matter, okay? Nobody does but you. This is your life and it's your decision and you are the only one who can tell you how to feel about any of it." Evie just stared at him, not even blinking. "If she messes with you—if anyone does—I got your back, Ev. I told you—whatever you need, I'm there."

Now she blinked, and the tears spilled. She said, "What makes you such a saint, Réal? I don't get it. You don't even know me."

He stared for a second, surprised, then looked away. "I'm no saint," he said. "Pretty far from it, actually."

Câlisse. What could he say? Everything honest was terrible. He slid his hands into his back pockets and told her, "Shaun was my best friend. My brother. I just want to do right by him, that's all."

She said nothing. And then, "Will you help me tell my mom on Saturday?"

"I will."

She smiled sadly. "And what about Sunny?"

He looked at her a long time, trying to figure out exactly what she was asking.

She is awfully pretty, he thought. She is all soft curves and eyes. The kind you wanna swim in, the kind that'd drown a guy if he wasn't careful. Her hair was always a wavy mess, and she wore boyish, oversized shirts, though that might have been just to hide her growing belly. She had pale freckles across the bridge of her nose that he'd only just noticed now, in this light.

She was the kind of girl you had to look at twice before you really saw her.

And she was a dreamer, just like him.

"Sunny and I are over," he said.

He could see the words take shape inside her, her heart jump up her throat. Maybe it wasn't what she'd been asking, but there it was, out loud. He almost laughed at how nervous he felt, how naked and silly and plain vulnerable those words had just made him. And then she threw out a rope and saved him—she smiled.

Not a huge, happy smile, not a gleeful, victorious one. One that barely touched her lips but reached all the way into her eyes, and he knew it was real.

He said, "Evie, I…" But the words got stuck partway. *That night, in my car,* he wanted to say. *And the way you look at me… I hope it's serious. It feels so fucking serious.*

"Me too," she said, and he fell right through the floor, into the basement, into the earth, all the way to China and out the other side. Flying in space. *Câlisse.*

He was so happy and so scared all at the same time. *Miigwech,* he thought, *miigwech, Gitchi-Manidoo.* I don't deserve this.

She took his hand and pulled him toward her. He swallowed. Magnificent strings of *sacres* flew through his brain as his mouth went dry. He licked his lips; he looked at her lips. She tipped her chin up and he ducked down, and he kissed her.

Instantly he was filled with the tingle and warmth of wine, and he was drunk. She put her fingers on his cheek lightly. He wrapped an arm around her waist, pulling her to him, feeling the curve of her belly press into him. Together they fell against the doorframe, her breath all over his neck, his hand in her hair. His joy was so heavy he didn't know if he could even stand up anymore.

He pulled away. "Ev," he said. "I—I don't do this. I don't just bring girls here."

"Okay," she said.

"I just want you to know," he told her. "I'm not like Shaun, like that."

"Ré," she said, "it's okay."

"I mean, I want to," he continued. "With you. I really want to." Her eyes were melting his legs out from under him. "It's just...I don't know if I want to *right now*. Is that okay?"

"Ré, please. Just shut up." She was grinning now.

He couldn't help but smile too. They were still bundled in each other's arms, smiling, pressed awkwardly against the doorframe. He ducked and kissed her again, and she made a little sound that nearly killed him. Good lord, he thought.

"Dude," came a voice behind them. Réal jerked back, almost dropping her from his arms. His brother Beni came down the stairs and passed them, looking deeply offended. "Get a frickin' room."

Ré chewed at the grin on his lips as he looked down at Evie. She was blushing furiously. He cupped her head in his hand and leaned his cheek to her hair. Beni disappeared into the kitchen.

"Do you want to go to my room," Ré asked, "and just hang out a while?"

She nodded, and he led her up the stairs and down the hall. The dog on his parents' bed barely raised his head as they passed, tail *wup-wupping* halfheartedly against the duvet.

They came to his bedroom door. No girl outside his own family had ever been in there. It wasn't any rule he had. It wasn't religious or anything. It had just never happened. Never been right. He pushed open the door and stepped in.

❖   ❖   ❖

Evie looked around, trying not to show her surprise. Réal's bedroom was nothing like she'd expected. It was smaller than her attic room, but it was immaculate. Almost military-tidy. The double bed was neatly made, striped sheet folded stiffly down. A dresser, a bookshelf, a night table with a lamp. Besides the bed, that's all there was. The closet doors were closed, everything else hidden away—if there even was anything else.

She didn't have so much experience with boys' bedrooms to have an opinion, but it was definitely a surprise.

He caught her eye as she looked around. "You okay?" he asked.

"Yeah, of course," she said. "It's just so clean."

He laughed shyly and looked around too. "The rest of this house kinda drives me crazy," he said. "I like things to be a little more..." He gestured vaguely with his hand.

"I can see that," she said. Since the bed was the only place to sit, she sat there.

"I have music," he said. "Wanna listen to something?"

"Sure." She watched him with a little smile on her lips. He seemed nervous, so unlike the Ré Dufresne people saw at school—cocky, silent and aloof. Toughest guy in the world. This guy's hands were shaking.

He went to the bookshelf, and she noticed a little black speaker nestled between the books. He flicked it on, then pulled his phone from his pocket and thumbed around, putting it down on the dresser as the speaker picked up the signal.

Ré liked heavy metal. He liked punk and thrash. He liked stoner rock. It was all that had ever played in his car, before Shaun died. Like Sunny had said, *dinosaur music*. But what came out of that little black speaker was another surprise— soft guitar, little drops of piano and a voice rasping quietly about the moon. "What is this?" she asked.

He sat next to her on the bed. He took her hand and pressed it between his, folding their fingers together, his leather watch pressing her wrist. "Nick Drake," he said, tracing her skin.

"I didn't know you liked stuff like this," she admitted.

"You don't really know anything about me," he said, smiling a little.

She smiled too. It was sort of true.

She looked at the side of his face as he looked down at their clasped hands.

Big brown eyes hidden by his paintbrush lashes. Nose bent where it had been broken, angling down toward his lips...She closed her eyes and breathed. When she opened her eyes, those lips were just as nice as they'd always been. Plum-colored and perfect. She wanted to run her fingers over them, trace them into memory.

She felt like she could really see him now, finally. Past his camouflage. Past the tough armor. Under the hard shell that kept his softest parts safe from other people.

Underneath all of that, he was just a normal boy.

It almost hurt, looking at him. He was not like Shaun at all. Shaun didn't have camouflage, he didn't have layers to dig through and peel back and etch away into something better than what he seemed. Shaun was loud. He was obvious and full of needs. He wanted everything.

But Ré never asked for anything, even when he needed it. All he did was give. True, she didn't know much about him, but she did know that.

And then she spoke very quietly, almost hoping he wouldn't hear. "I could love you, you know. If you asked me to."

He looked up, startled. Then his perfect, plum-colored lips curved into a sweet, surprised little smile, and he blinked at her like he was looking into the sun.

26

E

A picture of Shaun, standing in her driveway throwing stones. "Come down," he'd yelled. "Come on!" Waving her into his car.

That night he'd driven her to the Grains, not talking, eyes brimming with hot sparks. She'd been half asleep when they'd climbed the fence. And when she'd slid through the boarded window into the dark, he was already long gone up the stairs.

She'd heard the trucks of his skateboard rattle as he threw it down, the wheels whiz as he shoved off. She'd climbed the stairs after him, resentful. Why was she there if he wasn't going to wait for her, talk to her?

At the second floor, his shadow had arced around the farthest pillars. He'd been angry. It had made her angry—he'd got her out of bed just to ignore her. She'd stood there, thinking, Maybe if I close my eyes, I'll wake up in my own bed, dreaming.

Then she'd turned and gone up to the third floor, listening to the wheels curving close, then away, at the bottom of the stairs, no intention of following her up. *Let him skate all night for all I care.*

She'd gone to the hole in the wall and looked out over the broken fire escape, the tracks, at the stars cutting through blue velvet sky, and she'd imagined she was nothing, that she wasn't even there.

Evie stood in that broken doorway now, in bright daylight. In her pocket, she rolled a little silver bead between her fingers. She'd walked over the steps they'd taken that night, looking at the ground, the marks in the dust. They were almost clear. If you knew, you could see where he'd been, where she had been. All scuffs and scuffle, empty bottles, broken glass.

She sat down in the busted-out doorway, leaning against the frame. She'd written her last exam that afternoon. She should have been happy, but instead she was only jealous. After today, they'd all be free, Sunny, Ré and Alex. They could flee this town and never come back, if that's what they wanted. She dipped her toes into the loneliness and wiggled them around, testing the waters.

If Shaun were still alive, she would have at least had him. Deep down, she even thought that might be why he'd chosen her in the first place. That the answer to *why me, why now* was simply that she'd still be in school when he graduated. They might even graduate together, if he kept missing class. Then he'd never be alone.

Evie sighed. She looked at the drop below the broken fire escape to the second-floor landing, and through the rusted slats there to the scrubby grass below. Tomorrow, she'd tell her mom everything. Not just about the baby, but about Shaun too. The truth. Not Shaun the Invincible—the *real* truth. The one no one knew.

Evie swallowed at the lump in her chest, remembering Réal yesterday. His sweetness, his perfect lips, her hand in his, warm and secure. The word *love* out loud...

If he was serious about being there for her now, he'd hear the real story too.

She had no idea how he'd take it. How many times had he told her he and Shaun were like brothers? Grown up together, lives entwined, as good as blood, et cetera. Ré loved Shaun. They all did. He was the sun they had all spun around.

But that night, he'd been the other Shaun. The one that only she knew. *Pushy*. He was so pushy, always laughing at her when she pushed back, making her feel small. *Aw, come on*, always. It was just so much easier to let him crash over her.

Like that night, after the lake. Drunk, driving home. Her lip swollen and hot. He'd followed her up the attic stairs, lifting her clothes when all she'd wanted was to go to sleep, mad and alone.

"Shaun, stop it," she'd said. "You're drunk."

"Don't be so frigid." He'd laughed, not stopping.

Should she have bothered saying please? Did *please* work on freight trains?

She'd let him undress her, let him breathe and sweat. Because he wasn't always like that. He was nice, mostly. Not the monster you imagine boys who don't hear *no* to be. He was still *Shaun*, even when he hurt and when he wouldn't listen. It was all so confusing, she hadn't known how to feel, even though it had all felt wrong somehow.

Evie blinked tears from her eyes, staring out at the field where he was found.

Where should she have drawn that line, exactly? When did it stop being okay for him to always get what he wanted? He was her *boyfriend*, not some stranger climbing in the window. They'd had sex plenty of times, and it had mostly been nice, his face nuzzled into her neck, his heart beating fast against hers.

Just…sometimes it hadn't been like that. Sometimes he hadn't cared if she'd wanted it or not, and then it had felt like their whole relationship was just for him. Like she was hardly even there at all.

Inside her backpack her phone buzzed. Evie sniffled and wiped her eyes on her sleeve. She dug her phone out and read the screen. **Hey. You home?**

Butterflies flew out from under her ribs. She looked across the field. Réal's place was that way, just over the tracks and trees.

She typed back **At the Grains.**

There was no *dot, dot, dot* indicating a reply.

❖   ❖   ❖

R

At the Grains.

He lay on his bed, head propped on a bent arm as he stared at the phone in his hand, thinking, What in hell is she doing over there? He rolled and stood up, pulled his jean jacket from the back of his bedroom door.

Instead of replying, he went out to the Buick, a large paper bag tucked under his arm. He dropped it on the passenger seat, pulling the door closed behind him, then dialed Evie's number and put the phone to his ear.

"Hey," she said.

"Hey," he echoed. He cleared his throat. "Are you busy right now?"

"Not really." Her voice sounded heavy.

"Could I maybe come see you?" he asked, tapping his thumb on the steering wheel, hoping for a yes. There was a long silence, and he pictured that dreamy, other-planet look in her eyes, like his words had to leave orbit just to reach her.

"Okay," she finally said. "I'm in the storehouse. Third floor."

He shivered at the thought of that awful hole in the wall. "'Kay, don't move," he said. "I'm coming to you."

It was not even a five-minute drive. He parked on the street and jumped the rickety fence, leaving the paper bag in the car. He came up under the hole in the storehouse wall and looked for her. She leaned out and smiled. He blinked and smiled back. He pulled the broken board from the ground-floor window and climbed in, taking the stairs two at a time to where she was.

"Hey." His voice bounced off the rotten walls.

She sat cross-legged, leaning on the empty doorframe, looking like a rail rat, all scraped up and dirty, her clothes covered with grime. "Hi, Ré," she said, hair falling away from her tipped-up face.

"Why are you so damn close to that thing?" he said, jutting his chin at the gap in the wall. He crouched a few feet back from it. He wasn't a fan of heights, but he'd been Shaun's friend long enough to get used to them. She answered with a shrug. Maybe she was used to them too.

He looked around at the filthy floors, empty bottles smashed everywhere, fist-sized holes in the walls. He didn't like this place. It was dark. He hadn't been near it since that night, since the arc light. He didn't want to see the field below.

"So," he said, "remember when I asked if I could cook something at your place?"

She smiled, and he could tell she was sort of laughing behind it, but he didn't care. "Of course I remember," she said.

He jerked his thumb back the way he'd come. "It's in my car," he told her. "I was thinking I could drop it off at your house, then come cook it up tomorrow."

"Now?"

"Yeah, now," he said. "If that's cool?"

She nodded. "Okay." She shrugged her backpack up onto her shoulder and scooted toward him. He grabbed her by the ankle as if she were throwing herself the other way, out the window. "Thanks for saving me," she said sarcastically.

"Sorry," he said, letting go. They stood and went to the stairs, Ré casting a last, uneasy glance across the filthy room.

They walked back through the field to his car, evening sunlight cutting low and golden across the grass, crickets leaping out of their path.

"You shouldn't climb the fence," he told her.

"Why not?"

"Because of the you-know-what," he said. He didn't want to say *baby*. He didn't want to upset her.

She cocked her head defiantly. "I climbed it to get in here, didn't I?"

He jutted his chin farther east, toward the Grains' open front gate. "Just...will you walk down there and I'll pick you up, please? I don't want you getting hurt on my watch."

She rolled her eyes at him, but she agreed.

2 7

E

Evie walked around the nose of the Buick and got in next
to a large paper bag. In the closeness of the car, she noticed
he was wearing cologne, some kind of warm tobacco that
almost masked the car's natural smell. She smiled to herself.
And she didn't say anything when he U-ied back the way
he'd come, taking the long way to her house instead of going
past Shaun's.

He acted relaxed, but he looked nervous, shy. His dark
eyes sort of skittered over her but didn't settle, and he tapped
his thumb anxiously against the wheel. His silence made her
nervous, binding her tongue. He glanced at her as he drove,
but she couldn't tell what he was thinking. Then he said, "You
coming to Alex's tonight?"

She looked at him. "Are *you* going?"

He shrugged. "It's my grad party. Plus he asked me to.
I can't really say no, can I?"

"No, I guess not," she said. But she was surprised. Sunny would be there, obviously. And was he still friends with Alex after everything? Those seemed like dangerous, complicated waters.

"So are *you* asking *me*?" she said, after a pause.

He laughed quietly, glancing at her again. "Yeah, I guess I am."

"Well, then I can't say no either." She met his eye, and they both smiled. She felt the cabin pressure drop a little, as if he'd just been waiting for permission to land. He reached across the seat and took her fingers in his, squeezing lightly.

She pictured them arriving together, like this. Pulling into Alex's driveway hand in hand, all smiles and normal, like it used to be with Shaun, nobody even noticing how the furniture was rearranged. If only it could be that easy.

"Ré," she said, "what are we going to tell them? I mean, Sunny is gonna be mad, right?"

He didn't answer right away. He looked in all his mirrors first, and then he shook his head. "I want to say no, Ev. I want to tell you she'll be cool, but she probably won't be." He went quiet again, thinking. Then he said, "Maybe it's better if we don't say anything for a little while."

She knew he was right, but she still looked at him sideways. How long had he been with Sunny behind everyone's back? Did he really think he could keep Evie there too? But he was right, for now. For tonight anyway. It was safer, till the dust settled, not to say anything. And anyway, after tomorrow, after she told her mom, everything might change.

She swallowed. "So is there something to hide—with us, I mean? Are we...?"

He glanced at her, and she couldn't finish. The words got stuck in his eyes. He bit his lip, then let go of her hand and pulled on the steering wheel, bumping the car to a gentle stop at the side of the road.

He turned to face her, his arm draped over the wheel, little hairs catching sun like he was made of gold. "Ev," he said, looking not at her, but down, between them, "I hope you don't think that's all I am—just a guy with a lot of bad secrets." His eyes hid behind black lashes, keeping him safe, away. "I know I haven't been real good for a long while. And I done stuff I'm not proud of."

His voice was so quiet, his face so serious, she didn't know how to respond. Hadn't they all done stuff they weren't proud of?

Then he looked up at her, lashes fluttering open unexpectedly. "But I really do want to be good now, if you'll let me."

She flushed, embarrassed and a little confused. "I don't think it's up to me, Ré."

"No," he said. "I mean—I want to be good *to you*. Like what you said yesterday, about if I asked for it?"

His voice lifted at the end like a question, though it wasn't one. She remembered her words in his bedroom, of course, clear as a bell. But even in his asking, he still couldn't seem to get the question out. He still wasn't really asking. "I meant what I said," she told him, swallowing hard.

He reached to take her hand again, his fingers warm and firm, threading between her own, making her heart skip. "I want that," he said quietly. "I really do, Ev. But I don't want you to just give it to me 'cause I asked. I want to earn it. To be good enough for it. That's what I'm trying to tell you."

But she was still confused. Was he talking about Sunny? What could he possibly have done that was as bad as he seemed to think it was? Or that was in any way worse than the things she'd done? "So...for now," she said, "we say nothing, because there is nothing to say?"

His mouth quirked up at the corner, but she could see in his eyes how sincere he was. "It's not *nothing*, Ev," he said. "It's so, so much."

She nodded, throat closing on all her words, heart racing. He was right. It wasn't *nothing*. It was everything she'd never wanted to feel, and she wanted it more than anything.

Despite all her desire to disappear, to not exist, not feel, not let anything get too close or too real, there was Ré, sitting sideways on the driver's side of a shitty blue Buick, laying his heavy eyes on her and making her want it all.

❖   ❖   ❖

R

Réal eyed the car in Evie's drive as they pulled up outside her house. "Your mom's still home?" he asked, trying to sound relaxed.

Evie said, "She'll leave for work soon."

"Does she ever get days off?"

"Yeah, every two weeks she gets four days," Evie told him. "But almost never on weekends."

"You don't get to see her that much, huh?"

Evie shrugged. "Not really."

"That sucks," he replied, but it didn't seem to bother her. Family was important to Réal. But then, maybe a family as big as his swallowed you up, made you care, even if you didn't really want to. But if your whole family was just one other person you never saw, maybe it was easy not to care so much about them.

"Come on," she said, tilting her head. "She wants to meet you anyway." When his eyes went round, she laughed and got out of the car.

Ré didn't know why, but he was nervous as hell. Maybe it was the ten pounds of bear meat under his arm—*just the cure for cannibal demons, no big deal.* He was actually pretty good with parents when he wasn't worried about eating their daughters.

A middle-aged woman stepped out of a room at the back of the small house. She wore light-green scrubs and a pair of running shoes, and she was pulling her long brown hair up into a high ponytail. "Hi, Evie," she said, looking at him.

"Mom, this is Réal." Evie nodded over her shoulder at him. "The guy I told you about."

Câlisse. If he was nervous before those words, he was a catastrophe now. What, exactly, had she told her mother about him?

He shifted the package under his arm and stuck out his hand. The woman smiled, taking it. "Nice to meet you, Mrs. Hawley," he said, as politely as he could. He didn't even know where to look. He felt his cheeks flush red. Yeah, he was good with parents—you didn't half raise four brothers without meeting a lot of moms—but this was different. This was a *girl's* mom. He'd never done that before.

Catching the hint of his accent, Evie's mom said, "So you really are French, huh?" like she'd thought it was a hoax before he'd opened his mouth.

His eyes flicked to Evie's. "Ah...*oui*," he said stupidly. And then, like a dancing dog, "*Mais j'parle surtout l'anglais de toute façon*" But he could see she was impressed, and it made him feel slightly less idiotic.

"Ré's grad party is tonight," Evie told her mom. "He asked me to go, if that's okay?"

Mrs. Hawley stood back and looked him over. Ré stiffened nervously, wanting to clear his throat but afraid it would seem impolite.

"Okay," she said, poking a finger at him. "But don't stay out all night. And no booze if you're driving."

Ré was about to give her an answer she'd like when Evie rolled her eyes and said, "*All right, Mom*" and started pushing him through to the kitchen.

He glanced at Mrs. Hawley and could almost see her daughter in the wry smile she wore. "I'm trusting you, Réal," she said as he went by. "She's the only one I've got, so be careful with her."

"I will," he assured her. "I promise."

The kitchen was only big enough for the appliances and a small table, but it opened onto a dining room that was pretty and comfortable.

"Can I leave this in here?" he asked, raising the bundle under his arm. She pointed at the fridge, nodding yes.

He bent and put the package on a shelf. This is weird, he thought, pushing back the leftovers and half empty jars of mayonnaise. Nice weird. Like we're married or something.

He straightened from the fridge, not knowing where to look or what to touch. She stood at the sink, pouring a glass of water, and he couldn't help but let his eyes fall down the backs of her legs. Their shape made his stomach tighten, made him want to stand closer.

"All right, you guys." Evie's mom appeared in the kitchen doorway, keys in hand. Ré nearly jumped out of his skin at her voice. He turned, blushing, hiding his eyes. "Have fun at your party. Don't burn anyone's house down. Evie, can I have a little chat with you, alone?"

Evie groaned and followed her mom to the front door. Ré just lifted his hand in a shy wave and pressed his lips into a smile. He heard their murmuring voices and imagined what they must be saying about him. *Horny, pervert, sicko…*When he heard the car pull out of the drive, he felt a small weight lift from his shoulders.

Evie didn't return to the kitchen. She went straight up the attic stairs without a word, and it took him several minutes to realize she wasn't coming back. After a while he heard the upstairs shower running in the pipes above his head.

❖   ❖   ❖

"Ré?" Evie's voice rose from a distance. "Are you all right?"

Then her hand was on his shoulder, pulling him back from the dream.

He sucked a breath, startled awake in an unfamiliar room. When his eyes found her, he relaxed. He put his hand down on hers, patting it like he was comforting her, not the other way around. "Sorry," he said. "I guess I haven't been sleeping much lately."

He ran a palm over his face and felt a cold trail of drool. Jesus, he thought. Fucking embarrassing.

She plunked down on the other end of the couch, folding her legs under herself and looking at him with worried eyes. "What language was that?"

"Huh?" He blinked at her again.

"You were yelling in some weird language."

He flushed, remembering the deer, the dream. He said, "It's not weird. It's Anishinaabemowin."

"Seriously?" she said. "You speak *three* languages?"

He nodded. "I kind of suck at it, though. It's not like it's taught at school or anything. You gotta rely on family to keep it sharp, and we don't see my mom's side so much."

"It sounded pretty good to me," she said, and he smiled.

His heart had settled a little, the dream fading. He took another breath and told her, "My father's side are all from *Rivière des Outaouais*. They mostly speak *joual*—that's old-school Quebecois, not the French you learn at school. And my mom's side all speak Anishinaabemowin, with only a little French. You should see our family get-togethers. They're kinda nuts."

He shook his head, thinking of the chaos of two totally different languages, religions, cultures and traditions smashed together in one house, and the five wild, tough brothers it had made.

"Know how they say 'you're talking gibberish' in *joual*?" he asked. "*T'parle Algonquin.* 'You're speaking Algonquin.' *My mother's language.* How fucked is that, huh?" He shook his head again. "Talk about a culture clash."

They sat in silence for a while, cricket song rising from the empty field, sun almost down. "It's peaceful here," Ré finally said. "My place is so crazy." He thought of his bedroom, his only sanctuary. Even that never got as quiet as this. It was way too easy to feel good here.

And then she said, "My mom's an ER nurse. She takes the worst shifts, the bloodiest ones, 'cause the pay is better. Drunk drivers. Bar fights. Beat-up wives." Her eyes fell down to her hands. "That's why she's never here."

Ré pictured her here, night after night, all alone. He stayed put at his end of the couch, though he wanted pretty badly to slide over to hers, tell her, *J'suis là. I am here.*

She shifted, stretching her leg out, and he flicked a look at her, worried she was moving to sit closer, but she was only reaching into her pocket.

"What do you think this is?" she asked, opening her hand to show him a little silver ball. "I found it at the Grains."

He picked it up and rolled it between his finger and thumb. It was perfectly round. "It looks like a ball bearing," he said. "Like, from a wheel." He gave it back.

"Like a skateboard wheel?" she asked, examining it.

He shrugged. "Sure."

He sat back, resting his elbow on the couch, his cheek on his fist, watching her while she wasn't looking. Her wet hair had made shadows on her faded-soft plaid shirt, and her T-shirt just covered the rise of her little belly, poking out over her cut-off jeans. She looked cute, pregnant, but he'd never say that out loud.

He closed his eyes, thinking of her dangerously as his girl, that baby as his own.

Câlisse, it was easy to see...

Her toes pressed into his leg, and he opened his eyes, saw her grinning at him.

"Don't fall asleep again," she said. "I'll get bored and ditch you."

He smiled drowsily. "Where would you go?"

She looked out the front window, wiggled her fingers at the field. "Out there, somewhere," she said.

He looked down. Her toes looked like a little string of painted pearls pressed into his leg. His hand closed over them. "I'd just wait for you to come back," he said.

28

E

Alex's house was nothing like she'd imagined it would be. Nothing like Shaun's or even Sunny's. "Holy shit," she said, looking up through the cover of trees that hid it from the long driveway. "Is Alex *rich*?"

Réal laughed under his breath. "You could call it that," he said, ducking a little to look through the trees himself.

The house was a twenty-minute drive from town, east of the lake on a twisting, climbing, countryside road you might never find if you didn't already know your way.

It was after dusk, the woods just dark shadows, but winking between the trunks of oak and silver maple and birch were yellow lights from a house that seemed to go on for a mile. As the Buick came around a bend, she saw a massive triangle of windows, like an alpine lodge, that looked in on a double-height living room. Eerie blue light flickered up the endless walls from a flat-screen TV as big as a dining room table.

A huge wooden deck circled the house, and a few people were gathered there, drinking beer from tall cans. Evie didn't recognize them. They weren't from school. They were older, and they looked pretty tough—long hair, beards on some, dirty ballcaps. Even in the dark, Evie could see the ink decorating every inch of their arms. Their eyes all seemed to track the Buick as it came around the back of the house. Evie shivered and looked away.

Farther down the driveway stood a barn-shaped building with its doors flung open. Music and low light and voices spilled across the gravel drive, where cars were parked alongside a row of slick, black Harleys. Evie could see kids from school hanging out on a sloping lawn on the other side of the barn. A bonfire pit stood in the grass, but it was not yet lit.

Réal parked the Buick and they got out. Now that she was standing outside the car, Evie could hear the high, unsteady whine of dirt bikes not too far off. "Geez," she said, "they really like motorcycles, huh?"

Ré was bent into the back seat, grabbing a bag he'd picked up at the liquor store on the way, and as he straightened he gave her an amused look. "Just a little," he said, heavy on the sarcasm. He'd obviously been here many times. The place didn't seem to surprise him one bit.

She came around the back of the car, hoping he'd take her hand, knowing he wouldn't. For a second they just stood facing each other in the dark, nearly touching, nearly tipping their heads together, nothing but night between them. She could smell the warm tobacco scent of his cologne, his jean jacket, could almost smell the salt on his skin. All her senses exposed. She wished the whole night was just this, just them.

Then he cocked his head toward the barn. "You ready?" he asked. She nodded. He stepped back, and they crunched through the gravel to the open barn doors.

The building had to be a body shop, because the walls were hung with tools and engine parts, and the floor was smooth concrete stained black with oil. Evie was not surprised to find more motorcycles under the dim amber lights. These ones all looked pretty old, like they hadn't been ridden in a long time. Some were covered in canvas tarps or were lying in pieces on the floor.

Ré nodded to one that wasn't covered. "'43 Knucklehead," he said. "All original."

"What?" she asked, like he was speaking *joual*.

"That's a Harley Knucklehead," he repeated. "From 1943. It was Alex's great-granddad's. Not too many of them left these days."

Evie looked at it again, not as impressed as she guessed Ré wanted her to be. "Why do they call it a Knucklehead?" She pictured the rider, not the bike.

"The rocker boxes," he told her, like she knew what those were. "They look like knuckles." He made a fist and showed her.

It wasn't the most comfortable-looking bike. The tiny leather seat had no padding at all, worn cracker-thin by, presumably, Alex's great-granddad's butt. She remembered Sunny telling her that he was "full-patch." She didn't really know what that meant, but Sunny had made it sound pretty heavy. Those spooky, inked-up guys on Alex's back deck were probably all full-patch too.

"How come you know so much about motorcycles?" she asked Réal.

He shrugged. "My dad's a machinist," he told her. "Sometimes he makes custom parts for these guys." She didn't really know what a machinist was either, but the answer sounded like it made sense.

A framed picture hung on the wall behind the bikes. She stepped over to look at it. Three young guys leaning on long rifles, and one more sitting sideways on a motorbike with white numbers sprayed across the gas tank. They all wore military uniforms, and all were grinning at the camera. Time had yellowed the photo, but the boys looked so young, maybe only Ré's age. Handwritten across the bottom was the inscription *Stay out of the bathtub, Janeski!*

"Janeski?" Evie asked aloud.

Réal came up beside her, looking at the photo too. "Yeah, they changed their name," he said with a shrug. "Racism, I guess." He stood so close she could feel his shoulder move. It made her want to tip her head, rest it on his denim jacket, just lean into him. She swallowed and stepped away, careful not to back into the bikes.

Réal took his beer to a vintage-looking fridge. He pulled one can out, glancing her way as if to offer it, but she was already walking toward the back of the barn, putting some space between them.

The back doors opened onto the lawn, blue in the failing light and surrounded by a ring of trees topped with the night's first stars. To the right, the yard sloped off down a hill, toward the sound of the dirt bikes.

Kids from school were gathered around a big tin tub that overflowed with ice and beer. A picnic table by the barn was spread with food and bottles of liquor, and a keg sat in a big bucket of ice on the ground beside it, red Solo cups scattered around. Ré totally didn't need to bring his own. There was enough booze here to get the whole class drunk twice and then some.

She recognized a lot of the kids, but she didn't really know them. Familiar faces that Evie had never spoken to. Most were not in her grade—it was a grad party, after all, and she wasn't graduating. She was a little surprised Alex had even invited these kids. A few weeks ago, this party probably would have only been five people. And it might have been on a rooftop, or down at the riverbank, or at the lake. But things were different now that Shaun was gone.

The rattle and spit of two-stroke engines rose from the bottom of the hill. It broke through the tree line, drowning the music, yellow headlights bobbing up across the blue lawn. There were three of them. When they reached the barn, their engines skittered to a halt, and the quiet that followed made her wonder why she'd thought the music had been loud before.

Alex lifted his long leg over the lead bike. He pulled his helmet off and shook his hair out, every tooth he had glowing in the dark.

"What's up, yo!" he shouted at the crowd, which earned a cheer, red cups and bottles raised. "Let's get this bitch started!"

He pushed through the crowd to the fire pit, drawing a silver Zippo from inside his leather jacket. He knelt and lit the pile of wood and paper, and the whole thing went up instantly, probably doused with starter before anyone had arrived. Bright sparks popped and whirled into the sky. The crowd loved it, and they let him know.

Flames picked his copper hair out from the dark, the angle of his grin, his narrow eyes, shadows dancing up his cheekbones. Evie hardly recognized him. He looked half wild. Lord of the Flies. King Alex. She thought of that night, of him leaping over the flames, and of the hollow look on his face later, when the fire had died.

He backed off into the dark again, letting it swallow him, letting his guests fill the space he'd left behind.

Evie saw Sunny then, standing at the edge of the fire-light. Her arms were crossed over an artfully torn-up black sweater and an acid-green bra. Her face was blank as stone behind the heavy curtain of her hair. Evie couldn't see her eyes, couldn't tell if Sunny had seen her too.

Alex didn't go to her, but back to the two guys he'd ridden in with, slapping their shoulders and laughing. Evie had never seen them before. She was starting to feel like it was a mistake, coming here. The only person she could talk to was Réal, and she wasn't even sure that was a good idea, by the look on Sunny's face.

Someone came up beside her, putting a sweaty arm around her neck. "Hey, I know you," he slurred happily, breath stinking. "You went out with that dead guy."

Evie threw him a withering scowl. "He wasn't dead when I dated him," she muttered, trying to shrug his arm off.

"Duh," he said, laughing. Then he pushed the red cup in his hand at her. "Here. You look like you could use this."

She took it. Inside was something black. She sniffed it. Cola. And booze probably. She accepted it, and he wandered off, grinning.

She had every intention of dumping it in the grass, but it occurred to her that, at least for appearances, she should have something in her hands. Being the only person here not drinking would just invite more sloppy arms around her neck, more red cups pushed at her chest. She held it like a talisman to ward off others but didn't take a sip.

"You okay?"

Réal was beside her, like he'd always been there. "Yeah," she said, nodding, glad.

They stood shoulder to shoulder, looking over the crowd. It had filled out even more since they'd arrived. Theirs was the only high school for three towns, and the grad class was pretty big. Plus there were all those other guys, the ones Alex was with. He'd said he wanted this party to be epic, and it looked like he was getting his wish.

"So they really are bikers, huh?" she asked in a low voice. It felt like something to be whispered, even here, where it seemed like everyone knew. Ré nodded, sipping his beer. She said, "But what does that even mean?"

Réal thought about it. "It's a brotherhood, mostly," he said. "They have each other's backs, no matter what."

"But how does that make Alex so rich?" She looked around at the rolling property, the barn and the big house behind it. It was hard to understand why Alex even hung out with kids from the east side when he had all this. All those nights in Nan's tiny front room. It was like a dirty shoe box compared to this place.

"They sell drugs," Ré said, voice flat. "But I wouldn't mention it, if I were you."

"Holy shit!" she hissed, eyes wide.

He glanced at her sharply. "Seriously, Ev. Don't mention it. These guys don't fuck around. This isn't TV."

Evie zipped her lips. Pictures of Charlie Hunnam flashed through her brain, despite Ré's words. But this wasn't *Sons of Anarchy*. This was *the family business*—what Alex had told her he was destined for, that day in the cafeteria.

Of course, she'd met dealers before at school. Just punk kids selling dime bags and pills, mostly. She could hardly imagine the amount of weed you'd have to sell to get a place like this. Unless it wasn't weed they dealt in.

A picture of those guys lurking on the back deck, their eyes sliding sideways with the Buick. Evie felt a rock sinking fast in her gut. For no other reason than nerves, she put the red cup to her lips. The moisture was welcome, her throat suddenly parched. And she was right, it was cola, but there wasn't any booze in it, just sweet, syrupy fizz. Relieved, she took a bigger sip, letting it slide down her dry throat.

The music volume had swelled with the crowd. Kids pulled lawn chairs around the bright fire pit or sat on the lawn in small groups, the pounding bass keeping their words from Evie's ears. Every once in a while the fire would pop and crack, shooting a hail of sparks into the night sky, and everyone would cheer.

This is just like any old bush party, she told herself, trying to relax. Trying not to think about Satan's Own creeping at the edges. She'd been to dozens of bush parties. Bonfires in the fields at rural kids' farms. Parties you had to hike half a mile in the dark to get to. Wet feet and wet asses, eaten alive by mosquitos and hedges full of thorns, broken bottles everywhere, everybody wasted, bloody fistfights, and girls' shrill screams…

Yeah, she thought, red cup shaking in her hand. This party is just like that.

29

R

"What's up, Sun?" Réal lifted his chin at her as she came through the dark.

The look on her face said this was the last place on earth she wanted to be. She threw a disdainful glance at the kids crowding the fire pit. "Fucking amateurs," she spat. Then she turned back to Ré. "Where'd Evie go?"

He shrugged. "Bathroom, I guess?"

"So..." she said. "You and her, huh?"

Ré cleared his throat. He gave her a sideways glance but said nothing.

"Whatever, Ré, I really don't care." But she did, obviously. "You guys suit each other anyway. You're both quiet and sneaky."

"Sunny..." he started, searching for the right words. He was so bad at this. It was new territory, all of it. And no matter what Sunny might have thought, he wasn't actually trying to hurt her.

His eyes darted around for Alex. Not finding him, he hissed between his teeth, "You know we could never be a thing." He leaned in and spoke even lower. "You're his girl-friend. He's my buddy. We just…*can't.*"

Sunny laughed, tipping her head back and letting out that cackle that crushed everything in its path. "You are so full of shit, Réal," she said. "Shaun was your buddy too, in case you forgot. But that doesn't seem to keep you away from *his* girlfriend."

"Sunny, that's different—"

"How?" She cut him off, her voice too loud. "How is it different?"

He growled at her like a guard dog through a flimsy fence. "I'm not having this conversation again, Sunny," he warned, eyes slung sideways. "*Not here.* If you want to be friends, that's cool. But if you're just gonna pick a fight, then I'm gone."

"What, and leave poor Evie here all by herself?" Her voice was taunting, poking the dog. There was a ripple of laughter in it.

He turned to face her. "Don't start trouble with Evie," he said. It was as much a plea as a warning. "She's got enough to worry about right now."

Sunny closed her mouth and appraised him from behind her long lashes. He couldn't tell from her expression what conclusion she'd drawn, but it probably wasn't anything good. She pursed her pretty lips into a sneer, and the memory of her bare, hot skin sliding under his hands leaped up unbidden, her bones and breasts and tongue, memory of the *almost.*

Fuck Sunny, he thought, looking away. He took a gulp of his beer. He shoved his other hand in his pocket and made a fist. She just seeped in like nerve gas. Like sexy goddamn poison.

"I'm not the one getting Evie in trouble," she said, her voice slow and low and clear, pushing the knife in and pulling it back out again.

She stood there for a second more, then walked off, arms still crossed over her bright-green bra. He stared after her. What TF did that mean?

❖   ❖   ❖

E

Evie looked in the bathroom mirror. The light was awful. Way too bright, after the darkness of the yard. It picked out every flaw on her face, every blemish, every splotch of red. She'd thought she was going to puke when she got in here, but nothing had come up. Did you still even get morning sickness this far along? She dashed cold water over her cheeks and succumbed, finally, to the banging on the other side of the door.

"Took you long enough!" snapped a girl Evie didn't know.

Evie brushed passed her, mumbling, "Sorry." She went out to the picnic table and found the big bottle of cola. It was lukewarm now, but she was so thirsty she didn't care. She unscrewed the cap and refilled her empty cup.

Evie turned, looking for Réal, but he wasn't where she'd left him, and she didn't recognize anyone who'd taken his place. Everyone seemed to be looking at her, smiling, but when she blinked again, they weren't at all. They were just lumps of shadow in the dark, indistinguishable.

She shook the strange image from her head and stepped through the crowd.

People seemed pretty drunk now. They bumped into her as she walked, and the ground was surprisingly uneven. "Hey!" a girl yelped as she passed, but Evie didn't turn to see why.

She stopped at the thin edge of the firelight and looked at the crowd huddled near the flames. The heat was so intense. How could they sit so close to it? A sweat broke out along her scalp. She sipped again from her cup. Faces seemed to drift into focus, all staring at her, but just as quickly they slipped out again, leaving trails of smeary light behind.

She stepped back, heart racing. There was something wrong with them. People shouldn't look like that—smeary. Someone laughed, and it fell to pieces, her brain unable to make its proper shape. She caught more strange eyes looking her way, half moon faces trapped in amber firelight, smiling, laughing in weird, jagged pieces…

A picture bloomed and flickered on the other side of the flames. Sea-blue eyes. White teeth grinning ear to ear. Blond hair hanging limp and bloody beside a perfect smile. Shaun's voice echoed in her mind. *Do you remember, Evie?* it said. *Do you know what happened to me?*

She blinked down at the red cup and opened her hand. The cup slipped away, bouncing on the grass, sloshing black cola over her shoes. She stumbled backward, away from the fire. So *stupid*, she thought. Why did I drink from that cup? I didn't even know that guy.

She turned and stumbled back through the crowd. People's faces glowed blood red, toothy smiles crawling right up into their eyes. Laughter fell from jeering mouths. She fought through them and away, down the sloping lawn.

"Where are you going?" someone asked.

Evie turned, eyes struggling to make out a shape against the dark.

"Did you hear me? Why are you sneaking around down here?" The voice came closer, and then Evie could see her— black hair, black sweater, acid-green bra, with a crown of yellow bonfire.

Her heart snapped off at a gallop, remembering Sunny's hand on her shoulder, yanking her up from the bathroom sink at the Olympia. The fear that Sunny might fight her. *At least I waited till my boyfriend was dead.*

"*I'm* sneaking around?" Evie said, swallowing. Pictures of Sunny on the hood of the Buick, pictures of a switchblade smile. "How long have *you* been sleeping with Réal?"

Sunny laughed, a bitter green sound. "Is that what he told you?" she asked, crossing her arms.

"He didn't have to tell me." Evie knew she shouldn't, but the words wouldn't stop, whatever was in that drink letting them all spill out. "Anyone could guess. I bet even Alex knows."

"Oh, shut up, Evie," Sunny said. "You don't know anything."

"I know you're using them," Evie said, mouth barely working around the words. "Seriously," she slurred, "why don't you just break up with Alex already? Or is Ré too low-class for a rich girl like you?"

Sunny was silent, letting the noise from the party roll down the hill and fill the space between them, filling Evie's head with fizzy lights.

Then Sunny said, "You are an ice-cold bitch, Evie Hawley. Did anyone ever tell you that?" She turned and started walking away.

"At least I'm not crazy."

Sunny stopped. "What did you say?"

Evie's head swirled with pictures, words formed and fell apart—she wasn't even sure what was happening anymore, if any of this was real. "I saw you," she said, sticking a tack in the picture of Sunny at the medical center. "Leaving that clinic."

"What clinic?"

Evie's mind narrowed in on the sign beside the door. She read it aloud: *"The Cold Water Center for Mental Health."*

Sunny scoffed. "Oh, I see—you think I'm crazy because you saw me coming out of a mental health clinic. Stellar detection, Sherlock."

Evie said nothing. It had made perfect sense before, two and two together, but now that Sunny was challenging her, she wasn't so sure.

Sunny stepped closer. Evie shrunk into herself and squeezed her eyes shut, waiting for her to strike...

And Sunny hissed very quietly, "I have an eating disorder, you dumbass. I go there for counseling. You know— *to stay alive?"*

Evie wrapped her head around those words. Sunny was so skinny, she had nothing but bones in her clothes. Ribs and hips. She was like a wire hanger, just a collarbone with nothing underneath it. Evie had always been jealous of her— she made *thin* look so effortless. "Oh my god," she said, blinking. "I thought it was 'cause you're Asian."

"What?" Sunny blurted.

"You being skinny," Evie said. "I thought it was 'cause you're Korean."

"Jesus Christ, Evie," Sunny said, rolling her eyes. "Am I, like, the only Asian person you know? Not all of us are skinny, okay? And anyway, it's not even about my weight. It's about my fucking parents never being happy. It's about me not being a golden child like my stupid brother. So I go to a mental health clinic instead of bingeing on cheeseburgers and puking my fucking guts out till I'm dead."

The girls looked at each other. Evie wasn't sure they'd ever talked to each other like this. Honestly. How could they be the only girls in the group and not even really be friends, not even know each other? Evie almost said, *I didn't mean it. I'm sorry.* But she didn't speak.

After a moment Sunny said, "Are you really, for real pregnant?"

Evie couldn't answer. All she saw was Shaun, that night, his grin—

"God, he is *such* a liar!" Sunny said, looking at the sky and almost laughing.

The picture of Shaun skewered. "*Who?*" Evie said, confused. Her eyes tried to catch Sunny's shape, slippery in the dark. And then she understood. "Sunny—it's not *Réal's* baby."

Sunny's shape fell still again. She said nothing for a second, and then the pieces clicked together. "Oh my god. It's *Shaun's?*"

"Of course it's Shaun's!" Evie said. Guilt tapped at her chest. Shaun's face by the fire, all that blood in his hair. Nausea crept up her throat.

"Oh...*shit*," said Sunny.

"Ré was just trying to help is all," Evie slurred, feeling so, so tired now. She wanted to just sit down for a minute, maybe take a little nap. She flapped a hand at Sunny. "If you want him so bad, just take him."

Sunny laughed under her breath, and then she sighed. "Ev, I don't want Ré," she said quietly. "And I'm not using Alex. I just love them, okay? Both of them. They're my best friends. I can't help it."

Evie nodded. She understood. She really did. But she was just *so tired*. "Okay," she said. "That's okay, Sunny." She couldn't really tell if she was saying things out loud anymore, or if they were making any sense. "My drink..." she managed, swirling her finger to draw the mouth of a cup.

Then she turned and stumbled farther down the hill.

"Ev?" Sunny called after her. "Are you sure you're all right?"

Evie waved a rubbery arm at her. "Okay," she repeated. "It's okay."

But it wasn't okay. Sunny's words were like razor blades in her chest. Of course she loved Ré. Of course she loved Alex. She'd probably loved Shaun too. And they all loved her, obviously. The four of them had known each other for a long time.

Evie was the outsider. The fake.

I'm nobody, she thought. I'm *nothing*. Just some dumb girl King Shaun had picked to keep from being alone. A poison apple.

Well, look where that got him.

She reached the edge of the tree line, lawn dissolving into mulch beneath her feet, and the dark limbs of the woods gathered her in.

30

E

Evie stepped between the trees, sliding her hand along their rough trunks, feeling her way by their skins. She felt like she was floating outside of her body, looking down from above. An outsider, even to herself. Whatever was in that drink was strong, and the farther she got from the party, the more detached she felt.

She was dreaming.

She dreamed.

She dreams…

"I wondered where you got to," he says.

She smiles, turning. It's Ré's voice. Sweet.

No. Darker than that, lower.

Shaun's.

A hand closes on her wrist. Pulls her into a cloud of alcohol, boy sweat, hot, damp breath. "How you feeling now?" he says. Laughter, deep and muddy and mean. Hair in her mouth as he tries to kiss her. She turns away, spitting.

"Come on, don't be like that." He pulls at her again. "We're gonna have fun, I promise."

She stumbles, falls against his chest, pictures, pictures, like a deck of cards, *flipppppp*, together then cut, sharp. Shaun, that night. Crashing over her. "No!" she says, shoving back.

He grabs her other wrist, twisting hard. "Come on," he says. "Just be good. I'll go easy."

"Stop it!" she cries, drifting out of herself.

Shaun lunges, pushes her to the dirty ground. She kicks away, but he catches her, pulling her ankle hard toward him. "Shaun, stop!"

He kneels between her legs, one hand pushing her head into the dirt, the other hand sliding under her shorts. "Shaun…please…" Her plea muffled against his palm.

That night. He'd said, "It's my baby, too, Ev." And he wasn't stopping. He'd come up those stairs, sweating and drunk and mad as hell, skateboard in one hand, a bottle in the other. He'd thrown the board down by that hole in the wall at the Grains and smacked her so hard her skull had bounced off the doorframe. "It's mine too!" he'd shouted. "You can't do this."

He'd got her out of bed for this. Worked up his rage downstairs, skating and drinking, and then he'd heaved it all up here like a hurricane, ready to blow.

He'd pulled her back from the hole, dragged her kicking across the dirty floor, her shoes marking trails in the dust— they were still there, if you knew where to look. She'd screamed, and the scream had raced around the empty building unheard. It was still there too, if you knew.

"Please, Shaun, stop!" She cried, begged and twisted.

He laughed, pushing her down, booze seeping from his sweating pores, his stinking breath. Hands fumbled with the buttons of her cutoffs. Her stomach lurched. She twisted under him, shoving, and she puked sideways into the wood chips, into her hair, dark trees spinning, sour vomit up her nose.

She tried to crawl. He scratched her legs and back, tried to hold her still as she kicked.

The pictures in the deck had stopped making sense.

This piece doesn't fit. There are no wood chips at the Grains.

She turned, elbow raised, and brought it down hard against the boy's temple. He cried out, falling sideways. She turned again and kicked him in the balls as hard as she could. Booze-rotten air left his lungs, and he curled around his groin like a shrimp, whimpering.

She scrambled up, wobbling on her feet, backing into a tree. A picture of Shaun lying there, red in his hair. A skateboard in her hands with bloody trucks.

She staggered back. She couldn't breathe. Was this real?

Her knees ached, long scratches down her legs; cheek burning hot where he'd slapped her, temple pulsing bright where it had hit the wall. "Stop it, Shaun," she'd said through tears, "just stop it, please." But he'd never listened. Not when he was mad, not when he was drunk.

He'd pushed himself to his knees, one hand on his bleeding head. "Evie," he'd croaked, reaching for her again, and she had swung, grip tape tearing the pads of her thumbs.

"Don't touch me!" she'd shouted. "Don't touch me ever again!"

She'd known what those words would mean. No more King. No more front seat. No more fireworks on the roof.

She would no longer be part of the tribe. But she hadn't cared anymore. Tired of pretending it was always okay. Tired of Shaun always getting his way. Crashing over her, knocking her down.

She turned from the heap at her feet and ran until her feet splashed into water, ankle-deep.

Free from the woods, the moon hung low and not quite full overhead, pouring cool light over a pond as black as an endless void. Moon-white ripples circled out from where she had walked into the water. When it got too deep to walk, she swam, all her cuts and scrapes stinging like bright lightning in her skin.

She rolled onto her back, watching stars spin pale blue overhead. The ice-cold water calmed her racing heart till it stood, pawing and snuffling in her chest like a vexed horse. Then she tipped her head back, covering her ears, silencing the world, and let everything slide into black.

❖   ❖   ❖

Evie dreams she is the fetus inside herself. A Möbius loop. A dreaming thing in a black lake inside a dreaming thing. She gets to start over, at the beginning, before everything was irreparably fucked.

She sees Ré's goodness hidden under a silver shield, and now it's him driving past her house last summer, acting shy. And then someone good like him chooses her mom years before, and Evie is never born. None of this ever happened. There is no dreaming thing.

❖   ❖   ❖

Sunny's skinny arm slid under her rib cage and yanked Evie up into moonlight.

Water spluttered out of her lungs as she was dragged to shore.

Sunny threw her down, and she curled onto her side, coughing and shaking in the sand at the edge of the pond like some giant fish Sunny'd caught with her bare hands.

"What the hell are you trying to do, Evie? Fucking kill yourself?" Sunny snarled.

Evie just coughed, breathing wet sand and spit, her cheek pressed into the dirt.

"Are you seriously that wasted, Ev? I mean, come on! Aren't you *pregnant*?" Sunny had her head inside her black sweater, wrestling it back on over wet skin.

Evie rasped, "Someone…"

Sunny got her head out of the neck hole and stared at her, impatient. "Someone *what*?"

"Dosed me," Evie whispered. "Someone dosed my drink."

Sunny said nothing for second. "Fucking ketamine," she finally spat. She shoved her feet back into her black leather boots. "What a bunch of dead little ravers. This party is so stupid."

She stood and grabbed Evie under the armpits, hauling her up to her feet. "Come on," she said, "let's get Ré and ghost. Alex can apologize to us all tomorrow when he realizes what a loser he's being."

"Sunny," Evie said, wanting to tell her everything. To tell her about Shaun and the bruises, the skateboard, the Grains.

About the guy in the woods. Was he even real? "There was a guy…" Her voice trailed off, trying to remember.

"Okay," Sunny said, "a guy." She had her arm around Evie's waist, and they stagger-walked together, bumping three-legged into the woods again.

"He attacked me, I think," Evie said. "The guy who dosed me."

"Jesus," Sunny breathed. "Are you okay?"

Pictures flashed through her head. "I think I killed him…"

"Holy *fuck*," Sunny shot back. They stopped, and Sunny turned to face her, propping her up by the shoulders. "All right, tell me exactly what happened."

"He was mad about the baby," Evie mumbled.

"*What?*" Sunny shook her lightly. "What are you saying? Who is this guy?"

"I think…" Evie felt breathless, exhausted, confused. "I think it was Shaun. He was here. He was really mad."

Sunny just looked at Evie for a minute, then gathered her up under her swan arm, marching them both forward again. "I think you need some sleep, Ev," she muttered. "You're so high right now."

Evie could see splinters of amber light cutting through the black trees. The distance from the barn had felt endless before, going the other way. She saw now that it really wasn't so far from the barn to the pond. Maybe there hadn't been anyone in the woods after all? No one clawing her legs, knocking her down.

Tears suddenly spilled down her face. "I'm so sorry, Sunny," she said. "I didn't know about you and Ré. He was only trying to help me with the baby. And then I kissed him, and now everything is a mess."

She could feel the other girl stiffen against her, but Sunny only sighed. "It's okay, Ev. It was a mess before you got here."

"We aren't even anything," Evie went on.

"Yeah, okay," Sunny said.

"I don't even know if it's real. It's just how I feel." Evie sniffled, wiping her nose with her sopping-wet sleeve. A picture of Ré asleep outside her door, not asking for anything at all. "An anchor in the water."

"Okay, Ev, whatever." You could practically hear Sunny rolling her eyes.

They stepped out of the woods, at the bottom of the lawn. Above them, the bonfire still blazed, and music still thumped into the night, but there was no crowd around the fire pit. The whole place was empty.

"Where did everybody go?" Evie asked, blinking up at the hill.

Sunny's voice was wary. "I don't know," she said.

The girls picked up their pace, Sunny still guiding Evie, stumbling, her wet shirt balled up in Sunny's fist. They crested the hill and saw the fire pit deserted, red cups everywhere, spilled booze, cigarette butts, half destroyed bowls of chips. It was eerie. Like the party had just vaporized. Cars still peeked out from the other side of the barn, so no one had actually left. They were just *gone*.

Evie started shivering in Sunny's arms. "What's going on?" she asked, though it was obvious Sunny had no more clue than she did.

"How big is this property, Sunny?"

"Huge," Sunny said, her big black eyes sliding around, taking in the details, piecing things together.

And then the song on the boom box ended, and in the lull, the girls heard a sound that drove a chill up both their spines. In the not-too-far distance, voices were chanting. Some low, others high and shrill, saying one word, over and over. The girls looked at each other wide-eyed to confirm they'd heard it right:

Psycho, psycho, psycho...

And then the next song started, and the voices disappeared, washed up into a swirl of synthesized beats and bright loops and a voice cawing about Puerto Rican girls, all legs in tight skirts, all rising into the night sky like sparks from a dying fire.

31

R

Ré stood in a ring of faceless faces. White eyes peered through the dark. Black shapes of bodies all sharp-edged with excitement. Mouths twisted and jeering, like he was some kind of animal. *Psy-cho, psy-cho, psy-cho.*

But he didn't care about them. He worried about the ones circling just beyond the chanting crowd. The guys Ré didn't know. Alex's people. He could see them slipping like shadows, like wolves, just past the ring of rabid kids, weaving through the darkness, keeping it close.

Psycho Ré. It was a setup.

Inside the ring, Alex paced, seething, reckless. He was not a fighter. That worried Ré too. Guys who fought knew where and how hard to hit. Intended to win with the least amount of effort. And they knew when to quit. When they were beat.

Guys who didn't fight were just dangerous. Scared. Thought the point of fighting was to win at all costs, however violent.

And Alex was wiry, thin and lanky. He wasn't built, like Ré, out of muscle and steel, a machinist's son, fighting from day one. If this were *real*—if Ré was mad or had any right to be—he'd break Alex in seconds. The problem was, he wasn't, and he didn't. He stood in the circle, wary, ready, hands at his sides, lightly rubbing his fingertips against his thumbs, eyes jumping from dark wolves to bright Alex and back again.

Alex was talking to him as he paced, but it was meant for the crowd, the show. Ré wasn't really listening. At each pause, the kids all bayed for blood like cue cards had flashed the words *Applause* and *Make Some Noise*. But they didn't really hate Réal. They were just afraid of him and, like all fearful things, wanted to see him cut down, made weak. They'd get their wish. He wasn't planning on fighting back.

There was some movement to his left. Voices rose, and then the crowd parted and Evie and Sunny shoved through. Ré blinked like they were a mirage. *Why are they both soaking wet?* Mascara ran in sinister streaks down Sunny's pale face, transforming her into a sexy ghoul. Doesn't take much, he thought, with a twinge of that old desire.

Beside her, beautiful Evie shivered, eyes as big as saucers, as big as Jupiter, or maybe Venus, 'cause they were blue. Goddess of love, bellyful of baby. God, I'm greedy, he thought. WTF is wrong with me? About to get my ass kicked for these girls I can't resist...

Evie didn't look like she was really there, but then, she almost never did. And then he remembered something.

A word. The one he'd wanted the very first time he'd seen her, sitting in Shaun's car, dark hair veiled around her, shy Mona Lisa smile. *Ethereal*. She'd looked *ethereal*, then and ever since. Too delicate for this world—not to mention this particular moment. The word popped into his head now, and then it was gone.

"What the actual fuck are you doing, Alex?" Sunny shouted, a protective hand on Evie's shoulder.

Alex only laughed, turning on her slowly. "Oh, that's good," he said. "You're a good actress, Sunny. You should go to Hollywood." His hackles rose when he looked at her. He ground his boot heel into the gravel, skinny arms held tight. "How stupid do you think I am, Sun?"

If he expected her to shut up, to look shocked or humiliated, then he sure didn't know Sunny. "I think you're a brain-dead idiot, you zombie pothead," she replied. "You're so bombed-out all the time I don't even know you anymore. You're a joke, Alex. This party is a joke. Everything is a fucking *joke*."

Ré resisted whistling under his breath. He looked from Sunny to Alex and back again, swallowing hard. If she dished out much more of this, he'd have a *lot* more fight on his hands.

Alex straightened slowly. "Yeah? Is screwing Dufresne behind my back a big joke too?" he asked.

A shimmer of surprise went through the crowd. Gettin' more show than they paid for, Ré thought. And also, *Fuck*.

Alex raised his voice another notch. "Is that why I find his T-shirts under your bed? His damn car parked outside your house?" He was pacing again, working up his violence, letting the steam rise. "I'm tired of you yanking me around like a dog on a leash," he snapped. "Tired of you acting like I'm not even here. Like I'm too dumb to notice you screwing my friends."

Sunny's hand left Evie's shoulder, and Ré saw Evie wobble, fingers splayed for balance. More worry fled through him. *Is she okay?*

Then Sunny said, loud and clear, shoulders squared, "The only person I've *ever* screwed is too wasted to even get it up anymore."

A snicker and an *ohh* slid through the crowd. And then someone else was in the circle with them. He was tallish and had dark hair flipping over the collar of his black leather jacket. On the back of the jacket was a large woven patch: a white skull with red horns, a swirling, forked red tail, and the letters *SOMC*. Satan's Own Motorcycle Club.

He said, "You gonna let that little rice rocket sass you, young Alex Janes?"

Alex looked at him, red flames in his eyes, forked tail twitching. Ré could see his gears working, even in the semidarkness.

But before anyone could say anything, Sunny stepped up to the stranger, all jaw and jabbing fingers. "*Rice rocket?*" she said, head weaving like a cobra's.

He turned, unperturbed, and looked down on her. "Well, he rides your Jap ass, don't he?" He made a throttle motion with his fists and leered at her neon-green boobs.

"*Alex!*" She turned, daring him to stand up for her. But Alex was closed, his face shut, eyes dead. The gears had turned, and the brotherhood had won.

Sunny turned back to the big biker. "I'm fucking *Korean*, you sausage-eating monkey fart." She spat at his feet and turned, and the crowd parted for her like a holy sea. "Come on, Ev," she muttered, grabbing Evie's wrist. The smaller girl whirled with Sunny's momentum.

Ostie d'crisse, Ré thought. That girl is fearless. But the big biker only laughed.

Moments later, Sunny's pearl sedan sprayed gravel over the lawn, and the girls were gone. In a strange way, Ré was relieved. Even though he now stood here facing Alex alone, it was better that way. He didn't want Evie to see him so low as this.

He turned his attention back to Alex. Through all of this, Ré still had not said a word. Kept his cards close.

Alex jutted his chin, eyes blazing. "You gonna tell the same story, Dufresne?"

Ré tipped his jaw down and looked Alex straight in the eye. "No," he said. "I am not telling the same story."

Alex was visibly surprised. "So she's a liar? You really slept with her?" His pitch rose up and bounced over the crowd.

"No," Ré said again. "I did not sleep with your girlfriend, Alex. But I'd be lying if I said I didn't want to. If I told you I never touched her."

The big biker had stepped back into the crowd, arms crossed. This was between Ré and Alex now, nobody else. The boys began to sidestep within the circle, a slow, wary dance. Réal knew what was coming next. He held his abdomen tight, waiting for the lunge, the first strike. "You got every right to do this, buddy," he said. "I don't blame you one bit."

"I'm not your *buddy*, Réal," Alex spat, and the words hurt more than a fist. "You're nothing to me. You've always been nothing. Background noise." Alex was still circling, but he was starting to jump, fists ready. "You think you're so damn cool," he continued. "Shaun's little lieutenant."

Ré's ears pricked at Shaun's name. His eyes shifted from Alex in sharp flicks. He saw more dark shadows closing in around the crowd. Those guys who'd been drinking on the back deck. Maybe more than just them. Maybe even the whole club—or at least the ones tight with the Janes clan. Réal started to get a bad feeling that this wasn't about Sunny at all.

"I don't think I'm cool, Alex," Ré said warily. "And I'm nobody's lieutenant. Shaun and me were old buddies, that's all."

"He was gonna prospect for the club," Alex said bitterly. "Did you know that, *old buddy?*" Réal kept one eye on the shadows, listening very carefully now to Alex's words. "This summer. Me and him together. We were gonna be *brothers.*"

Brothers. How many times had Ré used that word to describe him and Shaun? They were practically blood. Raised together, in each other's homes as constantly as if they were family. They knew each other better than anybody. *Didn't they?*

Réal felt the ground go a little soft under his feet. He had been the first and only one Shaun had told about the baby, but *this*...Why hadn't Shaun told him? *Prospecting?* For Satan's Own? Sunny was right—it was a joke. A surreal, messed-up joke. And Réal felt a little bit like a punch line. "I didn't know that," he breathed quietly.

It all made sense now, this stupid party. It had nothing to do with graduation. It was an *initiation*. Alex proving himself to the brotherhood. And Ré had been carted out like an ox on a rope, his neck stretched out long for the machete. It wasn't about Sunny. It had *never* been about her.

All the fight went out of him at once. Letting Alex win a battle over a girl, letting him win back his sullied pride—that was something Ré could nobly do. He'd take those punches—even throw a few back for show, black up his eye maybe, just so it looked like he'd tried.

But not Shaun. Shaun was not something he could fight for. He couldn't even pretend.

"Alex," he said. He'd stopped moving, stopped the dance, let his hands hang loose at his sides. He swallowed hard. "I *loved* Shaun."

A childish snicker went through the crowd. They all were wound up tight as tops and wanted violence like they'd paid for it at the gate, but Ré ignored them. "Shaun was family," he said. "I never in my life thought I'd hurt him."

"Tell that to his fucking nan," Alex snarled, whipped up, still dancing. "Tell it to his fucking mother. Tell it to the brothers here tonight."

But Ré couldn't honestly say it to anyone. He knew deep down that he'd meant to kill Shaun. It was all over his dreams like bloody fingerprints, those fucking deer stalking him, filling him with evil. The fucking Windigo. Réal saw Shaun's torn belly, popped open like a bag of rotten noodles. He knew what he was. He knew what he'd done, even if all memory of it was gone.

"Tell it to his damn *girlfriend*," Alex said, and Ré's eyes went wide. *No!* She's not still here, is she? Unsteady, ethereal, other-planet Evie. Sweet, forgiving Evie. *No, no, no.* He searched the dark, desperate. He turned, hoping not to find her, but there she was behind him, all Venus-eyed.

"Ev…" Ré whimpered, thinking, Why TF didn't you go with Sunny, girl?

Then he heard her little voice in his head. *I could love you, if you asked me to.* And he wanted so bad to ask her now—*right now*—before he had to tell her everything else. Before the terrible truth was out.

But that would be cheating. Stealing the prize.

"Go on, Dufresne," Alex taunted. "Tell her what you did. Tell us all what you did to your so-called brother."

He sunk to his knees at Evie's feet. The words choked in his throat. They clicked, unsaid, as he stared at the ground, reeling with all of his demons. He couldn't breathe. His hands balled into fists. Tears spilled from his eyes. He whispered.

"What was that, Dufresne?" Alex called out like a side-show barker, like a man in a top hat.

Ré closed his eyes. Warm tears snaked down his neck into the collar of his shirt. "I ate him," he confessed, the words like chunks of flesh on his lips. Like stringy red arrows pointing to his guilty heart. "I killed him, and I ate him."

3 2

R

"*You what?*" Alex shrieked.

Réal slumped farther down on his folded knees, ruined, destroyed. *Sick, psycho, fiend.*

"*You fucking what?*" Alex bleated again. "Holy mother of God." He stumbled back, hands fisted in his hair, eyes wide and white, flashing firelight. He breathed like a broken bellows. This was clearly not the answer he'd expected, not at all the one he'd been teasing out for the crowd.

But there it was. Out loud. At last.

Ré could feel the crowd changing around him, the mood shifting. They stepped back, confused, frightened, knocking into each other, voices hissing and scared. Alex looked to the big biker for direction, but the guy just stood there with his mouth open, his meaty hands at his sides.

Réal was not the sacrificial ox they'd wanted—some poor, dumb creature Alex had dragged out here to destroy.

They'd asked for an animal. Ré had given them a monster—he'd given them the *goddamn devil.*

He could feel the ring widening, could hear people stumbling to get away. Car doors slammed, engines growled. He closed his eyes. He imagined he could hear *her* feet stepping away too. The sound of losing everything.

Feared, hated.

Just like Black Chuck.

Ré's picture next to Chuck's in the family book. Aunties telling his story to little boys who'd wet their beds, claw bloody any arms that tried to hold them.

Then he felt a hand on his shoulder, small and warm. He shivered like it was electric, opened his eyes and looked up. Evie stood before him, Venus blues, lips pulled in a frown. She was dripping water everywhere, and for one tiny moment all he felt was love and worry. "Why are you all wet?" he whispered.

And then the air left his lungs as he was kicked to the ground.

Alex stood behind him, cracking like lightning. "Get up, you psycho!" he screamed.

Pain lanced through his shoulders, down his spine. Evie scattered to the side. He sucked for air, tried to push up, but Alex was on him again, heavy boots striking his kidneys, neck and arms. He crawled on knees and elbows, coughing.

Alex kicked his ribs hard, knocking him sideways. *"Get up!"* he screeched.

Réal obeyed. He staggered to his feet, stumbling sideways, gasping for air. He cradled his shattered ribs under one hand. The other was held out for balance, defense, but it found neither.

Alex swung at his jaw, and Ré spun like a puppet, spitting blood into the cheering crowd.

There was no fighting back. Alex was on him too quick. The blows fell like bombs, lit fireworks in the air between them. When he fell, the crowd only dragged him back up, violence drawing them back to the circle. Through his bloody eye, Ré could see Satan's Own standing among them, looking grim. There was no escape, even if he'd wanted one.

Sparks lit out from the blows to his head. Constellations. One eye had swelled almost shut. He blinked blood from the other, tasted the tang of a cut lip swelling fast. Each breath filled his lungs with broken sticks. And the crowd howled at each strike like a piano split with an axe.

He could feel his body giving up.

He wasn't fighting it.

He was going to die.

This must have been what Shaun had felt that night, Ré coming at him in the dark. Pain squeezed Ré's heart, but it wasn't from fists or boots. He fell again to his knees, blood roping down from his open mouth, his hands limp at his sides. He was ready.

"Stop!" someone cried.

She pushed between them, her back to Ré. He blinked, tried to focus. "No, Ev..." he said, raising his hand to her. "Let him do it."

"No!" she shouted. Her hands were shoving Alex, feet bracing in the dirt. "It's not true!"

"Get out of the way, Evie," Alex warned through his teeth.

"It's not true," she said again. "He didn't kill anybody."

"He just confessed," Alex yipped, trying to shove her aside. She stumbled but wouldn't let go.

Alex was much taller than her and, despite his thinness, heavier, his angle better. She slid backward as he plowed her out of his way and she fought to keep her footing. "He didn't do it, Alex!"

"He's not saying he didn't!" Alex spat. He wasn't even looking at her. His eyes were over her shoulder, looking wildly at Ré, who was slumped on his knees behind her.

"Evie..." Ré groaned. He reached for her wet shirt, the soft, cold flannel grounding him like a bright light in the dark. "Evie, let him do it," he said.

"No, Ré!" She swung her face to his. Wet hair fell across it in dark brushstrokes. Her blue eyes flashed. "You didn't kill Shaun. And I am not letting Alex kill you!"

"I did, Evie," he said, his voice a reedy breath. "I killed him. I'm just like my uncle. I'm sorry. I didn't want you to know."

"No, Ré," she growled. She was shoving again, feet sliding. "*You* didn't do it. *I* did."

What the fuck? he thought. Has *everyone* lost their minds?

Alex wrapped his hand around Evie's wrist, twisting hard, eyes jumping from her to Réal and back. Ré still grasped her shirt, blinking up at her with his one good eye. She was trapped between them, saying words he couldn't hear, her attention drawn away from Alex, big eyes locked on Ré.

He saw the knife in slow motion.

The glint of dark metal in the shadows.

Alex's free hand had disappeared behind his back and reappeared, holding all the cards. The blade slid through the air at a low angle, its hard edge kissing the bone in

Réal's wrist. There was no pain, just a warm flood of blood down his sleeve.

Ré drew his arm out of the knife's path, shielding his face. He fell back and rolled sideways. All was confusion and sound. Then a numbing, unnatural silence. In the distance just the whine of a single, silvery bell.

Someone gathered him up under the arms and hauled him to his feet. The big biker who'd egged Alex on. When he spoke, Réal felt the thunder of his voice more than heard it. "That'll do, young Janes," he said. "That's just fine, boy."

Ré's good eye found Alex in the dark—panting, eyes burning, neck stiff, not yet willing to let it go. His hair hung lank and sweaty over his face. The knife shook in his fist, a snarl on his lips.

The boys looked at each other for one long moment, and they both knew it was over. All those years. No friendship could survive this.

And then Alex turned and pushed through the ring of leering faces. He disappeared into the dark beyond the circle, Satan's Own closing around him, swallowing him, ferrying him away.

The biker shook Ré lightly. "You did pretty good too, kid. Took it like a man. Now you and your little girlfriend best get the hell off this lot just as quick as you can." He laughed and slapped Ré's back, making him suck in air sharply. His ribs were broken for sure.

Ré touched the cut on his wrist. It was shallow, the blade just grazing the bone, but it bled through his fingers all the same.

He spotted Evie crouched at the edge of the ring, and he took her arm, pulled her to her feet. "Come on," he said through gritted teeth, leading her through the crowd. She stumbled silently along behind him.

They found the Buick and threw themselves in. It hurt to sit, bent over, busted ribs digging in his insides. His cut arm dripped little black patterns over everything, so he pressed it to his leg to close the wound. Evie had still not spoken. Ré threw the Buick in reverse and peeled out, turning the car around with just the heel of his good hand on the wheel.

He pointed the nose down the wooded driveway, head-lights bobbing through the trees. As they passed the big house, Ré took note of the guys on the deck, and they all took note of him. A chill ran through him, but he shook it off and pressed his foot to the gas till the driveway met the long dirt road back to town.

Finally, he glanced at her. "You okay?" he asked. He could see nothing in the dark but her huddled shape pressed to the passenger door. She didn't answer.

He sucked his cut lip, watched the road wind by for a while. He could feel the blood drying on his face. Pain began to chew on him like he was a spongy piece of meat. All the aches and bruises that adrenaline had pushed aside now creeping in.

"Evie," he said. He felt his guilt stretching the distance between them. "I didn't want you to find out that way. I was gonna tell you, I swear."

"You didn't kill him," she whispered.

"I did, Ev. I—"

"Stop talking, Ré. Please."

Her voice was dry and rough and smaller than ever. He glanced at her. "Hey. Are you okay?" She didn't answer.

Sticky blood had glued his arm to his jeans, and the wound peeled open again when he lifted his hand to take the wheel. He cursed, wincing.

With his good hand, he reached across the seat, searching for her in the dark. "Evelyn," he said. "Talk to me."

"Ré?" she whispered.

"Yeah, Ev, tell me." He'd raised his voice, nervous now. He only half watched the road.

"Did Alex..." Her voice frayed into nothing before she could finish her thought. Réal shook her shoulder, and she came alive again with a small gasp, and got the words out. "Did he have a knife?"

In the darkness he saw her splay her hands out, looking at them as if they belonged to someone else. Her clothes still dripped, and she had begun to shiver, though the night was warm.

"Evie, what's going on? Why are you all wet?" Ré was almost shouting, frantic. He shook her shoulder again.

"I think I should go to the hospital," she said, soft as kittens. "I—I think Alex might have cut me."

Ré's lungs failed. The floor of the Buick disappeared. And in the instant it took him to register that Evie was bleeding all over the seats, Ré missed the sharp left where the dirt road met the county highway. And then there was no road beneath them at all.

33

E

The car tore through the bushes, shattering saplings and green sumac, bucking sideways and sliding wildly down the hill beyond the road. A ballpoint pen skittered across the dash, lifting, drifting into the air just as the windshield cut into a thousand white spiderwebs. Airbags exploded, crushing Evie and Réal against blue vinyl.

A strange staccato sound rose as they careened down the hill—hundreds of tiny whips and stones hitting blue paint and underbelly. They turned, juddering backward, crashing through bulrushes toward a patch of black water. The rushes snapped and fell, grabbing the Buick like baleen, finally hauling it to a stop with a wet, heavy sigh.

Evie's ears rang. She choked on dust and smoke and plastic powder from the ancient airbags. Outside, water quickly rose in the wheel wells. It began to seep through the cracks at the bottom of the doors. She heard it hissing in the back seat.

"Ré?" she whispered, but he didn't answer. She leaned back and looked at the moonlight spidering through the broken windows, at the dark edge of the road above.

Will anyone find us down here? she wondered, feeling for the knife wound in her side. Probably not, she decided, and closed her eyes.

❖   ❖   ❖

Shaun kneels at her feet, hand pressed to the side of his head. Dark red slithers down his forearm, making a lacy cuff. Lucky Shaun, the invincible, trying to steal the future from her.

She stands over him, seeing stars, skateboard heavy in her hands. She was not marrying him, not having his baby. She was *not* going to end up like her mom.

She could smash his head in right now. It would be easy. All those months of feeling powerless catching up with her all at once, a storm pushing back against his force, blowing it down like a house of cards.

"I hate you, Shaun Henry-Deacon."

These are the last words she ever says to him. Maybe the last ones he ever hears. And in that moment, she means them with every piece of her soul, but they still punch a hole inside her.

Then she turns and swings the skateboard as hard as she can.

A picture of it spinning sideways in the dark.

It flies out the hole in the wall and disappears, Shaun's blood-laced hand reaching after it. "You fucking idiot!" he spits. The last three words she hears him say.

He gets up and goes to the fire escape, shaking the blood from his arm. She has seen him go out that broken door a hundred times. Monkeying down the busted escape, thrum of rusted metal under his hands. He doesn't think twice about it now, just leaps straight out into the black. And she just stands there, letting him go.

34

R

Ré dreams of a bright yellow bonfire. Hot sparks dotting the night sky. At his feet lies a red flannel shirt. He lifts it in his fingers; it's soft and sopping wet. He thinks, *Evelyn*, but there is no one else here and no sign that there ever was but for the shirt.

When he balls up the flannel in his fist, a sharp, familiar smell meets his nostrils, and fear slides like a blade in his gut. The shirt is soaked with blood.

He sees his shadow half crouched by the fire. He asks it, "What have you done?"

But it only asks him the same question.

Beyond the fire is a ring of trees, and he knows he's been here before, in this very spot, up to his knees in snow. Starving. Choking. Between the black tree trunks, white eyes stare. His heart skips like a fly on water, bright ripples vibrating in his veins, making him shiver though the fire is warm.

So here it is, he thinks. This I where I fall. Where I can't fight anymore.

There is no snow now, but it's as if the ghost of it is still there. A thin red trail stands out as cleanly as if there were snow to stand on. He swallows hard. The dream has never taken him this far before. He's always woken long before this part.

This time, he follows the trail.

When the white eyes see him coming, their owners turn and move deeper into the woods. Deer walking slowly on hind legs, hunched so their fur stands up at the shoulders, greasy and matted in small spikes, like soft armor.

He doesn't try to catch up to them but doesn't get left behind either. He can see his way by the moon, hear his way by the sound of antlers knocking on trees. A soft bone-orchestra, playing a path of hollow tocks, drawing him deeper into the woods.

As they cross an invisible line, the deer drop to their fore-feet, shaking off their strange illusion of humanness. They are animals again, not creatures, not monsters. When he steps on a twig, they leap on spindly legs, ears twitching, and he can't help but laugh, though it feels a little like crying. They seem so gentle now, not the fearful things he always dreams of. And if they're taking him to the demon, they are breaking his heart.

From the corner of his eye he sees the woods thinning, sees train tracks and a pale blue light hanging high, but it's not the moon. It's an arc light.

He goes cold.

His throat and gut begin to ache. He can't go any closer, can't move.

Because Shaun is standing there.

Ré's heart becomes a fist, becomes a flannel shirt dripping blood. Tears sting his eyes. He wants to wake up, but he thinks this might not be a dream. It might be a *memory*. The part he can't recall. The part he cut off so it wouldn't rot the rest.

Something grazes his arm, and Ré jumps. It touches his other side, nudging him toward the blue light.

Shaun is backlit, his long hair a golden halo over broad shoulders. He's wearing his leather jacket, hands at his sides, feet a little apart. He looks ready to fight, but Ré won't fight him. Can't fight him. Never again.

"Réal," he drawls out slow, his voice honey-gold and friendly. "What's up, bro?"

Ré can't see his face in the shadows, but his memory of it flickers in the dark—the broken jaw, teeth knocked out, eyes of pale-blue wax. "Shaun?" Ré says, but his voice breaks. He teeters on his legs like they're new. "Is this real? Am I dreaming?"

Shaun laughs, lifting his shoulders lightly. "You tell me, man."

Ré blinks at him, tears catching in his voice. "Shaun, I am so sorry. I never wanted this to happen."

"Nah," Shaun says, "we're cool, Ré." He runs a hand through his long hair, pulling it back. Ré can see the line of his jaw where the arc light touches it. It makes the same shape it always did, not broken at all, his teeth all where they should be, the shoes still on his feet.

Ré asks, "Are you okay? Are you...*alive?*"

Shaun thinks about it a long time, hooking his thumbs in the pockets of his jeans. "I don't know," he says. "Are *you?*"

Ré breathes out, heart dropping through his chest. He doesn't know either. Can't tell if he's alive—if this is a dream, a memory, or some kind of purgatory, a place where his sins still live. He says, "Shaun, I'm so sorry. I didn't want any of this to happen. I didn't mean for you to get hurt. You gotta believe me."

Shaun stares at him, saying nothing. Ré can almost see his sea-blue eyes working in the darkness. The weight of them pressing down so hard Ré can hardly breathe.

Then Shaun steps forward. Réal braces for the blow, for what he's earned. He squeezes his eyes shut. Shaun puts his hand on Ré's shoulder, making him flinch. "Ré," he says, voice close and low. "It's okay, man. Let it go." He gives Ré's shoulder a squeeze.

Ré's eyes flutter open, confused.

In the distance, a train whistle howls. It sounds mournful, lonesome, but Ré can hear along the tracks that it's coming fast. He swallows at the lump in his throat. He puts his hand down over Shaun's. "I love you, brother," he says, voice shaking.

Shaun grins, his bottom lip sliding up to touch his perfect teeth. He squeezes Ré's shoulder again.

The train whistle blows closer. Shaun looks toward it, his focus drawn away, and Ré can see now that he is bleeding from a deep cut on his temple, that the side of his face, his hair, is painted sticky red. Suddenly Ré can smell the stink of alcohol on him, a heavy, sweet, sweating smell, like he's been drinking for hours. Ré is confused—the smell wasn't there a second ago. "Shaun?" he says.

But Shaun has turned toward the tracks. Ré sees a shape lying in the ties. A skateboard. Shaun is heading for it, stumbling, arms held out for balance. Even in the dark, Ré can see that Shaun is trashed. He's muttering to himself as he staggers back over the rails.

This isn't the Shaun he's just been talking to, not sure if he's alive or dead.

It's the *real* Shaun, from that night.

Around the bend to Ré's right, the brilliant white light of a freight train appears.

"Shaun!" he shouts. "Get out of there!"

But Shaun doesn't hear. He trips over the rails, swearing, and staggers ahead.

Ré is stunned. He's never seen his best friend so graceless, so literally falling-down drunk. He's seen Shaun wasted before, acting like an idiot, having a laugh. He's never seen him acting like his mother—so trashed he doesn't seem to know where he is.

Shaun is so focused on the skateboard, he doesn't notice the train, or maybe he doesn't care. Playing chicken. Invincible. Ré's seen him do it before, laughing his damn head off. But this is no joke. Shaun can barely stand up.

"*Shaun!*" Réal screams, almost pissing himself, eyes darting from him to the massive black engine, the distance between them diminishing too fast. His heart falls through his shoes, his fists balled tight as hammers.

Shaun seems to wake up too late. He staggers back as the train bears down, dumb surprise all over his face. The engine hits the skateboard first, exploding it into a thousand pieces, and then it hits Shaun and does the same, throwing his body all the way back to the corrugated fence, a hundred yards away.

Ré squeezes his eyes shut, and his knees melt out from under him.

Hit by the night train to Belleville.

Not eaten. Not Black Chuck.

Ré buries his face in his hands.

Shaun was family. His pale fraternal twin. He used to cross these tracks to Ré's every time he had a need for getting lost, like whenever his mom was home. Shaun and Ré *knew* these tracks, like the veins under their skin. They'd never once come close to real danger, even when they were little and their legs could only take them so fast.

But seeing him drunk like that—it was like Alex telling him Shaun was prospecting for Satan's Own. Ré didn't know that guy. *That* wasn't his brother.

Réal feels the distance between them all now, him and Shaun and Alex. Even Sunny, even Evie. He feels a void opening, feels himself falling in: they can never go back. Nights laughing in Nan's front room. Fireworks from the Grains. High school. Who they used to be. *Kids.* It was always going to end. Shaun's dying had nothing to do with it.

Ré wonders if he too has changed, slipped away from the guy he thought he would always be...

And then a warm, wet breath falls on the back of his neck.

Ré jerks, kicking back.

In the dark behind him is a massive shape. The biggest bull elk he's ever seen. The span of its antlers is as wide as Ré's open arms, its shoulder taller than Ré himself. It sends goose bumps down the flesh of his ribs.

It can't be real.

For a split second Réal thinks, Is this *it*? Is *this* the Windigo?

But his heart knows it is something else.

This beast, as big as it is, is no demon. Its neck is stretched out. Vulnerable. Trusting. Inside Ré's chest, a thousand birds burst free, their wings thundering against his bones. He falls back on his elbows in the scrubby grass, heart and breath racing hard and fast.

"*What are you?*" he whispers.

The elk steps forward, bowing, sniffing. Ré can smell its damp breath, sweet as fresh cut grass. And then it backs away, raising its massive antlers into the night sky, scraping up the half full moon.

Beyond the creature, just inside the tree line, Réal can see the deer peering out, curious, shy. Ré can hardly breathe. Then the bull elk turns and walks back into the woods, silent and graceful despite its great size.

He watches in awe.

Inside his ribs, his heart burns pure white, melting everything else away.

Words come to him then, from his mother's tongue: *Omashkooz gidoodem, Réal.*

And he gets it, finally. At last he understands what the deer have been trying to tell him. What the creature has wanted, all this time. He almost laughs at how simple it is.

It's okay, man. Let it go.

He pulls himself to his feet and follows them all back into the woods.

35

E

Evie woke with a gasp, tail end of a dream slipping away.

She opened her eyes in a darkened room. An edge of light marked a half closed door, and a patterned curtain ran the length of the bed she was lying in. She blinked at these groggily, trying to figure out where she was.

She felt stiff and heavy all over. Something was jabbed in her arm, and a tube under her nose blew cold, dry air. It made her cough.

"Mom?" she croaked.

A voice replied from the shadows. "She'll be back."

Evie turned her head. There was a shape in the dark. It gathered itself up and rose from a chair, and the machine dotting out her heartbeat quickened as if it too was scared.

"It's just me," he said softly. A warm hand found hers, threaded their fingers together.

"Ré," she whispered. "What happened?"

The light from the doorway marked a pale outline of him. She couldn't see his face, but she watched his shoulders fall. "I totaled the Buick," he said. "And I nearly killed us."

She tried to remember it. Any of it. But all that sprang up was his arm draped over a steering wheel, golden sunlight painting each tiny hair. The look in his eyes, the shape of his lips, and then...nothing. "I don't remember," she told him.

"It's okay, Ev," he assured her. "No one's asking you to."

But she dug around for the pictures anyway, for all the snapshots leading up to that one, in his car. Images shuffled all out of order. Sunny's hair flung back, her dark and knowing smile. Alex's long legs leaping over a bonfire, all sand and spark. And Ré, of course, sleeping outside her door. If she took that old journal from her desk right now, its pages would be filled in an instant.

"I think Sunny hates me," she said.

Réal laughed. "Yeah, Sunny's got a weird way of showing how she feels," he said. "She was here though. She brought flowers." He jerked a thumb over his shoulder, and she saw the shadow of a vase by the wall, full of blooms.

Even though he was here, hand firmly in hers, Evie still felt a twinge of jealousy. Brittle, brash and scary as she was, Sunny was still the coolest girl Evie'd ever met. And no matter what, she and Ré had History. Evie could never blank that out or pretend it wasn't there, and neither could they.

Then she remembered Alex. Fire-lit flashes of his angular face, eyes like darts, like a snake's. She asked, "Does Alex hate *you*?"

Ré took a long, deep breath and blew it out slow. He said, "Me and him can never be friends again."

Evie squeezed his hand and felt his sadness.

She remembered the flicker of something else, before the darkness. *I should be thinking about Shaun, but I can't stop thinking about you…*

In her living room.

A small silver bead. A ball bearing from a wheel.

She heard those wheels whiz across the concrete floor of the Grains.

The skateboard flung from her hands, out that terrible hole in the wall. Shaun at her feet, hand pressed to the dark-red side of his head. It wasn't just a dream. That part had been real.

"Ré," she said, "you didn't kill Shaun."

"Yeah," he said quietly. "I know."

"It wasn't your fault."

"I know, Ev."

"You guys fought that night," she said, "and then he came to my house, all drunk. He took me to the Grains, and he hit me so hard I saw stars."

Réal flinched and sucked air in through his teeth.

"Ré…" she whispered. "*I did it. I killed him.*"

And she held her breath. But he didn't say anything.

He let go of her hand, and she thought, That's it. He's gone.

Then he turned and pulled himself up onto the bed, spongy mattress bowing under his weight. The movement made her ache all over, her wounds all waking up and crying out, but she didn't care as long as he wasn't leaving.

He eased himself down next to her and propped his head in the crook of his elbow. She could just make out the glint of hallway light in his eyes.

She remembered those same eyes from that night at the lake, alone with him. The way he'd looked at her like she was treasure. She'd died then, like she was dying now—heart stopping as she waited for him to say something, *anything*.

Dot, dot, dot...

"Ev, I didn't kill him," he said at last. "And neither did you. He was drunk. He played chicken with a train, and he lost. The police released the autopsy report. It was all over the news this morning."

She blinked in the dark at the picture his words made. Shaun, fearless, invincible. Staring down the bright lights of a train—he'd lived his whole life like that. Like he could stop the world from turning. Keep the future from getting anywhere near them, keep everything exactly the same, forever.

But you just can't stop a freight train.

❖   ❖   ❖

R

Ré had no idea where he was.

The carpet under his feet was cold and spongy-wet, and then he remembered: in the Buick, in a pond, slowly sinking.

He turned his head. Everything hurt. Evie was beside him, unmoving. He said her name, but she didn't respond.

He unclipped his seat belt, wincing at the pain in his side. "*Câlisse,*" he hissed, hand going to his broken ribs. His fingers came away wet, but he couldn't tell in the dark if it was blood or just water. "Evelyn, you have to wake up!"

He shuffled across the front seat and grabbed her shirt. She slumped forward, and for a terrible moment he thought she was already dead. "*Evie!*" he cried, shouldering her back against the seat, white lightning cutting through his side.

He tapped her cheek, and she gave a soft moan. "Evie, please," he whimpered. "Please wake up. We're sinking!"

Water trickled in through the rusted doors. The back end of the Buick was sunk almost to the trunk. He thought if it filled, the weight might drag them even farther into the pond. Ré felt for his cell phone. It wasn't in his pockets. It must have slid off the seat in the crash; it might be underwater now, useless. He felt like crying.

Instead he slapped at Evie's pockets and found her phone.

He thumbed the button to dial 9-1-1, but it wouldn't even turn on.

"*Fuck!*" He slammed the dash with his hand.

Evie moaned again quietly.

"Ev." He shook her lightly. "I have to leave you here. But I'll be back, okay? I'll be back soon as I can." He hoped that deep down, wherever she was, she could hear him. He hoped that if he couldn't get back in time, she'd wake and find her own way up to the road before the car was full of water.

He tried to see how deep it was in the back seat, but all was dark. He pressed his hand to her cheek and said, "Evelyn. I am coming back for you. *Do not die…*"

Waking in that car had been the worst moment of his life. Worse than fighting Alex. Even worse than finding Shaun. But he'd dug his strength out and crawled from the wreck and waved down help on the highway. There was no way in hell he'd let her die.

And now her body curved next to his in the hospital bed. He was glad for the darkened room. After the fight with Alex, and the crash, he was looking pretty rough. Six stitches in his arm, more near his eye, white tape around his ribs, purple ink everywhere. He'd definitely seen better days.

But still, Ré smiled. "*Omashkooz nindoodem*," he said.

"What did you say?"

"It's Anishinaabemowin. It means 'my clan is Elk.'"

"Okay." She said it slowly, like a question.

He eased onto his back, wincing as his ribs pressed into him, scratching at his lungs. He stared up at the ceiling in the dark. "My whole life I've had these nightmares," he told her. "Real bad ones."

He thumbed through the dreams as he spoke, projecting them onto the ceiling, letting their power burn out. "I thought I was a bad guy, just like my great-uncle. *Psycho Ré*." He swallowed hard. One image still hurt: blond hair in a bright halo. "When Shaun died, it seemed like I was right. Like, no matter what, I was always gonna be a bad guy."

"Ré..." she said, but he wasn't looking for comfort or sympathy.

"After I crashed the Buick, I had a vision," he told her, watching Shaun's shadow fade into the ceiling tiles. "An *omashkooz* came to me. An Elk Spirit." Ré still felt the tingle of pure wonder fizzing through his veins. The memory of those great antlers rising to the sky, and the deer nodding, inviting him in. His clan. He smiled.

She moved a little, and he could feel her looking at him, questioning.

"I thought I was seeing demons," he said. "That the dreams were all bad prophesy. But the whole time, it was just *me*, holding on too tight." The muscles in his arms flexed lightly at the thought.

"To what?" she asked.

He didn't answer right away. Instead, he rubbed his thumb against her fingers, thinking about it. "I guess to the way things used to be?" he said. "To the guy I thought I was. *Psycho Ré.* I know it sounds crazy, but I think those dreams were just trying to show me what I gotta let go of. Like"—he rocked his head from side to side—"I'm here, but I got to get to *there*, y'know?"

He fell silent, halfway to that other place in his head. It had been calling him this whole time. Not Black Chuck. The future. The *Omashkooz*.

The path he was meant to walk as a man, in the footsteps of the Elk.

Ré shook his head. "I was so scared of it before," he told her. "I was letting all kinds of dumb stuff get in my way. But I know where I'm going now, Ev, and I'm not afraid anymore."

❖   ❖   ❖

E vie couldn't help it—her chest squeezed tight.

She felt like he'd only just been found. Like, for a split second, everything she didn't even know she'd wanted was suddenly hers, and then it was gone.

She shivered. "What do you mean, *where you're going*? Are you leaving Cold Water?" She steeled herself for the answer.

Of course, he could go anywhere now. He was finished school. Free.

But he didn't answer. Tears slid into her hair, wetting the pillow.

She squeezed his hand. "Please, say something, Ré," she said. She heard him turn his head to look at her again.

"I'm not going anywhere," he said. He rocked their clasped hands lightly, reassuring her. "At least, not till after the baby."

Evie's eyes went wide, remembering. The distant star, the tiny alien. She pulled her hand from Ré's and touched her belly. "The baby," she gasped, feeling only cheap hospital blankets. The heart monitor skipped and raced as she jerked in the bed, trying to sit up. "Oh my god, *the baby!*"

She tried to breathe around the brick in her chest.

Until this instant, she hadn't felt anything for it. Not worry, and definitely not love. It was only stardust. It was only Shaun's. The last bruise to fade. But now it all boomeranged back, knocking the air straight out of her.

"Ev." He touched her arm. "She's fine—don't worry. You lost a lot of blood, but everything's okay now."

She stopped struggling and just stared at him, eyes wide. "Oh my god," she said again. "*She?*"

She could see him nodding in the dark. Could just make out his grin.

Then he shifted and with a breathless groan eased himself up on one elbow.

He ran his hand down her arm, sliding his fingers through hers over the little bump, still hiding safely away under the covers. A sleeping fox curled against her tail. A *baby girl.*

A flood of warmth began in Evie's chest and rippled outward, echoed by the skittish machine, *dot, dot, dot...*

She held his hand against her belly, against the strange universe growing there, still gathering itself to *become*. She had to fight her tears again, but these ones were happy, at least.

"Ev," he said again. This time his voice was very serious. In the dim light, she could see that he'd closed his eyes, too shy to look. "Do you remember that day we were in my room?"

She swallowed, nervous and embarrassed all over again. Of course she did.

She remembered the light along the side of his face. Lashes so long they kissed his cheeks. She remembered the song he'd played, the one about the moon.

She remembered his silver armor fallen away at last, and the tender heart that lay there, bare and sweet.

And the words she'd said. How could she forget?

I could love you, if you asked me to...

He cleared his throat. Opened his eyes, all liquid black, and looked at her again. A shimmering dark lake to go swimming in. A place she could probably drown. And maybe she already had. "Well," he said, so serious, so shy. "I was wondering, Ev...maybe could I ask you something now?"

AUTHOR'S NOTE

While writing this book, I reached out to many Indigenous people for their help in writing Réal in a sensitive and respectful way, and to them I am so grateful. It is a very tricky thing to write outside of your own culture—I only hope that I've done it with the care and respect it deserves.

I would be remiss in leaving out the influence my First Nations friends have had on me over the years, particularly Nadia McLaren, Ian Town, Jesse Chechock, and Rhea Doolan. Thank you for sharing your stories, and for opening my eyes (whether you knew you were or not).

Many languages thrived in Canada long before English and French. But as complex and ancient as those languages are, like Réal says, most now stand like newborn animals on skinny legs thanks to the residential school system.

In what is now accurately called "cultural genocide," generations of Indigenous children were stolen from their homes and sent to government-sanctioned schools in an effort to crush their languages, culture and traditions. The effects have been devastating and long-reaching.

The effort to revive these languages is an uphill battle, and I'm very grateful for the translations provided by Mskwaankwad Rice, who is deeply committed to teaching Anishinaabemowin to new generations.

In the storytelling tradition of the Algonquins, the Windigo is a malevolent spirit with an insatiable hunger for human flesh. Windigo stories serve many purposes, but most notably as a warning against cannibalism—as abhorrent in Algonquin societies as anywhere—during long, harsh winters.

For more about Windigos, I encourage you to read as much as you can, especially stories by First Nations writers. Nathan D. Carlson's *Reviving Witiko (Windigo): An Ethnohistory of "Cannibal Monsters" in Northern Alberta*, published by Duke University Press, has been a great help to me.

To learn more about Anishinaabemowin, email Mskwaankwad Rice at shki.nishnaabemjig@gmail.com. Also, check out his Rez 91 YouTube channel, or tune in to Rez 91 radio at www.rez91.com.

To learn more about the residential school system, look for Nadia McLaren's documentary, *Muffins for Granny*, read Monique Gray Smith's *Speaking Our Truth: A Journey of Reconciliation* or go to www.wherearethechildren.ca.

ACKNOWLEDGMENTS

Thank you to my sister Morgan, for telling me how a tiny universe feels. To my beautiful biker babe, Rayne Wildwood, many thanks for filling Alex in with all your sunshine. To Jaimie Dufresne, for lending me your language and your name. And to Waubgeshig and Mskwaankwad Rice, for helping Réal come to life with care.

Sarah Harvey, Andrew Wooldridge, Jen Cameron, Rachel Page, Greg Younging, Vivian Sinclair and the rest of the Orca team: Thank you all so much for making me feel like a real writer! It's a dream come true.

Many thanks also to Andrew Smith, Matt and Rebecca James, Michael Elcock, Evan Munday, Kate Brauning, Jackie Kaiser and Elizabeth Culotti, for guiding me up this strange mountain, and to Crissy Calhoun, for swooning first.

To Susan Stanton, Maisie Mulder, Nadia Kane, Mishelle Pack and of course Sylvia Knoll, thank you all so much for reading the roughest of drafts! Geneviève Scott—your eyes and encouragement were invaluable. Alaa al-barkawi, thank you for driving me back to an old idea; never give up on yours.

And huge thanks to Ronni Davis for your constant support, even when I'm invisible.

To the Booters, Campies and Corpies who keep me sweating, laughing, cursing and crying—you're all bananas. Never change.

To Ben Redhead, the valves of my heart. Thank you, and keep writing.

To my parents, Viv, Steps, Flashes, in-laws and all the littles, thank you for this big, ridiculous family. G&G (&G), I wish you were here to see this (sorry for the language). And to Derry, Risa and Morgan: you are my fortress. Nothing I am or do is possible without you.

Guy. As always, thank you for letting me close the door, and for listening, and for believing in me. I love you, Itch. And will still most likely kill you in the morning.

Finally, Northumberland County, with all your freaks and geeks...Cold Water couldn't exist without you.

REGAN MCDONELL studied poetry at the University of Victoria with Patrick Lane and Lorna Crozier, then promptly put the pen down to pursue a career in textile and graphic design. Now Creative Director at a Toronto-based marketing agency, Regan spends her days designing apparel for kids and her nights writing fiction for teens. She has no pets or children, but she does have a bass player, and is auntie, *oba* and *tädi* to four surprising, funny little humans. She also leaves love letters on subways for strangers to find.

This is her first published work. For more information, go to www.writerregan.com.

More **BOLD** YA from ORCA

9781459809765 • $14.95 PB

★
"HARD REALISM
WITH A HEART."
—*Kirkus Reviews,*
STARRED REVIEW

When Isabelle punches a girl at school, only one teacher sees past Isabelle's aggressive behavior. Challenged to participate in a group writing project, Isabelle tentatively connects with a boy named Will and discovers an interest in (and talent for) the kind of drama she can control—the kind that happens on the page.